Discover why everyone's falling in love with Happily Inc!

You Say It First

"The first in ever-popular Mallery's new Happily Inc series has the author's signature blend of humor, poignancy, and small-town charm." —*Booklist*

"The romance is sweet and hot, the writing is quick and easy… A great choice for a weekend read." —*Kirkus Reviews*

Second Chance Girl

"A heartfelt and genuine friends-to-lovers story fraught with emotional trauma that makes the happily-ever-after satisfyingly sweet… Sharp, well-drawn characters and a naughty beagle add depth to the story." —*Publishers Weekly*

"You can always count on Mallery to deliver warmhearted and quirky stories featuring emotionally dented individuals doing their best to survive and hopefully thrive…. A truly unforgettable read! Mallery is one of a kind!" —*RT Book Reviews*, Top Pick!

Why Not Tonight

"Verdict: Soul-crushing revelations and old resentments are tempered by whimsy, sass, and belly laughs in a scrumptiously sexy, playful story from one of the genre's best. Touching, refreshing, and fun." —*Library Journal*

"Full of blissful, sigh-inducing scenes and surprisingly complex characters." —*Woman's World*

"Delightful… A wedding destination hot spot in California is the perfect romantic setting for this tender story." —*Publishers Weekly*

Meant to Be Yours

"Marvelous… Many smiles and lots of laughs abound in this joyous romp… Susan Mallery is a treasure."   —*Fresh Fiction*

Happily This Christmas

"A heartwarming story about new love, new beginnings and new life, in the unique way that only Susan Mallery can write… A great holiday read."   —*Red Carpet Crash*

"*Happily This Christmas* had the lively banter and camaraderie I cherish in a Susan Mallery novel, plus it also gave that warm and fuzzy feeling the holidays bring that you want to wrap yourself up in all year long. Definitely recommended."

—*Harlequin Junkie*

SUSAN MALLERY

happily this
Christmas

HQN®

ISBN-13: 978-1-335-41877-7

Happily This Christmas

First published in 2020. This edition published in 2021.

Copyright © 2020 by Susan Mallery, Inc.

This edition published by arrangement with Harlequin Books S.A.

For questions and comments about the quality of this book, please contact us at CustomerService@Harlequin.com.

HQN
22 Adelaide St. West, 40th Floor
Toronto, Ontario M5H 4E3, Canada
www.Harlequin.com

Printed in Lithuania

Recycling programs for this product may not exist in your area.

MIX
Paper from
responsible sources
FSC® C021394

To my favorite marines: Will, Peter, Ben Z, John and Ben S.
We "met" under the most unexpected of circumstances,
a fact I will always treasure. Thank you for making me
a very small part of your deployment.

I think I speak for the entire country when I tell you
that I appreciate your service more than I can say.
Without your courage and dedication,
we could not be who we are.

happily this
Christmas

chapter one

Annoying other people was one thing. Wynn Beauchene could completely get behind that idea, mostly because more often than not, people deserved to be annoyed. But annoying herself? What was up with that? Not only was it a total waste of time, it made no sense. The only solution was to stop acting like a sixteen-year-old girl with a crush on the quarterback. She was a mature adult, a single mother with a successful business and a life she really liked. If she was attracted to her handsome neighbor, then she needed to stop hanging out by the front window of her house, hoping to catch a glimpse of him. She should march over to his place, knock on his front door and say… And say…

"I'm an idiot," she muttered out loud, not for the first time. No matter how she envisioned the "march over there" scenario, she couldn't figure out what she was supposed to say when he opened the door.

Hi, Garrick. I was wondering if maybe we could, um, well, you know, go out sometime.

Really? That was how she was going to start the con-

versation? Shouldn't she lead into it? Maybe mention she'd
enjoyed having him as her neighbor for the past year and
tell him how nice it was that he was a police officer and
the whole street liked the fact that he parked his patrol car
in the driveway. Not that crime was a problem in Happily
Inc, because it wasn't, but still, having a cop as a neighbor
was great. Although her interest was more personal, what
with how he'd looked over the summer, mowing his lawn…
shirtless. Not that she hadn't noticed him before—she had.
Until the lawn-mowing season, she'd managed to ignore
him, but now she couldn't and it was already November
and she'd done absolutely nothing to take their nonrelation-
ship past the waving and hi-ing stage, and here she was,
hanging out by her front window and she was ready to slap
herself upside the head.

It was the dating thing. She wasn't good at it because she
didn't do it very often. There were a lot of reasons, very few
of them interesting, but in the past five or six months, she'd
been thinking that maybe it was time to let the no-dating
rule go and have a personal life. But while she'd spent a lot
of time *thinking*, she hadn't done much on the *doing* front.

"I'm better than this," she muttered, ignoring the little
voice in her head whispering that she obviously wasn't.

It was just that in every other area of her life, she was
capable. Hunter, her fourteen-year-old, acting out in school?
She could deal with that five ways to Sunday. A printing order gone awry at work? Easy-peasy. A friend with
an emotional crisis? She was all about the hugging and
straight talk. But when it came to dating, or wanting to
date, or thinking Garrick was sexy and supersweet with
her son and lately she'd been wanting them to get to know
each other better, she was a mess. Worse than a mess—
she was pathetic.

As proof, she was standing in her living room, looking out the picture window, staring at his house, waiting for him to get home. It was Saturday afternoon. She had a lot of things she should be doing, and none of them included staring at some guy's empty driveway.

If only there weren't something about him. But there was. Not just the whole tall with broad shoulders thing, although that was very nice, as were his gray eyes and dark hair, but that wasn't really what got her attention. It was more the fact that while Garrick was always friendly and pleasant, there was a hint of something a little dark and dangerous lurking beneath the surface. Ridiculous, but true, and like most reasonably intelligent women who knew better, she couldn't help responding to the possibility of a great guy who just might have a whisper of a dangerous streak.

She turned away from the window just in time to hear a dinging sound. After walking into the kitchen, she pulled two cookie sheets out of the oven. Because she'd made chocolate chip cookies, if you could believe it. Things were that bad.

Oh, not the baking—she baked all the time for Hunter, and most likely she would pretend she'd made these for her son, as well. Only she hadn't. She'd baked them thinking she would take them over to Garrick, in a neighborly kind of gesture that—hopefully—would lead to some witty conversation, lots of laughter and him confessing that he'd spent the past few months wanting to ask her out.

It was a lot of pressure to put on chocolate chip cookies.

She slid in two more cookie sheets, reset the timer and had nearly moved all the baked cookies to a cooling rack when the doorbell rang.

Wynn walked through the living room and pulled open the front door only to find Garrick on her front porch.

He wasn't in uniform—instead, he had on jeans and a T-shirt. As usual, his mouth was curved up in a smile that left her a little breathless.

"Hi, Wynn," he said, his voice low and sexy—although that could have been wishful thinking on her part. "Do you have a second?"

"Sure."

She stepped back to let him in, wondering what on earth was happening. She'd just been thinking about him, and here he was. Weirder still, even though they'd been neighbors for a year, they'd never exchanged much more than a few passing comments, greeting each other and mentioning the weather. They'd certainly never been in each other's houses.

"I'm baking cookies and I need to get them on a cooling rack," she said, leading the way into the kitchen. "What's up?"

"I need your advice."

"Sure. I'm good at giving advice." She glanced at him as he slid onto one of the stools at the island in the center of her kitchen. "People are less good about taking it."

"Tell me about it." He eyed the cookies. "May I?"

"Help yourself, but be careful. They're hot."

He took one and blew on it before taking a bite. His eyes half closed as he chewed.

"Perfect," he told her, looking at her. "You're a great cook."

"Thanks."

Despite the relatively ordinary conversation, everything about the moment was surreal. Him sitting in her kitchen, them talking, all of it. Not that she minded his presence. Her kitchen didn't host many men, not counting service guys doing things like fixing her dishwasher and unclogging her sink, and the change was nice. Plus she couldn't help feeling she was being given the perfect opportunity to try one of the conversational threads she'd been practicing, where she mentioned them maybe, possibly, going out sometime.

"Joylyn's going to be moving in with me," he said, taking a second cookie. "It's going to be a new experience for me." He glanced at her. "We've never lived together before—not full time. There have been plenty of weekends and vacations, but this will be different. I want to make sure the house is comfortable for her."

Joylyn? Who was Joylyn and why was she moving in?

Even as the questions formed, the obvious answer popped into her rattled brain. He had a girlfriend. Of course he did. She'd been telling herself that two years after her last relationship ended she was ready to find someone new, and Garrick was about to have Joylyn move in. How perfect.

"I think I have the right furniture," he said. "It's the other stuff I need help with. Making the house seem…" He paused, as if searching for the right word. "Cozy."

Her mind went blank. Totally and completely blank.

"Cozy?"

Had he really just said that word? It didn't seem very Garrick-like, but then what did she know about anything? She'd never suspected there was a Joylyn, which pretty much confirmed the whole her being an idiot thing.

"I want the house nice when she arrives," he continued. "She's having a rough time of it, what with being pregnant and all. If she was older, it might be easier, but she's only twenty-one and—"

"Joylyn is twenty-one and pregnant?" Wynn asked, her voice a little more shrill than she would like.

Because him having a girlfriend wasn't enough of a hit, she thought grimly. Sure, make her a toddler and pregnant.

"What were you thinking? She's way too young to be your girlfriend. How did you even meet? Were you hanging out at the high school, hoping to get lucky?"

So much for her Garrick daydreams, she thought, wishing she hadn't been stupid enough to believe he was crushworthy. Yuck and double yuck. To think she'd wasted all that time thinking about him. No more sexy, possibly dangerous neighbors for her. That was for sure. She was going to go find a nonsexy, undangerous guy to fall for. She glared at Garrick, wishing she were physically strong enough to drag him to the door and throw him out. He was—

"My girlfriend?" Garrick's voice was nearly a yelp. "She's my daughter."

They stared at each other. Wynn had a feeling she looked as shocked as he did. On the heels of that revelation came the admission that she really had to start thinking before she spoke and maybe not be so hasty about assuming the worst.

"Oh," she managed to say, just as the timer dinged.

She busied herself removing the cookie sheets from the oven and setting them on the stove, then turned off the oven. She put down the hot pads, then drew in a breath and looked at Garrick.

"We should probably start over," she murmured.

"You thought I had a pregnant, twenty-one-year-old girlfriend? Wouldn't that make me a jerk?"

While she wanted to say that it would, she wasn't sure that was a good idea. "I'll admit to some disappointment," she said instead.

"I would hope so. I'm thirty-eight. I don't want to date someone in their twenties. What would we talk about?"

"Some guys aren't interested in conversation."

"That's not me."

They stared at each other. Despite her embarrassment and a sizable dose of chagrin, she found herself noticing that he had really attractive eyes. Not just the unusual gray coloring but the shape. They suited his face and, well, the rest of him. Without wanting to, she remembered the interesting scars on his torso. Not that she'd been looking—he was the one who had chosen to mow his lawn shirtless the previous summer.

She had no idea where the scars had come from. If she had to guess, she would say he'd been in more than one knife fight, but that wasn't possible. The man was a police officer in Happily Inc. Guys who did that didn't fight with knives.

She put the rest of the cookies onto cooling racks, poured two glasses of milk, took the stool on the other end of the island and then reached for a cookie.

"Hello," she said. "I'm Wynn Beauchene, your neighbor. We don't usually say much more than hi and talk about the weather."

Garrick smiled. "Hey, Wynn. I'm Garrick McCabe. I grew up here in Happily Inc and had my daughter when I was seventeen. I moved to Phoenix when I started college, mostly because Joylyn and her mom were there. I got on the Phoenix police force. When Joylyn went off to college a few years back, I returned to Happily Inc. Last year I bought the house next door."

"We all appreciate having your patrol car parked in the driveway."

"I'm glad." He grabbed another cookie. "My adult daughter is married to a deployed Marine. Her mom has three boys at home, and it's getting to be a bit much for Joylyn, who's due in about eight weeks, so right around

Christmas. Alisha, Joylyn's mother, thought it would be a good idea for Joylyn to stay with me until Christmas or until Chandler, Joylyn's husband, comes home, whichever happens first."

"I'm glad she's going to be with family during the holidays."

"Me, too." The smile faded. "Joylyn and I went through a rough patch when she was about fifteen. We used to be close, and then one day she didn't want her dad around. I'm hoping to use her time with me to reconnect." One shoulder rose and lowered. "To that end, I want the house to be comfortable for her."

"Cozy?" she asked, her voice teasing.

His smile returned, which made her unexpectedly happy. "That would be it. I don't know anything about decorating or, you know, plants, and I don't cook. Her being pregnant adds stakes to the game for sure. That's why I want your help. I've seen your graphic work around town, and it's always exactly right for whatever business it is. The colors, the tone, all of it. You're a real professional. You have excellent taste and style, and I was hoping to get your advice about what I should have around." He waved his hand. "Maybe some more dishes and throw pillows and stuff."

That was a lot of information to process, she thought, slightly off balance from the unexpected compliment. She always worked hard to please her clients, and she was happy to know her work was appreciated, but it was strange to consider that Garrick would look at a sign in a window and think of her. Did he think of her in other ways or was that her hoping a little too much?

Regardless, she liked that he cared about his kid and that he wanted to make his house nice for her. She also felt bad about assuming the worst about him, so even if she hadn't been inclined to help—which she was—that would have pushed her over the edge.

"I'll give you whatever advice you'd like," she told him. "But my style might not be hers. That could be a problem."

"No, you and Joylyn have a lot in common design-wise. You have a good eye for space and color, and she would like what you do."

His words made her feel a little floaty, which was silly. She was in some serious trouble here—she hadn't been this flaky even in high school. If she wasn't careful, she was going to start flipping her hair and saying "like" in every sentence.

"If you're all right with me adding fringe to every surface in your house, then I'm in," she told him.

He chuckled. "Fringe would be a look."

"But not a good one?" she teased.

"I'm not a fringe kind of guy."

"Good to know. Tell me about Joylyn."

Something sad flashed through his eyes. "I don't see her much anymore. In fact, I haven't seen her since the wedding. Like I said, we used to be tight." One corner of his mouth turned up. "She was my best girl."

"I'm sorry that changed."

"Me, too." He was silent for a second, then drew in a breath. "As I said, she's married to Chandler, who is currently deployed. Alisha says he'll be back before the baby's born because first babies are always late." He shook his head. "I can't believe my little girl is going to be a mother. It all happened so fast."

"Children grow up even when we don't want them to. I'm figuring that out with Hunter."

"He's a good kid."

"Thanks. I like to think so." She wrapped her hands

around her glass of milk. "I'm happy to help with whatever you need, and I'm sorry for jumping to conclusions."

"Thank you for the offer. As for the rest of it, I can see why you'd think what you did. In my own defense, I'll admit it never occurred to me you wouldn't know about my daughter, what with Happily Inc being a small town and all."

"This might shock you, Garrick, but we don't spend a lot of time talking about you."

He stared at her in mock surprise. "Now you're just being mean."

She laughed. "We have our own lives we discuss."

"But hey, it's me."

They smiled at each other. Wynn wondered if there was a way to ask about any other women that might be in his life, but figured she shouldn't press her luck. She was going to help her neighbor, and in the helping, she might get a chance to probe into his personal life. If he was single, she would try to find a way to suggest they go out to dinner and get to know each other. Of course the more likely scenario was that they spent some time together, and then she discovered he was annoying. Because that seemed to happen a lot. Her friends said she was too picky, while she thought of herself as careful.

"When is she going to move in with you?" she asked.

"Next Saturday."

"Then we should probably take a look at your house and make a plan."

"When's a good time?" he asked.

"I'm free now."

"Me, too," Garrick said, coming to his feet.

Wynn rose and smiled. "Let's go."

She picked up her cell phone from the counter and tucked it in the back pocket of her jeans, then led the way to the front door. He followed, trying to keep his gaze in the neutral position, which was tough. He kept finding himself checking out her long legs and her butt. She had a great butt—all curves with a little bounce. It was a butt a man could grab hold of for all kinds of reasons.

Down, boy, he told himself. Yes, Wynn had the requisite parts, and she was one of the most beautiful women he'd ever seen, but there was no way he was going to do anything about it. He didn't do commitments anymore and doubted Wynn was the kind of woman who wanted anything else. In the year they'd been neighbors, he'd never seen her bring a man home. He had a feeling some of that was about her standards, and a lot of it was about being a single mom. She took her responsibilities to her son seriously.

Thinking about Hunter made him think about Joylyn. He was glad she was going to come stay with him, even for a few weeks. All these years later, he still didn't know what had gone sideways between them when she'd been a teenager, but whatever it was, he wanted to make it right. She was his daughter and he missed her.

They crossed her lawn and driveway before walking up to his porch. He stepped around Wynn and opened his unlocked front door.

"This is me."

She went into the house.

Their neighborhood in Happily Inc was older, with family homes on good-sized lots. The trees were mature, the streets wide and the houses all around two thousand square feet.

Wynn paused in his living room and looked at the black

leather sectional, and the seventy-five-inch TV mounted on the wall.

"That is a very large television," she murmured.

He suspected she didn't mean the comment as a compliment, but he was good with that. "I like sports. Bigger is better."

"With the players practically life-size?"

He grinned, unrepentant. "It's a guy thing."

"No wonder Hunter is always begging me to let him come over and watch the game with you."

"You should say yes. I'm good with kids." He always had been. The skill probably came from having a child when he'd still been in high school. He'd been forced to learn fast. He'd spent much of his after-school hours during his senior year studying while looking after Joylyn. He'd learned how to manage feedings, diapers and colic. He might have been a kid himself, but he'd done his best to be a good dad.

"I'll keep that in mind." She pointed to the walls. "You don't have any artwork."

"Should I?" He studied the bare space. "Doesn't it look clean just plain?"

"There's clean and then there's sterile. A few inexpensive prints would add a little color. Maybe distract from the continent-size television."

He grinned. "But why would you want to do that?"

"There is something strange about your gender."

"I've heard that."

She smiled as she walked around the room.

"Ignoring the black leather sofa, to which I would ask, 'what were you thinking,' the space is good. I like the end tables."

He glanced at the wood-and-glass cubes. They were

more modern than he usually liked, but they were well made and the wood was mahogany inlaid with ebony.

"I'm pretty sure they're custom," he told her. "I know they're handmade. I found them at an estate sale. They were pricey, but worth it."

"They're gorgeous." She pulled out her phone and took a few pictures. "Maybe we can find some pieces that link back to the pattern on the wood. You never know." She looked at him. "Kitchen next?"

He led the way.

One of the reasons he'd bought the house was the fact that it had already been updated. He liked working with his hands, but he preferred projects to be things he wanted to do rather than things that were required to make a place livable. He'd wanted three bedrooms, and the pool out back had been a plus. The kitchen was big with a lot of windows and good-quality cabinets. His real estate agent had gone on about the appliances and counter space, but he didn't cook, so none of that mattered to him. He was more of a takeout kind of guy. He worked long hours, he lived alone—getting food to-go was easy.

He waited while Wynn looked around. Her brown eyes were large and expressive. He liked her eyes. And her hair. It was dark and long and curly. Like, really curly. He often found himself wanting to touch the curls to see if they were as soft as they looked.

Of course he also thought about other kinds of touching—not that he would act on those thoughts, either. But a guy could dream, and Wynn was definitely dream material.

She pointed to the empty space by the bay window. "That would be where a table and chairs would go. Unless you eat in the dining room."

"I didn't furnish the dining room."

Her eyebrows rose. "So you eat…" She put her hands on her hips. "No. Do *not* tell me you either eat standing up at the counter or while sitting on the sofa."

She was an intriguing combination of annoyed and amused.

"You're not speaking," she said.

"You told me not to."

She laughed. "You're right, I did. My mistake. So you do eat at the counter or on the sofa."

"It's easy."

"You are such a guy. Fine. You need a table and chairs. Joylyn will not think standing while dining is the least bit cozy." She walked over to his cabinets and glanced at him. "May I?"

He nodded.

She began opening doors, then closing them. He knew she wouldn't find much inside. He owned a handful of plates, a few bowls and mugs, some flatware. His cooking supplies consisted of a couple of pots, one with a lid, and a cookie sheet he'd never used.

She glanced in the large pantry, where he kept his coffee and a few boxes of cereal. When she closed the door, she turned to him.

"You don't cook."

It wasn't a question, but he answered it anyway. "Nope."

"Joylyn is going to need healthy food, which means cooking at home. Does she know how?"

"She does."

Alisha had taught her. He still remembered the first time Joylyn had made him dinner. Spaghetti. She'd used every pot and pan he'd owned and the kitchen had been a mess, but she'd been so proud of herself and he'd been impressed as hell.

Recalling that made the ache of missing her a little more intense. He supposed some fathers wouldn't be thrilled to have their pregnant daughter moving in, but he couldn't wait. They would have time together—time for him to figure out why he'd lost her and how to get her back.

Wynn glanced around. "You're going to need dishes, flatware, serving pieces, pots and pans. Actually, everything." She shook her head. "Shall we go look at her bedroom?"

On the way to the bedrooms, she ducked into the hall bathroom.

"It's empty," she said, reappearing in the hallway. "You're going to need supplies in there, too. Towels and soap and a bath mat." Her eyebrows rose. "Maybe some kind of artwork on the wall."

He groaned. "In a bathroom? Is that normal?"

"It is. Trust me. Now where's the bedroom?"

He pointed to the larger of the spare rooms. He used the smaller one for an office. He'd set up a folding table and chair and used a moving box as a file cabinet. He only had a laptop and a printer—he didn't need anything more.

Wynn walked into Joylyn's room and came to a stop. Her eyes widened and her lips parted. "Oh, Garrick, where did you find this?"

"A guy I knew back in Phoenix was selling it. The set belonged to his great-grandmother. It's not too much?"

"No. It's perfect."

Wynn crossed to the large four-poster bed. The wood, also mahogany, was intricately carved with flowers and fairies and leaves. The dresser and nightstands had the same design.

Despite their size, all the pieces seemed light and whimsical. The second he'd seen the pictures, he'd known that

Joylyn would love it. Before handing over a check, Garrick had examined every inch of the furniture and had quickly figured out the set had been made by a master craftsman. He'd bought it, thinking he would give it to her when she and Chandler got settled after Chandler left the Marines. Now she would get to see it before that.

"What are Joylyn's favorite colors?" Wynn asked, running her hands across the carvings.

"Purple and blue."

She smiled. "We'll get a really great comforter. A thick one that's soft. And lots of pillows." She glanced at him, her eyes bright with excitement. "The hall bathroom is pretty plain, so we can continue the color theme in there. Extra thick towels with a matching bath mat. Maybe some accessories."

"And artwork," he said dryly. "Don't forget that."

She grinned. "I won't." She looked at the walls. "Maybe a fairy print. We'll have to see what they have. Or maybe I can find something online and have it printed on canvas. It's a great look and not that expensive. We can decide as we go."

"We?"

She returned her attention to him. "I assumed you weren't just asking for a shopping list. You have great taste in furniture, but you seem lacking in the softer touches. Unless you want to do it on your own?"

"Absolutely not. I appreciate your willingness to see this through." He hesitated. "I asked for your help because I knew you'd make her room look good, but I didn't mean for you to take on a whole project."

She smiled. "It's a challenge and I love a challenge. Plus I'm committed now."

Her voice was teasing, her expression happy. As she'd

said, he'd only known her well enough to say hello and comment on the weather. He'd noticed her, of course. No straight guy could be within twenty feet of Wynn and not notice her, but that was physical. He hadn't thought much about who she was.

Now he found himself enjoying her company and wanting to know more about her.

"With Joylyn arriving next weekend, we don't have a lot of time," she added. "How about going shopping tomorrow?"

"If you're available, that would be great."

"I'm free." The smile returned. "You're going to have to brace yourself. This is going to be a big hit on your credit card."

"Not a problem." He had plenty of savings, and except for food and an occasional guys' night out, he rarely spent any money. "I want Joylyn to feel good about staying here. Thanks for helping me, Wynn."

She smiled. "You are going to owe me big time."

"You name your price and I'll pay it."

Something flashed in her eyes. For a second he wondered if she was going to suggest something he would find intriguing, but then she looked away.

"I'll let you know what I decide. In the meantime I'll get going on the shopping list. I'm going to start in the kitchen."

She walked down the hall. He allowed himself to admire that view of her, then shook off any lingering desire. Wynn was his neighbor. She was helping him when she didn't have to, and he would respect that. As for wanting anything else—he knew better. Relationships always ended badly for him. He'd been through enough to know he was done with trying to make one work.

If he wanted to repay her for what she was doing, he would build her a gazebo or expand her back deck. Nothing else. Anything romantic would only be a disaster.

chapter two

Wynn was surprised to realize she'd never been shopping with a man before. It seemed an odd kind of event to have missed in her life—after all, she was a business owner and single mom. She'd dated men—sort of—and had been in a couple of semiserious relationships. She'd had sex with men, had dinner, gone to bars, concerts and completed a whole list of normal activities with the opposite gender, but she'd never gone shopping of any kind.

"Thanks again for helping me with my project," Garrick said, glancing at her briefly before turning his attention to the road.

They were in his ridiculously large black SUV, heading to the outlet mall about forty miles from Happily Inc where there were a couple of big bed-and-bath kind of stores, along with a few furniture places.

"I'm looking forward to it," she told him with a grin. "I'm going to test your ability to handle fringe."

"You keep mentioning that. I'm starting to think you're not kidding."

"You're going to have to wait and find out."

She pulled a list out of her handbag. "We should get the kitchen table and chairs first. Once we have that, we'll deal with linens and kitchenware, leaving the artwork for last." She glanced at him. "In case you flake out, we'll have the most important items taken care of."

"Flake out? I'm the one who came to you. I want to make this happen."

"You say that now, but let's see how you handle all the shopping."

The corners of his mouth turned up. "Maybe I like shopping."

"Oh, please. If you did, you'd have more stuff in your house. Most guys don't like shopping, which I've never understood. All you have to do is pretend you're hunting. You stalk, you pounce, you strap it to the car and take it home. A total win, but men don't see it that way."

He chuckled. "There are a lot of gross generalizations in those few sentences."

"I'll admit that's true, but how many of them are wrong?"

"Not as many as I'd like."

She smiled. This was nice—being with Garrick in the not-quite close confines of his SUV. He had a very commanding presence she found appealing, along with the subtle scent of freshly showered man that she'd been missing in her life. Today would be a great opportunity to figure out if they had any kind of chemistry and if there was any "there" there. Of course given her sucky personal life, there was every chance she was going to end up being ready to try a little kissing action about the time he was ready to head home and watch the game.

"What's Hunter doing today?" he asked.

"Hanging out with a friend. He couldn't believe I was letting him out of his Sunday chores."

"That would be a sweet victory. He's in what, ninth grade?"

"Uh-huh. Ninth grade is middle school in Happily Inc, so he's in high school next year. I can't believe how fast he's growing up."

"They do that. Enjoy every second while he's still living at home."

"I do my best."

She pointed to the off-ramp for the outlet center up ahead, and Garrick moved into the right lane of the freeway. They quickly found a parking space and walked into the furniture store. Wynn headed for the dining room and kitchen tables, Garrick keeping pace with her.

"No one needs this much stuff," he said as they wove their way through a massive display of sofa and recliners.

"Maybe not, but people like choices. What if your sofa had only come in purple?"

His cool gray eyes shifted to her face. "Was it a toss-up between saying purple and pink to get your point across, or did you go right for the purple?"

She grinned. "I went right there. It's not too girlie, but there's a message."

He surprised her by laughing. She liked the sound of his amusement, the way he relaxed when he laughed. Something stirred to life low in her belly, reminding her it had been a very long time since her last relationship and that she would very much like to be in one again. The boy-girl kind, she added, just to be clear. With lots of touching and kissing and naked time.

But that wasn't on the schedule for today, she told herself, pushing the whisper of anticipation to the back of her mind. Shopping and getting to know Garrick came first. She would enjoy her fantasies about her neighbor later.

They circled the dining room sets and headed for the more casual kitchen tables and chairs. Wynn stopped next to a round oak table with four chairs.

"It's very classic," she said. "And wood, which you seem to like. What do you think?"

Garrick walked around the display a couple of times before picking up one of the chairs and studying the underside. "They're not very well made and the style is kind of boring. Let's see what else they have."

"The alcove is big enough to take a table for six, if you want to do that," she said. "I don't think the shape of the table will matter, so if you want square or rectangular instead of round, we can do that. I have the measurements with me, so we'll be able to double-check that it fits."

"A table for six might be better," he said. "I'm hoping Joylyn will have some friends come by to keep her company. She doesn't know anyone in Happily Inc, and I don't want her to feel isolated."

They walked around the various displays. Garrick spent time studying a simple rectangular table and chairs in the Shaker style, then surprised her by stopping next to a round glass-top table with a wrought-iron base. The pedestal base was made up of curving iron bars that wove around each other, almost like a braid.

"That one?" she asked, not keeping the surprise out of her voice. "But you're all into wood and handcrafted."

"I know, but this one is interesting. I like that there aren't fifty like it in the store."

"I think it's great. The glass top keeps the look open, and it's easy to clean. They have chairs over there. We could go find something fun to go with the table."

They carried several chair options back to the table. Garrick considered plain wooden chairs painted black, several chrome and suede styles.

"None of these are right," he said. "The table needs something more."

Wynn eyed the chair selection before pointing to a set of lacquered red chairs with black-plaid seats. They were contemporary, unexpected and, when she sat on one, surprisingly comfortable.

"I know they're not traditional," she said.

"Let's try them."

He carried two over to the table and slid them into place.

The proportions were perfect, she thought. The red was a pop of color, while the black base grounded the look.

"I'm sure we could find white plates with a bit of red and black in the border," she said, walking around the table. "A pattern would be too heavy with the plaid cushions."

She looked at him and smiled. "There's a whole Christmas plaid thing. Tablecloths and napkins, with green instead of black in the pattern. That would be beautiful for the holidays." She paused. "If you like the chairs."

"I do. I have no idea why, but I like them a lot."

He used his phone to take a picture of the sales tag for the table and one of the chairs, then he suggested they look at outdoor furniture.

"I don't have much by the pool," he said. "I thought Joylyn might enjoy being outside in the afternoons. Right now the weather is perfect."

"Good idea. You have a lot of patio area. You could get two or three loungers and still have room for a table and chairs."

They made their selections quickly. Garrick went looking for a salesperson to write it all up. Delivery was arranged for the following Tuesday. As they walked back to the car, Garrick glanced at his watch.

"Less than thirty minutes," he said, his tone approving. "I like how you shop."

"Wait until you see me stocking your kitchen. I'll be a blur of activity."

They went into the home goods store. Wynn collected a shopping cart for herself and had Garrick take one, as well. As she'd promised, they moved quickly.

"Linens," she said, pointing to the far side of the store. "Bedding, towels and accessories." She smiled. "This time I think we really are going to be looking for anything purple."

"It's her favorite color."

Wynn found a pretty bedding set with a soft comforter and good quality sheets in various shades of purple and lavender. For the towels, she went for a soft shade, then found a set of bathroom accessories in lavender with a pop of silver. She added a half dozen throw pillows to the cart.

On their way to the kitchen department, they swung by a display of prints. Wynn held up a set of adorable fairy prints.

"Too young? They'll look great with the furniture, but I don't want her to think you forgot how old she is."

He shook his head. "Not too young. They're perfect."

Wynn added them to her cart, then steered into the middle of the displays of dishes.

Garrick looked at all the options, then took a step back. "There are too many. Nope. Not going to do this."

She grinned. "Chest getting a little tight?"

"I'm fighting the urge to bolt. I'm man enough to admit it."

"Just remember we want white dishes with just a touch

of red and black. It can be a border or a subtle pattern. If we can't find that, we can go for white with red or white with black."

He relaxed a little. "You're right. That helps."

They left their carts and wandered up and down the aisle. Garrick walked over with a dish in his hand.

The round plate was white with a swirl of black in the middle and a single spot of red by the rim.

"What about this?" he asked.

"Do you like it?"

He looked at the plate. "Not really. But the colors are right."

"They're only right if you like them. You're going to be eating off these plates for the next however many years, Garrick. You need to want to have them in your life."

He looked at her. "I don't think about wanting dishes in my life."

She smiled. "Yes, I know, but for today, let's pretend."

She found a couple of patterned dishes, but Garrick shook his head at them before surprising her by holding up a simple red plate.

"This," he said.

"It's red."

"Yes, I knew that. I like it. The mugs are a good size, the bowls work for me and there's no pattern. I want these."

"And you said you didn't think about wanting dishes in your life," she teased. "Let's get two sets. That's service for eight."

As Garrick put the boxes of dishes in the cart, she spotted a Betty Boop canister set across the aisle. The colors were perfect, the style retro. She picked up the smallest canister.

"Too much?" she asked.

Garrick shook his head and grinned. "I'm in. I love Betty."

Less than a half hour later, they had picked up glasses, cookware, flatware and a baking set. By then they were up to four full carts, and Wynn was thinking it was really good that Garrick drove a big SUV. She didn't think she would have gotten everything into her car.

"Thank you," he said when they had checked out and loaded everything. "I couldn't have done this without you."

"You're welcome. I enjoy spending other people's money."

He pointed to the steakhouse across the parking lot. "Can I buy you lunch?"

"I'd like that."

They were seated at a booth by the window. Wynn scanned the menu, her mouth watering when she read the description of the steak salad. Her decision made, she put down her menu.

Garrick was still studying his. She took a second to admire the strong lines of his face and the unfairness of men having thick lashes. Why did that always happen? Was it the Y chromosome? Did it come with naturally thick lashes?

Garrick looked up and smiled at her. "What's so funny?"

"Nothing. I was just thinking about eyelashes."

His brows drew together. "I wouldn't have guessed that."

"I know. My mind can be an unusual place." She glanced around at the ceramic turkeys on every table. "It's nice to see a place celebrating Thanksgiving. Too often we seem to go right from Halloween to Christmas."

"I agree. When Joylyn was little, we always made a big deal out of Thanksgiving. We would put together those funny paper turkeys and pilgrim paper dolls a few days before. The morning of, I made her blueberry pancakes. Then we'd head over to her mom's for a big dinner."

"That sounds nice. You were still in high school when she was born?"

The server appeared. Wynn ordered her salad and a diet soda while Garrick got a burger and iced tea. When they were alone, he looked at her.

"I'm a really great guy."

She did her best not to smile. "Okay, sure."

One corner of his mouth turned up. "I only say that to state the obvious before telling you about how Joylyn came to be."

"You're not the hero of the story?" she asked, not concerned about what he was going to say. However things had started for him and his daughter, his affection for her was clear.

"I tried to be." He leaned back in the booth. "Alisha and I were both juniors in high school. I had a thing for her best friend and foolishly asked Alisha's advice on how to win her."

Wynn winced. "No girl likes that."

"I know that now, but at the time I was an idiot. I also didn't know that Alisha had a thing for me."

Wynn would guess Garrick had been one popular guy back in high school. No doubt he'd been just as handsome, with a little teenage edginess for extra appeal.

"Which made your request doubly painful for her."

"It did." He smiled. "She said she couldn't recommend me to her friend unless she went out with me first. To see how I was as a boyfriend."

Wynn raised her eyebrows. "Impressive. Go Alisha."

"We agreed to date for a month. At the end of that time, I was totally into her and she had come to see I was not all that."

Wynn smiled. "You got your comeuppance."

"You could sound a little more broken up about it."

"I could, but I won't."

He flashed her a smile that nearly made her swoon. She told herself it was because she hadn't eaten much for breakfast, but knew she was lying.

"While I was still trying to convince her I was worthy boyfriend material, she turned up pregnant." He glanced down at the table, then back at her. "Neither of us saw that coming. The parents were unamused."

"I can imagine. Did you get married?"

"No. Neither of us wanted that. By the time Joylyn was born, we were happy to be good friends, and that's the way it stayed. Alisha's a great mom, and I did my best to be a hands-on dad."

"So you had a baby while you were a senior in high school."

He nodded. "It was harder for Alisha than me, of course. She was the one who was pregnant. Once Joylyn was born, we worked out a schedule. Our moms did the lion's share of the work. We didn't realize it at the time, but they were there for us. After high school Alisha and her family moved to Phoenix. I didn't want to lose touch with my daughter, so I applied to ASU and got in. Joylyn and I kind of grew up together."

She liked how he'd been involved with his daughter from the start. A lot of guys his age would have done the least they could or walked away completely.

"You became a police officer in Phoenix?" she asked.

"I did. Alisha got married and had three boys, one after the other. It was a lot for her to deal with. I saw Joylyn as much as I could."

Their server brought their drinks.

"We did everything together," he said, reaching for his

iced tea. "Hung out after I got home from work, went camping, horseback riding."

His tone was wistful. There was lots of love there, but also the fact that he missed what he'd had.

"You were a good dad," she said.

"I hope so." He sipped his tea. "What about you? Is Hunter's father around?"

"No. He died right around the time Hunter was born. He had an insurance policy and I was the beneficiary. The money allowed me to go to trade school and learn graphic design, then move here and buy the business I have now."

There was a lot more to the story, but this was the version she told people.

"Where did you grow up?" he asked.

"Oakland. So a fair distance from Happily Inc." She smiled. "I'm liking small town living very much."

"There is a different rhythm here. It's a good place to raise a family. I enjoyed growing up here and I'm glad to be back."

"You never had more kids?" she asked.

"Nope. Just Joylyn. I thought I'd have more. I was married for a while and we talked about it, but somehow it never happened."

"You're divorced?" she asked.

He nodded. "It was unfortunate but not dramatic. We were both busy with our jobs. I was gone a lot and we drifted apart."

"How were you gone a lot?" she asked. "I thought police officers worked regular hours."

Their server brought over their food. Garrick thanked her, then looked at Wynn.

"I took on a few special projects. For several years I was part of a task force with the DEA. I did a little undercover work, and that meant being gone for several weeks at a time."

Wynn stared at him. "You were an undercover agent for the Drug Enforcement Administration?"

He picked up a french fry. "It wasn't like the movies. I went undercover locally a few times, then had a couple of assignments in Colombia. That's about when my marriage hit the skids, which was bad, but losing Joylyn was worse."

Wynn did the math. "That's the rough patch you mentioned, when she was fifteen?"

"Yeah, and that was not an easy transition. She got very independent very quickly and told me she didn't need to spend time with me. Every time I came back from an assignment, I hoped she had changed her mind, but she never did." He sighed. "Teenagers aren't easy."

"Don't say that. Hunter's fourteen."

"Brace yourself."

"I don't want to. I want him to be eight forever."

Garrick laughed. "Sorry. You don't get to make the rules." He picked up his burger. "All right, I've been doing all the talking and I've surprised you with my dark, dangerous past. What don't I know about you?"

"Nothing that exciting." Garrick an undercover agent with the DEA. And now he was a cop in Happily Inc. That must have been quite the journey.

"You were married to a rock star?" he prompted. "Once stole artwork from the Louvre? Have a tattoo of a cobra on your back?"

She started laughing. "So you have an imagination. That's interesting. And sadly, no to all of them."

"You're sad you're not a tattooed art thief?"

"A little. My life is fairly ordinary. I have a business, I'm a single mom and that's about it." She paused when she realized how boring that sounded. "I mean I have friends, of course, and there have been a few men in my life."

"Anyone I know?"

"I dated Jasper for a while." She knew he and the local thriller writer were friends.

Garrick's eyes widened with surprise. "When?"

"Maybe three years ago. We broke up before you moved back." She held up a hand. "It's fine. I'm close friends with his wife Renee, and Jasper and I have stayed close. It's very civilized."

"I guess, although he and I hang out and he never said anything to me."

"How much time do you and your friends spend talking about the women in town?"

"None. You're saying that's why he never mentioned you. I get that. It's good you two get along. My ex and I didn't stay friends." He paused as if he was going to say something else, then shook his head. "I'm okay with that." He looked at her. "No kids other than Hunter?"

"No, although I think you would have noticed them hanging around the house. I'm not the type to keep children locked up."

"Good to know. Did you want more kids?"

The question surprised her. "I never really thought about it. I adore Hunter and having him has been wonderful, but it's not easy being a single parent. I think having a partner and a support system would make things go more smoothly. I guess I was never in a place where that happened, and now it's too late."

"Why is it too late? You're what? Thirty-two?"

"Thirty-four."

"Still young enough to have a few more kids."

He took another bite of his burger. Wynn stared at her salad as she tried to absorb what he'd so casually pointed out.

She *wasn't* too old to have more children. Lots of women her age got pregnant. The concept shouldn't be startling, but it was. Somehow she'd decided that part of her life was over without asking herself if that was what she wanted.

Not a conversation to have with herself right now, she decided, but something to think about later.

"What about plants?" he asked.

She had no idea what he was talking about. "Plants instead of kids?"

He chuckled. "No. What about getting some plants for the house? Don't women like that? Something—" he waved his hand "—I don't know. Leafy and green. For Joylyn. Can pregnant women be around plants?"

"They can, and if you'd like, we can go to the nursery after we empty out your SUV. I'm sure they have a nice selection of leafy green things."

"You're making fun of me."

"Only a little."

"Captain, do you have a second?"

Garrick looked up from his computer and saw Phillips, a relatively new officer, hovering outside his office.

He waved the younger man in and saved the email he'd been working on. His recent promotion had come with a lot of paperwork and responsibility. He disliked the former, enjoyed the latter and knew that if all went according to plan, both were going to increase.

After he'd returned from his last task force assignment in Colombia, he'd taken a few weeks to clear his head. He wasn't going to say he had anything like PTSD, but weeks of being held hostage by an angry, vicious drug lord had left a few scars—some physical, some less visible. His job in Phoenix had been waiting for him, but Garrick had felt he wanted some kind of a change. The call from Frank Dineen, known to all in Happily Inc as Grandpa Frank, had offered an unexpected career path.

The current chief of police was looking at retiring in a few years, and the town wanted to hire an heir apparent. Garrick was a known entity with the right skill set. He'd been recommended by his boss in Phoenix and the task force commander. Three regular-length interviews and one two-day-long interview later, he'd been hired and had moved back to his hometown.

He'd come in as a sergeant and had been promoted to captain about six months ago. His "career development plan" included him getting more involved with community outreach, including the city council and other governing boards.

He wasn't excited about the politics in the position, but understood that a part of good policing was understanding how government worked and knowing his department's place in the overall structure of the town. He'd just wrapped up an online college course on city management. Last year he'd studied human resources as it related to law enforcement, and he still had three or four more courses he wanted to take. So much for his homework days being behind him.

He motioned to the chair next to his desk and waited until the young officer took a seat before asking, "What's up?"

Phillips was a good kid—maybe twenty-five or twenty-six. Married with a two-year-old. He had a four-year degree in criminal justice. A year into law school, he'd decided to become a cop instead.

He was decent officer—a little impatient, but that came

with his age. He was well liked and had no trouble working with female bosses. That was one of Garrick's tests of new recruits—have them report to a woman. New hires tended to come to the job either cautious and willing to learn or arrogant as hell. Garrick wanted to weed out the jerks as quickly as possible. Happily Inc wasn't a big metropolitan area. The force was meant to be part of the community, not an adversary.

Phillips had done well with everyone he worked with. The only negative reports were that he kept to himself a little more than was socially acceptable for such a close-knit group.

Phillips glanced at his hands, then up at Garrick. He cleared his throat. "I wanted to let you know that I'm, ah, gonna be moving out of my house. I'll be staying with a friend for a few weeks while things get straightened out at home."

Garrick's radar lit up and his body tensed. Trouble on the home front was never good, but in a kid this young, with a baby, it could be a disaster.

He got up and closed the door, then resumed his seat. "I'm sorry to hear that. What seems to be the problem?"

Phillips looked startled by the question. "Just some personal stuff."

Garrick waited. Phillips had come to him. He could have moved out without saying anything, but he hadn't, which led Garrick to believe he wanted advice rather than to make an announcement.

"Angie's being so difficult," he said, his jaw tightening as he spoke. "When I get home from work, I'm tired. All she wants to do is talk to me. I need time to unwind, but I don't get a second. She's always asking me questions and wanting me to take care of the baby. It's not that I don't love her and Bailey, it's just, I can't be her entertainment every second I'm not working. She's complaining we're not going to have any family with us for Thanksgiving. It will just be the three of us." He looked away. "Maybe marrying her was a mistake. It's too much."

Garrick took in the information, trying to decide how to handle the situation. With some men, it helped to berate them into seeing sense. Others needed to be led to the truth.

"You and Angie moved here from where?" he asked.

"New Mexico."

"That's a long way from home. Does she have a big family there?"

Phillips nodded. "A couple of sisters, her folks, all her friends. She was a nurse there, but with Bailey and all, she hasn't had time to get her license here."

Garrick leaned back in his chair, his posture relaxed. "You moved your wife away from her family, her home and her job to a town where she doesn't know anyone. She's caring for your daughter twenty-four hours a day, and when you get home, she wants to have a conversation with you and have you take part in raising the child that is half yours. At the same time, you have a new career that is interesting and meets all your social needs. You're going and doing all day long, so much so that when you pull into the driveway, you just want to be left alone. Do I have that right, Phillips?"

The officer flushed. "It's not like that."

"Isn't it? Tell me what I got wrong."

"She wanted to come here, too. It wasn't my decision."

"And why is that? To further her own career?"

Phillips looked away. "To help me with mine."

"Do you love her?"

Phillips pulled his head back to stare at Garrick. "What?"

"Do you still love your wife?"

"Of course I do. It's just—"

Garrick held up a hand. "No. Whatever you're going to say, don't. It'll only make you look bad." He leaned close. "Here's the thing. You're an idiot. You're married to a smart woman who had a great career. She gave that up for you. She moved to a strange place where she has absolutely no support system, for you. The way I see it, the woman gave up pretty much all she had and here you are, complaining like a little boy."

"I'm not complaining."

Garrick let the words hang there for a second before speaking.

"Don't move out like some indecisive whiner. Man up or let her go."

Phillips's eyes widened. "Let her go? You mean divorce her?"

"Why not? It would solve all your problems. She could move back home and be with people who actually love her. You won't have to deal with your wife and kid. Didn't you just tell me getting married was a mistake? So undo it. Sure, your daughter will grow up without you, but hey, that's the price of freedom, right? Besides, if Angie is all you say she is, she won't be single long. Bailey will have a new dad, and you won't have to worry about her at all."

Phillips balled his hands into fists. "Sir, I don't want a divorce. I don't want her leaving. Why would you say that?"

"I think the bigger question is why aren't you on your knees every damn day saying a prayer of gratitude that you have a woman willing to do what she did for you? A woman raising *your* kid, taking care of everything while you live out your dream job. She wants to talk, then you talk. She wants you to take care of your daughter, you say thank you for the privilege of spending time with the most amazing human being you've had the good fortune to have in your life. Give Angie flowers, hire a babysitter and take her out to dinner. Talk to some of the guys you work with and find out who would like to have you three with them for Thanksgiving. I'd say invite them to your place, but that's just more work for your wife. Take time off work so Angie can do what she needs to do to be licensed in California. Make this right, Phillips, or I will start to think you're not the man I thought you were."

Garrick waited, not sure if he'd gone too far or not. He knew that a few of his HR professors wouldn't approve of his style, but he was okay with that. He had a feeling Phillips didn't want a divorce—he just needed to see what he was so blithely tossing in the trash. And if Garrick was wrong, well, he would deal with that, too.

Phillips stared at him. "I've screwed up with her, haven't I? I messed up everything. I made her feel awful. You're right. She's been so great this whole time. I know she's lonely—anyone would be. I have to do better." Tears filled his eyes. "I don't want to lose her. I don't want her to leave me."

Garrick pointed to the door. "Then go fix this. Take the rest of the day off and make things right with your wife. I'll see you tomorrow, Phillips."

The kid nodded as he sprang to his feet and ran to the door. "Thanks, Captain."

Garrick nodded, watching him go.

Hopefully the situation would work out between them. Thinking about Phillips and his wife made Garrick feel old and maybe a little bit broken. It was easy to give someone else advice, but much harder to know what to do yourself. He'd screwed up with his daughter, and he still had no idea what had gone wrong. His marriage to Sandy had failed, although there it was easier to see how things had turned and why they didn't make it. As for Raine…

He drew in a breath, determined not to get caught up in the past again. It was done and there was no do-over allowed. Knowing what he knew now, he would have walked away as soon as he figured out the truth—assignment be damned. But he hadn't had the benefit of foresight, so he'd gone on thinking he could handle it. That somehow he would keep it all from being a disaster. And then she'd died.

She'd died because she'd broken the rules. Their undercover fake relationship was never supposed to be more than a means to an end. They weren't supposed to cross that line, and while he hadn't, she had and in the end, she'd paid with her life.

chapter three

"It was so gross, Mom," Hunter said cheerfully as he unpacked pots and pan from the box and put them on the counter. "Jimmy threw up everywhere. His desk, the floor. He barfed all over Penny and she started crying. Then a couple of other kids barfed, and everyone started screaming and running out of the classroom."

Wynn did her best not to picture the event. She was feeling perfectly fine and wanted to keep it that way. "What had he eaten?"

"An egg salad sandwich he'd had in his locker for three days!" Hunter sounded both shocked and impressed. "He said it smelled funny, and I told him to throw it out because you always said stuff with mayonnaise has to be kept cold, but he didn't listen."

"While I live to be proven right, I'm sorry about what happened."

"The room still smells. We had to move to another classroom. They took Jimmy to the hospital. Byron texted and said he's okay. They'll keep him overnight and let him go home in the morning."

"I feel sorry for your teacher. That isn't something anyone wants to deal with."

Hunter finished emptying the box. He flattened it and added it to the pile. "The person we should feel bad about is the janitor. He has to clean it all up."

"An excellent point," Wynn said, making a mental note to stop and get the janitor a Starbucks gift card on her way to work in the morning. "That's not an easy job."

"Especially when teenagers do dumb stuff like that."

She held in a smile. "I'm glad you see it that way."

Her handsome, fourteen-year-old son grinned at her. "I'm maturing, Mom."

"I can tell."

Hunter reached for a box of flatware. They were spending the afternoon at Garrick's house, unpacking all the purchases while she waited on the furniture delivery. She had an easy week and had offered to accept the delivery scheduled between three and six. She already had the sheets in the dryer and a load of dishes going through the dishwasher.

She didn't mind being neighborly, but she had to admit it felt a little strange to be in Garrick's house, which was why she'd asked Hunter to help her with the unpacking. Having her kid around made the situation a little less weird. Plus now that he was, as he'd put it, "maturing," she didn't see him as much as she used to.

"Aside from the throwing up thing, it was a good day?" she asked.

"Uh-huh. I did great on my algebra test. I might even get an A."

"Impressive."

He glanced at her from the corner of his eye. "I was

thinking, I need to be more responsible around the house and stuff."

Wynn carefully put down the mixing bowls she'd just unpacked and tried not to shriek, *You are an alien! What have you done with my son?*

"In what way?" she asked, careful to keep her tone conversational rather than incredulous.

"Like I said, I'm older now and I should be a more well-rounded human being. Maybe help out in the community."

She busied herself flattening the box so her shock wouldn't show. "Okay, what does that mean in English?"

Hunter laughed. "I want to start volunteering, Mom. You know, doing some good. I want to talk to Carol and see if she needs help at the animal preserve. My science class went there last semester after the baby giraffe was born. It was supercool."

"Carol always has work for volunteers," she told him. "She holds orientation classes every few months, and people sign up to help feed the animals or clean up after them. It's not glamorous work."

Hunter surprised her by smiling. "Mom, if it was glamorous, they wouldn't need volunteers."

"Let's go there over the holiday break," she said. "You can talk to her and get a feel for the work. If you still want to volunteer after that, we'll look into the necessary steps."

"Thanks, Mom."

The dryer buzzed. Wynn left Hunter unpacking the rest of their purchases. She walked into the laundry room and put the clean sheets into the basket and moved the towels from the washer to the dryer.

Once she'd started the dryer, she went into what would be Joylyn's room and started making the bed. The sheets were soft and the pillows fluffy. Wynn smoothed the blanket into place, then tucked in the edges and reached for the comforter. She'd just flipped it onto the bed when Garrick walked into the bedroom.

"Hi," he said, smiling at her.

He looked good, she thought, taking in the dark hair, gray eyes and the perfectly fitting uniform. Really good. Swoon-worthy good.

Nerve endings started a conga line in her belly and began hopping and cheering all through her body. Heat flared, not wanting the nerves to get all the attention.

"Hi, yourself," she managed to say, pleased that her voice didn't crack.

"I was able to move a few things around on my calendar and get home a little earlier than I'd thought." He smiled again. "I still can't believe you took off work to help me with the delivery."

She smiled. "Happy to do it. So far, no large truck has pulled into the driveway, so you haven't missed the excitement."

"Let me go change my clothes, and I'll join you to finish up what needs to be done."

She nodded, afraid that if she tried to speak she would offer to help with the whole changing thing, and that would just be embarrassing for both of them. Well, not if he didn't say no, but what were the odds?

Once he'd left, she drew in a couple of deep breaths to calm herself, then went back to work on the bed. With the throw pillows in place, she folded a blanket across the foot and smoothed it.

The space was calming, she thought. Light came in through two large windows. The bed frame was beautiful, the bedding complementing the exquisite carving. There was plenty of storage space in the dresser, and Wynn had remembered to buy hangers on Sunday so the closet was good to go. Joylyn had a TV on her dresser and a nice desk in the corner where Wynn had placed a couple of paper turkeys along with a little fabric gourd to remind Joylyn of the season.

Across the way, the bathroom looked welcoming. There were new rugs in front of the sink and the toilet. Soap, body wash and a loofah were placed on the shelf in the walk-in shower. She still had to hang the prints they'd bought and add the towels when they were out of the dryer, but otherwise, the bathroom was practically picture perfect.

She returned to the kitchen. Hunter had finished unpacking everything.

"I'm going to take the boxes out to the recycling bin," he said, picking up the stack.

"Thanks. After that, would you like to head home?"

He glanced longingly toward their place. "I have homework I want to do before dinner."

"Then go do it and thank you for your help."

He grinned at her and bolted for the back door. Wynn chuckled as she began measuring shelf paper.

"Put me to work," Garrick told her as he walked into the kitchen.

She ignored how good he looked in jeans and a T-shirt. "Hunter and I have unpacked all the kitchen stuff." She motioned to the stacks of dishes, pots and pans and utensils on the counter. "The first load is already in the dishwasher. Once that's done, these have to be put through a quick wash cycle. The bed is made, the towels are in the dryer and I'm about to put shelf paper in the cupboards."

"I was going to ask Jasper and Cade to come help with all this, but you've already finished it." He gave her lopsided grin. "I'm going to owe you big time."

"Yes, you are, but no doubt some roof or plumbing crisis is looming in my life and you can help with that."

"I will be there." He made an X over his heart. "Until then, what can I do? Want me to measure? Cut? Place? Sweep?"

She laughed. "No sweeping until we're done. Why don't you—"

She paused when she heard the sound of a big truck pulling up in front of the house.

"Why don't you go deal with the delivery and I'll keep doing this?" she said.

"Consider it done."

He walked toward the front door. Wynn watched him go, thinking the more she got to know her neighbor, the more she liked him. Which was both happy news and just a little terrifying.

Garrick stood in the center of his kitchen and took in the changes. A table and chairs stood in front of the big windows facing the front of the house. Some tall plant-tree thing was in the corner, the red and black of the decorative pot picking up the colors of the chair cushions. There were place mats on the table, along with an odd little gnome salt-shaker. Sadly there had been an unfortunate unpacking accident with the pepper gnome, but Wynn had said he could buy a small pepper grinder to replace it.

Behind him, the cupboards were full of dishes and pots and pans, while the drawers held flatware, spatulas, knives and other things he couldn't identify. The Betty Boop canister set sat on the counter.

Small changes that made all the difference, he thought. It was the old cliché about a woman's touch—especially a woman with style. The right woman. He'd noticed the same thing after Jasper and Renee had gotten together. Subtle additions to Jasper's house had transformed it into a home. The same with Cade and Bethany. The old ranch house was more welcoming now.

He wasn't sure how women made that happen. He supposed it was an attention to detail that came with an ability to nurture. He'd been a good dad to Joylyn, but he'd been focused on her, not the surroundings.

He moved to the living room where two big abstract prints dominated the wall behind the sofa. There were more plants and a couple of vase things. Down the hall, Joylyn's bathroom was fully stocked with towels and shower stuff and soap. A new heating pad sat on the counter.

He walked to the bedroom. The sense of empty furniture with no purpose had been replaced by something more warm. And cozy, he thought with a smile. Fluffy pillows covered nearly half the bed. Fairy prints decorated the wall. The drawers were lined, the closet filled with hangers. The last touch, a rotary dial phone he'd found a couple of years back and had bought for his daughter, was on the desk.

He stared at the plain black phone and wondered if she would remember how much she'd loved rotary dial phones when she'd been a kid. Whenever they'd taken their road trips, she'd always run into the coffee shops they'd stopped in and checked out the public phone, hoping to find a rotary dial one.

Things had been much simpler then, he thought to himself. His relationship with Joylyn had been easy—filled with love and laughter. Now they rarely spoke and she almost never answered his texts.

Hopefully that was going to change, he told himself. Once she got here, they would have a chance to talk. She would understand that he loved her and wanted her to be happy. If he could get through to her, then maybe their relationship could be restored.

He glanced at his watch, then returned to the kitchen where he picked up a bottle of wine before heading next door. On her way out of his place earlier that afternoon, Wynn had invited him over to dinner. At this rate he was going to owe her forever.

As he crossed the driveway and lawn between their houses, he smiled. Maybe she would let him pay her back with some kind of service. Very inappropriate thoughts filled his mind, most of them having to do with Wynn naked and on her back, while he had the delightful task of evening up the score.

He quickly pushed those images away and rang the bell. Seconds later Wynn let him in.

"Hi," he said, holding out the wine. "I hope you like red."

"I'm actually not picky when it comes to wine."

She stepped back to let him in.

He'd been in her house before, when he'd come over to ask for help. Back then he'd been focused on needing to get things right for Joylyn, and he hadn't paid attention to his surroundings. Now he had a moment to take in the differences between their two places.

Her living room was about the same size as his, but there was no massive TV or leather sofa. Her furniture was all fabric covered, done in earth tones of brown, teal and blue. There were rugs on the floor, and a fireplace. Books were stacked on shelves and pictures lined the mantel.

Plants with long vines and dangling leaves nestled with the books, and there were little knickknack thingies all around. A pair of Hunter's shoes were by the door, along with a basket containing reusable grocery bags.

Not his style, he thought, assuming he had a style, but

still nice. Everything felt right and comfortable. The space suited her and he liked being in it.

"Where's the TV?" he asked.

She laughed. "You are such a guy."

"You have to watch sports."

"Technically, I don't, but when I want to watch something, it's in there."

She pointed to a cabinet in the corner. The doors were closed, hiding the TV from view.

"But it's so small. Poor Hunter."

"Yet he continues to thrive."

"Children are so resilient."

She smiled. "If it makes you feel better, we have a family room at the back of the house and there's a much larger TV in there."

"I'll sleep better tonight knowing that."

They passed a large dining room with a big wood table, then went into the kitchen. Here the layout was similar to his. Like the living room, this space had plenty of personal items everywhere, including a *Star Wars* canister set. There was a round wood table with four chairs by the big bay window. A wicker cornucopia decoration overflowed with apples and oranges.

Wynn motioned to one of the stools at the island. "I just need to pull together a salad and dinner will be ready."

As she spoke, she put a tray of rolls into the oven and set the timer, then pulled a corkscrew out of a drawer and handed it to him.

"I made a stew." She pointed to the Crock-Pot on the counter. "It's really easy. I prep everything the night before, then toss it into the pot before I leave for work. When I get home ten hours later, the meal is ready."

He opened the wine, then poured. "You sound like you're strongly hinting at something."

"I am. A Crock-Pot would be good for you. Better than takeout. Plus all the recipes make a lot of food, so you could fill your freezer and have easy dinners later."

He handed her a glass. "You can't help yourself, can you?"

"What do you mean?"

"You're a caretaker. It's nice."

"I'm not. I'm just saying—"

"I'm never going to use a Crock-Pot, Wynn. Or bake."

Amusement danced in her pretty brown eyes. "You're saying I should stop trying to convince you?"

"You can try all you want, but you're destined for disappointment."

"Fine." She touched her glass to his. "I'll say it again. You're such a guy."

"I am."

For a second their gazes locked. Something flashed between them—something with a little sizzle and promise. Or maybe that was wishful thinking on his part.

Once again he wanted to bury his hands in her curly hair, only this time the image had a little more detail to it. He didn't just want to feel the softness of the curl, he wanted to cup her head and draw her close and kiss her until…

She turned away. "I should start on that salad."

He carried the wine bottle over to the table, then returned to his seat at the island.

"How do you do it all?" he asked. "You got Hunter off to school, went to work yourself, were at my house by three, unpacked everything, washed it, and here you are, making dinner."

She waved away the compliment. "I was happy to help.

As for the rest of it, that's a regular day. I'll admit when Hunter was younger, there were times when I didn't think I could keep it all together, but now it's much easier. He takes care of a lot of things himself. Sometimes he even does his own laundry."

"Impressive."

"I want him to be a good boyfriend and husband with a reasonable set of skills." She grinned. "I never want to catch my future daughter-in-law looking at me with a 'what were you thinking' expression."

"That's a long-term plan."

"I know, but time goes quickly. You have to know that with Joylyn being married and pregnant."

As she spoke, she pulled out ingredients for salad and put them on the counter.

"It did happen quickly," he admitted.

Just then Hunter ran into the kitchen. "I'm right on time, Mom."

She glanced at Garrick. "He has a way of going down to the minute."

Hunter hurried over to the sink where he washed his hands. "Why be early for chores?"

"We are a work in progress," Wynn murmured.

Garrick listened as the pair teased each other. They had a good relationship, he thought wistfully, remembering when it had been like that for him and Joylyn.

Mother and son worked well together, Hunter setting the table, then pouring himself a large glass of milk. When the timer on the oven dinged, Wynn took out the rolls while Hunter got down a small wooden bowl. He put a cloth napkin in place before handing the bowl to his mother. She dropped in the hot rolls, and he took the finished salad to the table. He carried over the rolls while she ladled out a rich, thick stew.

Once they were seated, Wynn stretched out her hands to him and Hunter. He had a brief impression of soft, warm skin before she bowed her head and softly said grace.

Hunter mumbled a quick "Amen" when she was done, then reached for a roll before passing the bowl to Garrick.

"This is one of my favorite dinners," Hunter told him. "It's really good and there's a lot of it."

Wynn smiled. "He's in the middle of a growth spurt so volume, when it comes to food, is really important."

"I want to be tall, like my dad," Hunter said. "At least six feet. Six-three would be better."

"Six-three is going to be tough," Wynn told him.

"You're tall, Mom. For a girl."

Conversation flowed easily between them. Garrick listened rather than join in, liking the dynamic. He was hoping he and Joylyn would get to be that comfortable together when she moved in. He knew things would be awkward at first, but he was determined to restore his relationship with her.

Less than twenty minutes later, Hunter pushed away his bowl. "I'm done, Mom," he said, his tone faintly pleading.

Wynn held his gaze for a second before sighing heavily. "You used to like to talk to me."

"Mom!"

She laughed. "Fine. Go. Clear your place first, though."

Hunter grabbed his dishes and raced into the kitchen. He dumped them into the sink, started out of the room, stopped, turned back and said, "It was nice to see you again, Garrick," before disappearing down the hall.

Wynn sighed. "Tonight is his computer game night. He gets two a week, and it's a big deal to him."

"I wouldn't want to stand between him and his computer games."

"You'd get run over."

He picked up his glass of wine. "I envy your closeness. Joylyn was only a year older than him when our relationship fell apart."

Wynn looked at him expectantly, but didn't say anything.

"It was about the time my wife and I split up. I asked Joylyn if she was upset by that, but she said she wasn't." He shook his head. "I don't know what happened. One day she was my best girl and the next she refused to see me."

"That must have been really awful."

"It was. I didn't know what to do. Alisha, her mom, said to let her work it out. Looking back on the outcome, I think that was the wrong decision. I should have insisted I have my time with her. Even if she sat there, not speaking to me, I would have still been spending time with her."

"Do you think she was testing you?" Wynn asked.

"I don't know. I never thought of that." He frowned. "She knew I loved her, so I'm not sure why she would want confirmation."

"People get strange ideas about things. Maybe you can talk about it when she's here."

"That's what I thought. We'll be in the same house, so we'll have to communicate."

Wynn sipped her wine. "Her baby is due around Christmas?"

"The twenty-fifth is her due date. Alisha said Joylyn's not happy to have her son's birthday so close to the holiday, but there's nothing to be done about it. Aren't first babies usually late? Maybe he'll be born in the new year."

"Not a big difference, but maybe it will help," she said.

"Did Alisha mention how Joylyn feels about being away from home for the holidays? That might be hard for her."

Something he hadn't thought about. "You're right. I'll ask her when we talk. I should probably go all out with the decorating and stuff."

"How much do you usually decorate?"

He thought about his empty house. "Not, you know, a lot."

Her mouth curved up in a smile. "As in none?"

"Yeah. That. I mean I used to, when she was little. I still have all the ornaments we would put on our tree. But that's about it."

"I'll help."

"While I appreciate that, you've already done so much."

"That's what neighbors are for."

"You're going to have to let me build you a bigger back porch or something to make up for everything."

"I think the porch is okay the way it is, but if I think of a good project for you, I'll let you know."

"Please do." He thought about how he and Joylyn had celebrated the holidays. "I need to get some of those paper turkeys. Do they still make them?"

"They do. I put a couple in her room already. Maybe you could get some more gourds and the little pumpkins for a centerpiece. Hunter and I are having a few friends over for Thanksgiving. You and Joylyn are welcome to join us." The amusement returned. "What with you not cooking and all, I honestly can't see you pulling together Thanksgiving dinner. No offense meant."

"None taken." He lightly touched her arm. "Thank you. I mean it. Thank you for everything."

For a second he would swear her gaze dropped to his mouth. He told himself he was imagining things—or getting caught up in wishful thinking—a theory proven when she said, "The holidays nearly always mean a plumbing emergency. If that happens here, you should expect me to remind you of what you owe me."

"I will keep my toolbox handy."

Joylyn Kaberline pulled open the drawer and grabbed clothes by the armful. She carried them to the open suitcase on her bed and shoved them inside, pausing only to wipe the tears from her eyes.

"I understand you're upset," her mother said from her place in the doorway. "Please don't be mad."

There wasn't a part of Joylyn that didn't hurt. Her back ached constantly, her feet hurt because her ankles were swollen. Her butt hurt because she was getting hemorrhoids, her eyes were gritty because she wasn't sleeping. But most of all, her heart was broken. Not only was she in her eighth month of her pregnancy, her husband was thousands of miles away, deployed. While he was supposed to get home before her Christmas due date, they weren't sure that was going to happen. And because that wasn't enough suckatude in her life, her very own mother had thrown her out of the house.

Joylyn sniffed. "Don't be mad, but don't let the door hit me in the ass on my way out."

"Joylyn, please."

"Please what? Stay? We wouldn't want that. Why would you want your only daughter around in the final months of her pregnancy? Better that I go live with my father because that's going to go well. I wonder if he'll bother to look up from his life enough to notice that I'm even there."

Her mother, a pretty blonde, sighed heavily. "Your father is very excited about having you stay with him."

"None of us believe that, Mom. You don't want me here. Just admit it."

Joylyn brushed away more tears. All she did these days was cry and hurt. She loved Chandler, but maybe everyone had been right. Maybe they had gotten married too young. Even if that hadn't been a mistake, she'd accidentally gotten pregnant. They'd wanted to wait, but the stick had turned blue and now she was going to have a baby. She was twenty-one years old—it was all too much.

"You know you've had a problem with the boys," her mother said quietly. "They're really bugging you."

Joylyn ignored that. Yes, her half brothers were loud and messy and drove her crazy, but she'd never thought complaining about them would cause her to be banished.

"You'll be here for Christmas," her mother offered. "Chandler gets home from his deployment the week before, and he'll drive you back here."

Yes, that was the reward that was supposed to make up for what was happening, Joylyn thought bitterly. If she went quietly and stayed with her father, then gosh, golly, the week before Christmas, she was allowed to come home.

"If I really behave, maybe I'll get some gruel to go with my bread and water."

Her mother shook her head. "Joylyn, it's not a punishment."

"What would you call it? You're sending me away, Mom. You're forcing me to leave. I'm going to miss Thanksgiving and all our traditions before Christmas. I'm getting ready to have a baby, all on my own. I'm going to be by myself at my birthing classes."

"I wanted to go with you months ago, but you kept putting it off."

"Because I thought there was time. It never occurred to

me that you'd be kicking me out. I still can't believe it. I can't believe you're sending me away. It's horrible and I'll never forgive you. Whatever happens for the rest of our lives, you will always have done this to me."

Her mother's expression was weary. "I'm sorry you feel that way."

But she wasn't sorry enough, Joylyn thought, her anger fading as sadness took its place. Nothing was going to change—her mother was tossing her out on the street, and the only person willing to take her in was her father. She was going to have to go live in some hideous little town where she knew no one, and then she was going to have a baby.

All her friends were in college or back on base in San Diego, and her husband was on the other side of the planet. Joylyn had thought she could count on her mom to be there for her, but she'd been wrong about that.

Fear joined the other emotions swirling inside her. More tears fell. She waited for her mom to walk over and give her a hug, but she didn't. When Joylyn turned back to the doorway, she saw her mother was gone and she was alone.

chapter four

Wynn sat on the porch next to Garrick. They were close enough that their shoulders brushed every now and then. She felt foolish for noticing but so what? No one had to know about her borderline schoolgirl crush on her hunky neighbor.

"Nervous?" she asked.

Garrick kept his gaze on the street in front of the house. "Yes. Excited, too." He glanced at his watch. "She should be here by now."

"Don't start worrying. She's not late. Pregnant women have to pee a lot. I'm sure she's made at least three stops on the drive from Phoenix."

His mouth twisted. "I shouldn't have let her come out by herself. I should have driven out to Phoenix, then brought her here. What if something happened?"

"What if something didn't?" She smiled at him. "Let's wait for the crisis before we panic."

"You're not panicked at all."

"It's important that one of us stay rational."

He drew in a breath. "You're right. Did I mention I'm nervous?"

"You did. It's going to be okay."

She hoped she wasn't lying about that, Wynn thought, not sure how Joylyn's visit was going to go. She didn't understand why Garrick's daughter would have suddenly refused to see her father. Maybe she'd been in a snit for a few weeks, but surely that would have blown over. And where was her mother in all this? There was no way Wynn would have let Hunter act that way. Family was family. Even if things were difficult, you made it work. Of course that was easy for her to say—Hunter was her only family. She wouldn't turn her back on him regardless of what he did. Nor would she let him turn from her. But she knew it was easy to have an opinion when she wasn't intimately involved in the situation.

A light blue Prius pulled into the driveway. Garrick was instantly on his feet.

"That's her."

He crossed to the car in three long strides and pulled open the door. A very pregnant young woman slowly got out.

"Hi," he said with a smile. "How was the drive?"

Joylyn was pretty, with blue eyes and medium brown hair. Her eyes were red, and if Wynn had to guess, she would say that Joylyn had spent much of the drive in tears.

She looked at her father without returning his smile. "How do you think it was? Awful. My back hurts, my feet are swollen and every driver on the road is an idiot. I can't believe I'm going to be stuck here until Chandler gets home."

Garrick took a step back. Wynn saw the confusion on

his face, followed by hurt that he quickly hid. She stood and approached them.

"Hi," she said, holding out her hand. "I'm Wynn, your neighbor to the south." She shook hands with Joylyn. "Look at you. You're what? In your eighth month?" She grimaced. "Your back's a mess, huh? I have a fourteen-year-old, but I still remember how much my back hurt toward the end of my pregnancy. What works for you, ice or heat?"

Joylyn looked startled by the question. "Uh, heat."

"For me, too. There's a heating pad in the bathroom. It's the extra big kind so you can cover a lot of area." She smiled. "Your dad came to me for advice so he'd have what you'd need to be comfortable. Be sure to tell me if I forgot anything."

"Thank you."

Garrick moved closer. "Let me show you around. You must be tired from the drive."

Her expression returned to peevish. Wynn expected another outburst, but she only pressed her lips together and stared pointedly at the house.

Garrick quickly added, "I'm really glad you're here, Joylyn. You look great."

"I look hideous and I feel worse. Being pregnant sucks." With that, she pushed past them and walked into the house.

Wynn glanced at Garrick, not sure what to say. He had to feel terrible about what had just happened. From an outsider's perspective, Joylyn was trying to be as difficult as possible.

"Don't take it personally," she said quietly. "It seems like she's mad at the world."

"I'm part of that."

"Maybe, but right now she's lashing out. Try not to engage."

He looked at the house. "I really want her here. She's my daughter."

"Keep telling yourself that."

He nodded, then collected the luggage and carried it inside. Wynn followed, a sinking sensation filling her chest. Joylyn stood in the middle of the living room.

"Why aren't there any Christmas decorations?" she asked. "Are you planning on ignoring the holiday? In case you've forgotten, it's my favorite time of year." Tears filled her eyes. "Or are you going to ruin that, too?"

He put down the suitcases. "It's a couple of weeks until Thanksgiving. We never decorate for Christmas until the Saturday after, and we don't get the tree until at least ten days into December. Honey, I remember all of our traditions and I want to enjoy them with you, like we used to. I'm glad you're here."

She responded by sighing heavily. "Which room is mine?"

"The one across from the bathroom."

Without saying anything else, she walked away. Seconds later a door slammed. Garrick stared after her.

"She hates me. I'm screwed."

Wynn privately agreed, but knew saying that out loud wouldn't help the situation. "What did her mom say when she asked if Joylyn could stay here?"

"She said the boys were a problem." He looked at Wynn. "Alisha's three boys are between the ages of fifteen and eleven."

"Yikes. That *would* be a lot for Joylyn to deal with."

"That's what Alisha said when she asked if Joylyn could come here."

Wynn wondered what Alisha hadn't told him. "Did she mention her attitude at all?"

"No, although Joylyn seems really upset."

"Like I said, it's not personal." But it was going to be a problem.

"She's still mad at me and I don't know why."

"It's been six years, Garrick. A lot has happened. Give her a little time to adjust."

He glanced down the hall. "I will. I just hope…" He shook his head and turned to Wynn. "You've been great and I appreciate all your help, but I've got this."

She knew that he was giving her a polite escape, but wasn't sure he was going to be all right on his own. From Wynn's point of view, Joylyn was making things more difficult than they needed to be.

"Tell you what," she said. "I have to do my weekly grocery shopping today. Why don't I pick up some steaks and chicken and a few salads? You and Joylyn can come over. You'll man the barbecue and I'll ask Hunter to try to make friends with your daughter. I know there's a big age difference, but she's used to teens his age. Plus she might want to play video games with him or something. I know he'd love an extra night of playing."

Garrick's gaze met hers. She saw both desperation and gratitude. "You don't have to do that."

"I want to help. Plus the wine you brought last time was really good."

He surprised her by wrapping his arms around her and hugging her tight. The unexpected contact flustered her a little—not that she was complaining. Being close to a big, strong man was really nice. He was warm and solid and he smelled good. She relaxed in his embrace and put her arms around his waist, wishing the act had been fueled by a little bit more than gratitude.

"Thank you," he said, resting his chin on her head and proving her point. "I mean it. Thank you."

Tingles began floating through her body. If he kept up the hugging, she would pretty much agree to anything.

"You're welcome."

He released her.

For a second she didn't want to let go, but figured he had enough on his mind without dealing with her wayward advances. In his present state of distraction, he might not even notice if she came on to him, and she doubted her ego was up to that kind of rejection.

She stepped back. "Feel free to show up early. Anytime after four. And if you and Joylyn work things out and want a quiet dinner alone, just text me and let me know."

His mouth twisted. "I don't see that happening."

She didn't, either, but you never knew. "Think positive and know that if nothing changes, you have a steak to look forward to." She smiled. "And pie."

He raised his eyebrows. "Pie?"

"I'm in the mood to make one. I'm thinking berry."

"Is there anything you can't do?"

"I have flaws, but I like to keep them hidden." Along with a couple of secrets from her past, she thought as she waved and headed for the front door.

Joylyn sat at the desk in the bedroom, trying not to give in to the rising panic she felt in her chest. No matter how much she felt as if she'd been exiled, she wasn't trapped and she wasn't in prison. She could leave anytime she wanted.

Not that she had anywhere to go, she thought, wiping the tears from her cheeks and wondering if it was possible to cry so much that a person got dehydrated. No matter how she felt, no matter how alone or scared or rejected, she had to remember the baby and do her best to do right by her son.

She placed her hand on her belly, trying not to think about the fact that if she wasn't pregnant, she wouldn't be suffering like this now. She would be back in San Diego, going to college and working part-time. She would still be missing Chandler, counting the days until he was home, but everything else would be easier.

If only she hadn't panicked, she thought regretfully. She could have stayed on base and continued living her life. Except once Chandler had left, she'd gotten scared. She'd felt so alone that moving back in with her mom had made the most sense. But that hadn't worked out, what with her brothers and having no support system. Her mom was busy with her new family—she hadn't had time for Joylyn. And then her mother had thrown her out.

Her phone buzzed. Joylyn picked it up and read the text from her friend Holly.

You get there okay?

At least someone remembered she was alive, she thought.

I'm here and it's awful. I should never have left San Diego.

What did your dad say?

Nothing.

He's not happy to see you?

Why would he be? He basically ignored me for years. He's only letting me stay because he doesn't have a choice.

Joylyn, give him a chance to explain. He's your dad.

Probably good advice, Joylyn thought, not that she would take it. Holly didn't have a father, so she looked at things differently. She was always telling Joylyn to give her dad the benefit of the doubt.

A subject change seemed in order. How are things in SD?

Good. Rex is being especially sweet. I wish he wasn't going away.

Rex was Holly's boyfriend. They were both Marines and had been dating about a year. Joylyn had met Holly two days after Chandler started working with her. He hadn't wanted his new wife to worry about his female coworker and had brought her home to dinner. Joylyn and Holly had become friends in maybe twenty seconds.

It's hard when they're deployed, Joylyn typed.

You know that one, don't you? I gotta go, but I'm thinking of you. Kisses to my favorite baby.

Joylyn smiled at that and sent back a baby and a heart emoji. As she put her cell on the desk, she noticed an old, black rotary dial phone. Despite everything, she smiled. Where on earth had her dad found one? They were practically extinct.

She'd always loved the stupid things when she'd been a kid. She'd looked for them in old diners or bowling alleys and had kept a log of where she found them.

She rested her fingers on the dial. Things had been easier back then. Simpler. She and her dad had been tight—

a team in a way. No matter what, she knew he would be there for her.

Not anymore, she thought grimly.

She rose and looked around the room. It was a nice size, with a pretty four-poster bed. There was a dresser and matching nightstands. The comforter was nice, and there were lots of pillows.

She thought about lying down and taking a nap, but decided it was too late in the day. She was already having trouble sleeping at night. Better to be tired for a little longer.

She opened her tote bag and took out a little Winnie the Pooh music box. When she and Chandler had discovered they were having a boy, they'd spent nearly a month trying to figure out the theme for their baby's room. Eventually they'd settled on Winnie the Pooh, done in light blue and pale yellow. Right after that, she'd found the music box and had bought one for herself and had sent one to Chandler.

She'd brought it with her to feel more connected and because she had nowhere to put it. Once Chandler returned, they could move back into base housing, but right now she was pretty much homeless.

And stuck, she thought. Stuck where she didn't want to be.

She rested her hand on her belly. "It's just you and me, little one. I swear, no matter what, I will never do to you what your grandmother did to me."

She felt the baby stir. The baby with no name, she thought, smiling. "Once you're born we'll name you," she whispered. "Your dad and I have a list of names, but we want to see you first. We love you very much."

She left the bedroom and walked into the living room. Her dad was still there, hovering by her luggage. He looked a little stunned, which almost made her feel bad. She knew she was being awful, but so what? He deserved it.

"Could you bring my bags in?" she asked, carefully avoiding looking at him.

Her dad picked them up as if they weighed nothing and started down the hall. When they were in place, on the bed, he turned back to her.

"Joylyn, what's wrong? Why are you so mad at me? I meant what I said—I'm happy you're here. I want us to be close again, but I don't know what happened."

For a second she wanted to say it didn't matter and throw herself into his arms, the way she had when she'd been little. But she didn't—partly because she was still mad and partly because she didn't know if he would catch her and hold her tight. He'd let her go so easily before. Why should she think he cared about her now?

"What happened is you abandoned me, emotionally and physically. You went away. One day you were there and then you were gone. Wow—that's what Mom did, too, just now. Is this part of a master plan?"

His confusion was nearly comical. "I never abandoned you. *You* refused to see me. You told me you didn't want anything to do with me. I showed up week after week and you slammed the door in my face."

"So? You're the parent. You're not supposed to give up. If you cared, why didn't you *make* me hang out with you? Why didn't you insist I stay with you on the weekends? You could have forced me, but you didn't. You were happy to have your time back. You never wanted to spend time with me."

She felt tears forming and willed them away. The ache in her back got a little worse, but she ignored that, too.

"That's not true. I wanted our time together. That was

important to me." He stared at her. "Joylyn, you're my daughter and I love you. I've always loved you."

"Oh, please. You disappeared for weeks at a time. When you came back, you weren't interested in me at all. Then you went away again for like a year."

"I was working."

"On some secret assignment. I know. As if." The man worked for the Phoenix Police Department. What kind of "secret assignment" would have taken him out of the city? "You could have seen me if you wanted to."

"Joylyn, I wasn't around because of my job."

She held up her hand. "Whatever. I don't want to hear it. Fine. You were working, but what about later? When you were back. You didn't want anything to do with me. You moved away, leaving Phoenix for this crappy town."

His confusion deepened. "I continued to show up every weekend until you left for college. I tried to see you a few times in San Diego, and you were always busy. You told me to stop bugging you. Why would you care that I left Phoenix?"

She didn't have an answer for that. Or any of it.

"If you wanted to see me, you only had to tell me," he said quietly. "I would have been there."

"I didn't," she said, pointing to the doorway. "I have to unpack and I'd like to be alone."

He hesitated. For a second she thought maybe he was just going to grab her and hug her. Longing swept through her. She needed a familiar Dad hug that would ease the ache in her heart and let her think everything was going to be okay. But instead of pulling her close, he simply walked out of the room and shut the door. The tears returned as she realized nothing had changed. Her dad was willing to be there for her when it was easy but the second it got hard, he walked away.

* * *

The distance between his house and Wynn's had never seemed so long, Garrick thought as he led the way, Joylyn trailing behind him. He was confused, angry, hurt and a dozen other emotions he couldn't name. Most of the time he didn't care that he was a typical guy with a limited vocabulary to describe his emotional life, but every decade or so he thought maybe women were smarter with their ability to understand what they were feeling. Although given how badly things were going with his daughter, maybe ignorance was the safer path.

Since he'd delivered her luggage, she'd ignored him, keeping to her room and refusing his offers of food. When he'd knocked on her closed door to mention dinner with Wynn and Hunter, she'd surprised him by agreeing to join him. His first thought had been disappointment that he wasn't going to escape her for a few hours. That had led to guilt and other feelings he couldn't name and here he was, walking up Wynn's porch and hoping she could make some sense of the situation.

Wynn opened the door seconds after he knocked. Relief swept through him as he stared into her beautiful eyes.

Help me, he mouthed.

She smiled but didn't say anything as she turned her attention to Joylyn.

"How are you feeling?" she asked. "Achy?"

Joylyn nodded. "The drive was really hard."

"I'll bet. Did you take a walk this afternoon? The movement might help."

"I didn't think about that." Joylyn shot him a glare. "I had other stuff on my mind."

He wanted to protest he hadn't done anything wrong,

but knew there was no point. Rather than say anything, he walked into the house and greeted Hunter.

"This is my daughter, Joylyn. Joylyn, this is Hunter."

"Hey," Hunter said, staring at her belly. "You're going to have a baby. No one told me that."

"He's due on Christmas Day."

Hunter's whole face lit up. "That's great. A Christmas baby! That happens all the time in the movies, so it's kind of a thing. And, you know, Baby Jesus."

Joylyn laughed. "Baby Jesus is a lot to live up to."

Wynn touched Joylyn's arm. "We're going to barbecue chicken and steak. I have several salads to choose from, so you should find something that tastes good and sits well in your stomach. There's plenty of time. Would you like to take a walk now? Just a short one? Hunter will go with you."

Joylyn glanced at the teen. "You sure?"

Hunter nodded. "I wouldn't want you getting lost. Plus Mom said you have brothers around my age. We'll figure out something to talk about."

"A walk would be nice," she said, and they headed for the door.

When they were gone, Garrick followed Wynn into the kitchen and collapsed on one of the island stools. "You're amazing."

Her gaze was sympathetic. "That bad?"

"Worse. She hates me. She practically said it. She blames me for not seeing her when she was in high school. I pointed out that I showed up every week and she slammed the door in my face, but that doesn't seem to count for anything. I called Alisha."

Wynn got a beer out of the refrigerator and handed it to him. "What did she say?"

He took a couple of big gulps before setting down the

bottle. "She admitted she hadn't been honest with me when she asked if Joylyn could stay with me." He looked at Wynn. "Apparently the problem isn't the boys, it's our daughter. She's turned into, and this is a direct quote from her mother, 'a raving bitch with psychotic tendencies.' Nothing makes her happy, she's unreasonable, demanding and horrible to be around. Alisha couldn't stand her anymore and sent her here."

Wynn's eyes widened. "That's not happy news."

"I agree, but what can I do about it? I can't throw her out. Despite how she's acting, I don't want to get rid of her. I love her. I just wish she wasn't so difficult."

"I want to say Alisha should have warned you, but I'm sure she was afraid you wouldn't agree to let Joylyn come stay."

"Being prepared might have made a difference, but I doubt it. Right now Joylyn is mad at the world."

And him. He supposed he should be grateful that some of her attitude wasn't personal, but it didn't feel that way. The great relationship they'd had before had been lost, and he still didn't know how to get it back.

"She is dealing with a lot," Wynn said. "She's newly married, pregnant and her husband is deployed. That would be hard on anyone."

"I don't know why she didn't stay on base in San Diego. She had friends there and support from the other Marine wives. Going back to live with her mom isolated her."

"She's stuck now." Wynn's tone was sympathetic. "And now you are, too."

He appreciated the understanding, but before he could say anything, the front door opened.

"We're back," Hunter called. "We saw Jackson's new

puppy. It's a Great Dane. She's really big already and her feet are huge."

Garrick glanced at his daughter and was relieved to see her eyes were bright with amusement. "They said she would be over a hundred pounds when she was grown. That's a lot of dog."

Hunter grinned. "That's a lot of poop to pick up."

Wynn sighed. "You're never going to outgrow the bathroom humor, are you?"

"Nope." He waggled his eyebrows. "Sorry, Mom. You should be used to it by now."

"I keep hoping for improvement."

"Not gonna happen. Oh, Mom! Joylyn plays Fortnite. Can we go play before dinner?"

"Sure."

He took a step, then glanced at her. "Does this count as part of my game time for the week?"

"No. You may have a guest exception."

Joylyn made a fist and gently hit Hunter in the upper arm. "Girls rule, boys drool."

"It's not because you're a girl," he said, leading the way back to the family room. "It's because you're a guest. And I don't drool."

"You do in your sleep."

"Na-uh."

Their voices faded as they entered the family room. Garrick stared after them for a couple of seconds before looking at Wynn.

"She's transformed."

"For the moment. I'm sure she feels better after moving around and Hunter's good company, but I wouldn't hold my breath thinking it will last."

He knew she was right. "At least I know the real Joylyn is buried in there somewhere. It gives me hope." All he had to do was figure out how to reach her. Maybe then they could talk and their relationship could be restored.

Wynn sighed. "You look optimistic."

"I have a sunny disposition."

She laughed. "Even if that's true, I would remind you to be cautious. And maybe learn how to play computer games."

chapter five

Tuesday morning Wynn woke up a few minutes before her alarm. It was still dark outside and the room felt a little cool. Winter, she thought, standing and stretching. At least as much of a winter as Happily Inc ever got. Not that she'd ever experienced real winter. Oakland, California, where she'd grown up, also had temperate winters.

She used the bathroom, then brushed her teeth before walking toward the kitchen. As she turned on the coffeepot she'd prepped the night before, she glanced out of the living room's side window, toward Garrick's house. She hadn't seen him in a couple of days and wondered how things were going with Joylyn. Their dinner together had been relatively pleasant. Hunter was an excellent buffer, and the two got along well. Joylyn had been less pleasant when it came to her father. There was definitely something going on there, although Wynn couldn't say what it—

Something moved in the living room. Something large that seemed to get bigger. Her heart thundered and her body went cold as she realized there was a strange man in her house. Panic gripped her. She had to protect Hunter—that, she knew for sure. Should she run or scream or—

"Sorry, Wynn. I didn't mean to frighten you."

The man stepped out of the shadows and she immediately recognized Garrick. He had on jeans and a T-shirt, and his hair was mussed, as if he'd been asleep.

Adrenaline poured through her, making it hard to focus. Her mouth was dry and her head was spinning. Her heart continued to race, making it difficult to talk.

"You scared me!" she gasped. "What are you doing here?"

He shoved his hands into his front pockets in what she would guess was an attempt to look nonchalant.

"I slept on your sofa."

The statement was so incredible, she couldn't begin to understand what he was saying.

"What is wrong with you?" she demanded. "You don't sneak into someone's house and sleep on their sofa. You can't just be here, lurking in the darkness. It's not right."

She thought longingly of the self-defense class she'd taken years ago and wished she could remember a few moves so she could break his nose or something. She pressed a hand to her chest only to realize she was wearing an oversize T-shirt, panties and nothing else.

"Dammit, Garrick."

"I'm sorry."

She stalked away, hoping the back of the T-shirt covered her butt. After pulling a robe out of her closet, she slipped it on and tied the belt at the waist. Only then did she return to the kitchen where she found Garrick seated at the island, sipping on a mug of coffee.

She poured herself a cup, then leaned against the counter and eyed him warily.

"Sorry," he said, before she could speak. "The light was

on late last night and I knocked. Hunter let me in. He said you were in the bath. I thought he told you I was here."

"He didn't. He was in bed when I got out of the bathroom." Having never said a word.

Garrick drank his coffee. "I really am sorry."

"I believe you. Now, why did you spend the night on my sofa?" She looked at him as she spoke, trying not to notice that despite the casual clothes and mussed hair, he looked good. Men, she thought humorously. It was always that way with them.

He sighed heavily. "I had to get away. Your place is right next door. I could have gone to Jasper's or Cade's but they're both a few miles outside of town."

"Okay, that explains why you picked my sofa over theirs, but not why you left your own bed in the first place."

He glanced away from her. "Joylyn's a nightmare. I know it's wrong to say that, but she is. Sunday she mostly stayed in her room, but every time she came out she was complaining about one thing or another. So I tried giving her a little space, and then she complained I was abandoning her all over again. When I tried to talk about what it was like when she'd been a kid, she said she didn't remember any of it."

He clutched his coffee in both hands. "Last night I offered to take her out to dinner. She said she didn't want to. I said I could get takeout or go to the grocery store, only she said she wasn't hungry. Thirty minutes later, she accused me of trying to starve her and wanted to know why we weren't going out to dinner. I don't know if she's torturing me or if she's having some kind of breakdown."

She relaxed. "You're afraid of her."

"You would be, too, if you had to live with her."

"Poor Garrick."

"It's awful."

"How can I help?"

"You can't, but I appreciate the offer. I'm sorry I scared you." He looked at her. "It was dumb to come here and I apologize. Tell me how I can make it up to you."

She instantly thought of her still-warm bed and how good he would look in it. She liked the idea of them together, naked and touching. There were complications, however. Hunter would get up in less than a half hour and Joylyn was right next door. Oh, and the fact that Garrick had never once hinted he thought of her in a boy-girl way.

"Next time leave me a note," she said. "By the coffee-pot. That way I'll see it right away."

"I promise." He drained his coffee and stood. "I need to get back and make sure she's all right. With any luck, she's asleep."

"And you can sneak out to work before she wakes up?"

"I wouldn't say sneak. Want to come over for dinner tonight? Hunter, too, of course. I'll be serving the finest takeout in town."

She laughed. "That would be nice. Thank you."

"You're the one doing me a favor."

"Acting as a buffer?"

"Something like that. Although I do enjoy the company." He paused, then smiled. "The T-shirt was cute."

She flushed. "Pretend you never saw that."

"Too late, but how about if I don't comment on it again?"

"That would be good."

He put his coffee mug in the sink, then left. Wynn stayed where she was, wishing she wasn't wondering what he'd thought about seeing her in the T-shirt. What did *cute* mean? And why did he have to say cute? Sexy would have been more interesting. Appealing was good, too. But cute? Men were just so annoying.

* * *

Wynn's morning flew by as quickly as always. Work was busy with new orders coming in and completed orders going out. A little after eleven, her friends Renee and Natalie walked in.

Natalie, a pretty brunette with curly hair and bright red glasses, was several months pregnant. Her visible happiness and sweet disposition were a stark contrast to Joylyn's sullen nature. Wynn wondered how much of Joylyn's attitude was about her circumstances and how much of it was because of her personality. Not a question she would get answered today, she told herself.

While Natalie wore a flowy maternity dress, Renee, a petite redhead, had on a dark suit and three-inch heels.

"Work or play?" Wynn asked, hugging her friends.

"Work," Renee said. "We need some help with a couple of weddings."

"Then let's go to my office."

Renee was a partner in Weddings Out of the Box—a destination wedding venue in town. She'd worked in the business nearly two years and had bought in last year. Renee was organized, creative and fiercely loyal. She was also married to Jasper Dembenski, a successful thriller writer and Wynn's former lover.

Wynn had ended things a few years back for reasons that seemed really silly now. Not that she wanted him back. She and Jasper had both been more interested in the convenience of their relationship rather than any romantic connection. He was much happier with Renee than he'd ever been with her.

As for what Wynn wanted—well, that was less sure. Someone she could love with her whole heart. Assuming she let herself go there, she thought sadly. Because most days it seemed that she wouldn't.

"What's up?" she asked when her friends were seated.

"There's a wedding," Renee said. "In fact there are several."

"People love to get married at the holidays," Wynn said, then turned to Natalie. "If you're involved, then I'm guessing there is some kind of art project."

Natalie was a gifted artist who worked with different materials, including paper.

"There is," Natalie said. "We're going to need to special order some paper, and it has to be a rush."

Renee opened her briefcase. "I have the specs here." She flipped through several folders. "We have a Hanukkah wedding coming up. That's keeping me awake at nights worrying that we're getting it all right. I was totally freaked because I don't know much about Jewish traditions, but then the bride mentioned that her aunt was a rabbi, so we've been emailing nearly every day. She's been amazingly helpful."

She set one folder on the desk, then pulled a menorah out of her briefcase. It was gold with blue enamel accents.

"We want to match the place cards to this color blue."

"Are the menorahs going to be part of the centerpieces?" Wynn asked.

Renee nodded. "We're debating lighting versus not lighting. The bride is still deciding."

"It makes a difference," Wynn said as she pulled out her paper samples to match the color. "If they're lit, you can't have anything close to them. If they're not lit, you could cluster flowers around. Either would be pretty."

"That's what I said," Natalie told her with a smile.

Wynn held out a couple of color samples. They all stared at the small pieces of paper.

"That one," Renee said firmly, pointing. "The usual card-stock weight. Can you print them?"

"If you get me a list and a font." Wynn grinned. "I'll even fold them for you. Okay, not me exactly, but the machine that does it."

Natalie laughed. "I love office equipment. I have no use for it, but I love it."

"Me, too." Renee made a note. "Thanks for the folding. I gave the bride a ballpark price for the work. Assuming there's nothing extra pricey about the paper and the printing, then we're good to go."

"The only cost difference would be if they use an expensive font I don't already own."

Renee made more notes on her tablet. "I'll be in touch with the bride as soon as I'm back in my office. She's fairly responsive so I should have an answer today. Next." She scanned her list. "We have two Christmas weddings that are mostly planned. I've already placed my orders for those, which leaves us with the snowman wedding."

"Snowman? You mean snowflake wedding."

Renee shook her head. "Snowman. As in snowmen as a theme."

Wynn looked at Natalie. "I've never heard of that."

"Me, either," Natalie said. "But apparently it's a thing."

Renee sighed. "Less of a thing than I would like. We're having a lot of trouble finding appropriate decorations that aren't too kids party. Natalie is creating a whole snowman village scene out of paper."

Natalie eyed Renee's tablet. "I'm not as organized as she is, but I brought in the different paper weights I want and the colors." She smiled at Wynn. "Mostly everything is white, but I do want a little contrast. Green for trees, some red and a little pale gray for shading."

She pulled a small box out of her tote bag and removed several paper samples. Wynn took them and flipped them over. Sure enough, the weights were on the back.

They discussed the different suppliers Wynn used. She went online to see who had what stocks and who could deliver overnight.

"I'm going to need some heavy paper for the base of the project," Natalie said. "I couldn't find a real sample of what I wanted, but it's this weight."

She handed Wynn an old library card. The paper was thick, but not coated, with a heavy fiber content.

"Thicker than card stock," Wynn murmured, rubbing it between her fingers. "But with more give. This used to be popular, but now it's more of a specialty item. Give me a second."

She went into her big storeroom and dug around on several back shelves before finding a half ream of the paper she'd been thinking of. It was heavy, and the paper wrapping was dusty. She blew it off before carrying it back to her office and setting it on the table.

"What about this?"

Natalie pulled out a sheet and smiled. "This could work." She counted the sheets left, then smiled at Renee. "I've got my base for the winter scene."

Wynn pointed at the notes on the side of the package. "I've got a price for you."

Renee added the information to her tablet, then they placed the order for the paper Natalie was going to need.

"It will be here tomorrow," Wynn said. "I'll text you when it comes in."

Natalie glanced at Renee who nodded encouragingly.

"So would Hunter be interested in a part-time job?" Natalie asked.

The question surprised Wynn. "He's only fourteen."

"I know. It's nothing big. Just making these." She pulled a four-inch paper snowman out of her tote. "They're made with a combination of cutting, gluing and a little origami. I need a thousand."

Wynn stared at her. "Seriously?"

"Unfortunately. I wasn't thinking when I came up with a really cute idea for the centerpieces for the wedding. It's four weeks away, and there's no way I can put them together myself. Not and do everything else."

"A thousand?" Wynn couldn't get past the number of snowmen required. "How long does each one take?"

"It's slow at first, but then it gets quicker. I would say the average is probably five minutes. The bride's budget is a dollar fifty a snowman for the work."

"She must really want the snowmen for her wedding."

Wynn did the math. Assuming five minutes per snowman, that was only twelve an hour. It would take over eighty hours to complete the job.

"How many are done?" she asked.

"I've done a few samples to figure out the best way to put them together." Natalie dropped her gaze. "And that's kind of all."

"You're in trouble." Wynn looked at Natalie. "You need help. Lots of help."

"We're just about to put out the call."

"I'll ask Hunter," Wynn told her. "Oh, and let me talk to Joylyn."

Her friends stared at her blankly.

"Who?" Renee asked.

"Joylyn." Wynn tried to figure out the easiest explanation. "You know Garrick McCabe is my neighbor, right? He has a grown daughter who's staying with him until the holidays. She's pregnant and doesn't have any friends in the area, so she might be looking for something to fill her day."

Given that Joylyn wasn't working and that her husband was in the military, Wynn would assume they weren't rolling in money. The extra cash might help.

"You'll talk to her?" Natalie asked. "I'm pretty desperate. This is all my fault. I really should have thought through the centerpieces."

"You artist types," Renee said, hugging her. "With your head in the clouds. You can't help being so talented."

Renee's phone rang. She pulled it from her bag and glanced at the screen.

"It's a bride," she said, getting up from the desk. "I'll be back when I've calmed her down. Feel free to chat among yourselves."

She left. Wynn smiled at Natalie.

"Are you in a panic?"

"Pretty much." She pulled one of the little snowmen out of her bag.

The simple design was adorable, with a folded body and cute face. A tiny stovepipe hat sat on his head.

"There's a girl one, too," Natalie said, setting her down. "I've worked up instructions, and I thought I'd hold a quick class for anyone interested in helping."

"I can do some in my free time," Wynn said, not sure how quickly she could get hers done. She'd never been great at crafts. She could design an invitation or a sign with no problems. She enjoyed playing with color and space, but folding and gluing? Not so much.

"How are you feeling?" she asked her friend. "Aside from the snow person crisis."

"Good. Ronan is turning into a worrier. He monitors my every breath."

"Your husband loves you."

Natalie smiled. "Yes, he does and I like that in a man."

Renee walked into the office and collapsed in the chair. She looked shell-shocked.

"What?" Wynn asked. "Are you all right?"

Renee blinked a couple of times. "We have a cancellation. The wedding on the eighteenth isn't going to happen. The bride ended things and is going back to her old boyfriend. The groom is taking a job in China where he's apparently kept a mistress for two years. The parents are the most upset, but I don't have to deal with them."

Wynn knew that weddings got canceled at the last minute. It was rare, but it happened. "Good news or bad news?" she asked.

"I can't answer for them, but for us, it's kind of not a bad thing." Her mouth curved up in a smile. "We have a very well-designed contract that protects us from absorbing any costs when there's a cancellation. And that was going to be our last wedding before the holidays." The smile widened. "We're going to get an even longer break than we'd thought."

"Good for you," Natalie said, before winking at Wynn. "She wants time at home to have more sex with Jasper."

"I do like the sex," Renee said as she picked up her phone. "I need to text Pallas and let her know what's happened. I can't believe we're going to get almost three weeks off work and over the holidays. Yay us!"

Natalie looked at her. "You're just going to say you like the sex and move on?"

Renee didn't bother looking up from her phone. "Oh, please. As if you don't like making love with Ronan. It's one of the perks of a great marriage. I'm not going to apologize for enjoying it."

"Me, either," Natalie said with a sigh.

Wynn didn't enjoy feeling like the odd friend out, but there was no getting around the fact that she wasn't having sex with anyone. Even more significant—she was ready for that to change. She wanted a man in her life. A good guy who cared about her and wanted a real relationship. It was time. Probably past time. She'd had her reasons for avoiding anything significant in the romance department, but she was starting to think it was time to forgive herself and move on. Yes, she'd been awful, but she'd learned her lesson and she was a better person now. Wasn't she allowed to let go of the past and start something new and wonderful? Didn't she deserve a second chance at happiness? And if she believed all that, shouldn't she get off her butt and do something about it?

"Can I talk to Natalie tomorrow?" Hunter asked eagerly, as he walked next to Wynn. "I want to get going on the snowmen, Mom."

She smiled. "I've texted her to ask when she can meet with you. I'll let you know as soon as I hear."

"I thought I'd have to wait until I was sixteen to get a job. Earning some money would be great." He looked at her. "You know, it's less than two years until I'm sixteen."

She pretended confusion. "What does you turning sixteen have to do with anything?"

"Mo-om! I want to get a car. A guy needs wheels."

"I can afford the wheels," she told him. "It's the rest of the car that's going to be more complicated. You should have told me you only wanted the wheels."

They climbed the three steps leading to the porch of Garrick's house. While Hunter sighed heavily, Wynn rang the doorbell.

"You're not funny," her son told her.

"Actually, I think I have a great sense of humor."

Joylyn opened the door. "Hi." She stepped back to let them in. "My dad just left to get the takeout."

"Did he say what we're having?" Hunter asked. "I hope he got a lot. I'm starved."

Joylyn looked pale and unhappy, Wynn noted. "You're always starved." She smiled at Joylyn. "He's in the middle of a growth spurt. I'm sure you know from having brothers that boys can pretty much eat a grocery store when that happens."

Joylyn nodded listlessly. "There should be plenty. Dad always buys too much." She led the way into the living room and flopped down on the sofa. "I'd rather have something from home but of course he doesn't cook."

"Do you?" Wynn asked, trying to sound curious rather than judgy.

"Of course I can cook." Joylyn gave her a superior look. "I'm also pregnant."

"Oh. I didn't know you were a high-risk pregnancy."

"I'm not." She sat up straighter. "Why would you say that?"

Wynn smiled. "Now *I'm* confused. You said you couldn't cook because you were pregnant."

Hunter glanced between them, but didn't say anything. He took a seat on the edge of the sofa and watched Wynn, as if trying to figure out what was going on.

"I'm tired a lot," Joylyn said. "My back hurts. I don't want to be on my feet."

"It's nice to have an option," Wynn told her. "When I was pregnant with Hunter, I was on my own. It didn't really matter how I felt, I had to keep working to save as much money as possible." She smiled at him. "I worked until I went into labor."

He closed his eyes and groaned. "Mom, please don't talk about giving birth."

"I won't." She looked at Joylyn. "I'm simply pointing out that a lot of pregnant women don't get to spend the last couple of months of their pregnancy living off their parents while neither working nor going to school. You're lucky."

She kept her tone light, wanting to get the message across without being mean. Joylyn flushed and looked away. Tears filled her eyes.

Wynn braced herself for the explosion, but Joylyn only sniffed and said, "It's not what you think."

"I'm sure that's true. But it would be nice if you helped around the house."

Joylyn's expression turned sullen. "I don't want to be here."

"You have made that clear, haven't you?"

Joylyn opened her mouth—no doubt to shriek—but before she could say anything, Garrick walked in the door. He held up two overflowing bags.

"I hope you're hungry. I got plenty."

Hunter shot to his feet. "Chinese! My favorite."

Wynn shook her head. "Everything is your favorite."

"That's because I'm easygoing and a happy kid. You should be grateful. What if I were a picky eater?"

"I'd have more leftovers in my refrigerator."

They walked into the kitchen. Wynn saw the table wasn't set, so she washed her hands, then started collecting dishes and flatware. Joylyn watched her for a second before joining in. She poured lemonade for herself and Hunter, then got out wineglasses for Wynn and Garrick.

When they were seated at the table, Wynn held out one

hand to Hunter, the other to Garrick. Hunter did the same, grabbing Joylyn's hand. Joylyn hesitated a second before reaching for her dad. Wynn said grace, then looked at the cartons of food.

"A lot of choices," she said. "Thanks, Garrick."

"You're welcome." He motioned to the star on the side of several of the containers. "The marked ones are low sodium and less spicy." He glanced at Joylyn. "I got the chow mein the way you like it. Combination meat and extra vegetables."

She pressed her lips together before murmuring a reluctant, "Thank you."

Hunter looked pleadingly at his mother. She began opening cartons and handing them to him. "No more than a small serving of everything the first time around," she reminded him. "Everyone else wants to have some, too."

He sighed heavily before pulling an egg roll out of a container and setting it on his plate.

Garrick grinned at him. "I remember the feeling of always being empty. I don't think moms get it."

"Girls," Hunter grumbled.

Wynn instinctively glanced at Joylyn, prepared to share the moment. But instead of meeting her gaze, the young woman was staring at her dad with an expression of sadness and longing. As if she remembered a time when she and her father had joked around and she missed it.

Wynn quickly looked away, not sure what to make of the moment. She served herself some Kung Pao Chicken before asking, "Joylyn, have you had a chance to drive around town yet?"

"Not yet."

"It's not a big city but we have some interesting areas. Happily Inc is a destination wedding town. There are several venues that cater exclusively to people getting married. A couple of friends of mine own a place called Weddings Out of the Box. It's an interesting building, with one entrance looking like a villa while another is a castle."

"Why?"

"A lot of the people who come here to get married have theme weddings. A princess wedding, a *Lord of the Rings* wedding."

"Remember a few years ago?" Hunter asked. "That wedding based on a computer game. That was so cool. They had a zip line and I got to use it."

"Why not just have a regular wedding?" Joylyn asked.

"Sometimes the bride and groom want something else. Oh, we also have a game preserve on the edge of town."

"There aren't any predators," Hunter told her. "Just grazing animals. There's a herd of giraffes and a water buffalo and zebras and stuff. It's pretty cool. We go there a lot on school trips. A baby giraffe was born a few months ago. He was nearly a hundred and fifty pounds when he was born."

Joylyn's eyes widened. "That big?"

"Uh-huh. Baby giraffes fall to the ground when they're born. That's a hard way to start your life." Hunter sounded more impressed than upset. "They stand in about an hour. You never want twin giraffes, though."

"Why not?"

"Because when a mother has twins, the two babies are small. A newborn giraffe has to be tall enough to nurse." He grinned proudly. "Our class had to write a report. I got an A."

"I wouldn't mind seeing a giraffe," Joylyn admitted.

"I can check with Carol to see if she can give us a tour," Wynn said casually, as she glanced at Garrick. "Want to join us?"

"You know I have a soft spot for the giraffes."

Joylyn's mouth tightened, but she didn't speak. There was something, Wynn thought, with no idea what it was or how to fix it. But maybe, just maybe, Joylyn wasn't as unreachable as she wanted everyone to think.

chapter six

Conversation flowed easily through the rest of dinner. Garrick allowed himself to relax, at least for the moment. Every now and then he caught glimpses of the daughter he used to know, and that gave him hope.

Having Hunter and Wynn around made a big difference. Too bad they couldn't be there every night because Joylyn had changed in the past few years, and not for the better.

"I have a question," Wynn said when even Hunter couldn't eat anymore. "There's a snowman wedding coming up before the holidays." She glanced at Garrick. "Apparently it's a thing."

"Snowmen?"

She nodded, and turned back to Joylyn. "My friend Natalie has designed centerpieces using paper snowmen. The problem is she needs a thousand of them in a very short period of time."

"She needs help making them," Hunter said. "She's paying a dollar fifty a snowman, and you can make like ten or twelve in an hour!" He sounded delighted. "I'm going to make some. You should do it, too, Joylyn. It's not hard. Mom, did you bring a sample?"

"In my bag."

Hunter raced into the other room and returned with a small paper snowman. He handed it to Joylyn.

"You're not doing anything all day. You should make a lot of money."

Joylyn flushed. "I'm pregnant."

Hunter shrugged. "I know that, but you just sit around. Why not make these?"

Joylyn studied the small snowman. "I guess I could help."

"Good," Wynn said. "I'll give her your contact info. I'll be getting the paper in first thing tomorrow and I can drop it off."

"Why will you get the paper?"

"I have a graphics and printing business in town. Natalie is ordering the supplies through me."

Joylyn stared at her. "You own your own business?"

"I have for about ten years. Ever since Hunter and I moved here."

"But you're a single mom."

"That's true. I was never married."

Hunter looked at his mom. "She does great, but if she wanted to get married, that would be good, too." He grinned. "Maybe you'd like to date someone who lives by the golf course." He turned to Joylyn. "Most of those houses have big swimming pools."

She laughed. "So you don't care about your mom's happiness—just getting a pool?"

"Why not have both?"

"You are weird." She stood. "Come on. Let's clear the

table, then we can go play video games. I bet I can beat you again."

"You didn't beat me. I let you win because you're new. Tonight there's no mercy."

Garrick was more caught up in the fact that Joylyn was being pleasant and voluntarily helping.

It took them only a few minutes to get the leftovers into the refrigerator and disappear down the hall. He watched them go before returning his attention to Wynn.

"You worked a miracle."

"I'd love to take credit, but I didn't do anything."

"She was almost nice."

Rather than smile, Wynn shifted in her seat. "I'm going to say something that may get me in trouble."

"I doubt that."

"You haven't heard what it is yet." She moved her wineglass around the table. "Garrick, you need to have expectations when it comes to your daughter. Joylyn is pregnant, but she's not sick. She can do something around here. Tell her she has to cook two meals a week and, I don't know, manage the grocery shopping. Whatever. You can come up with the list, but don't let her just sit on her butt and brood all day. It's not good for her."

"You're right," he said, wishing he'd thought of that himself. "She should do more. I don't look forward to the fight, but it's the right thing to do."

She stared at him, as if waiting for more. "That's it?"

"What else do you want me to say?"

"I don't know. I thought you'd be mad."

"Why? You're helping. You gave her a job. You have good advice." He held up the wineglass. "I have dishes because of you. Even more important, you're raising a great kid. Of course I'm going to listen to you."

"Thank you. I just think she'll be happier when she has more to do."

"I'd like that. Not just for me but for her. She's really different these days. She's constantly in tears. I know she misses Chandler, but I worry she's too emotional. She was always so easygoing as a kid."

"I think the word you're looking for is indulged."

"So harsh," he teased, then glanced at her empty glass. "More wine?"

"Thanks, but I need to get Hunter home. It's a school night."

"For us, too."

They both stood. He reached for her empty glass at the same second she reached for his. Their hands bumped and their arms tangled. They both pulled back, and he looked at her.

She was beautiful, he thought absently. High cheekbones and a full mouth, the soft glow of her light brown skin. Plus all that long, curly hair.

Without considering he might be crossing a line, he reached out and fingered one of the curls. Her hair was as soft as he'd imagined. Her gaze met his, and he read interest in her brown eyes. The kind of interest that got a man's attention and turned any day into a very good one. Awareness crackled between them.

He released the curl and drew her close, then slowly, deliberately settled his mouth on hers.

Her lips were soft and warm, igniting heat in his body. She put her hands on his shoulders and leaned into him. He felt the imprint of her breasts on his chest, the brush of her thighs against his. When he touched his tongue to her bottom lip, she parted and he eased inside.

It was a great kiss. All sexy and hot as they discovered

the rhythm of the dance. He teased her tongue, liking the heat flaring and the way she hung on.

He wanted to pull back just enough to kiss his way along her jaw, then down her neck. He wanted to lift her up on the table so he could move between her thighs and start to explore her incredible body. He wanted to move her toward the bedroom and figure out at least fifteen ways to make her come before burying himself inside her and finding his own release.

And none of that was going to happen.

They broke apart at the same time. Her eyes were slightly glazed, which was gratifying considering his massive erection.

"If only we didn't have kids in the next room," she said, then cleared her throat. "Why is life all about timing?"

"Rain check?" he asked.

"Absolutely."

Joylyn carefully applied a thin layer of glue on the tiny black hat, then set it on top of the snowman's head. She held it in place for a count of ten before moving her fingers and studying the finished snowman.

The work wasn't very interesting. She'd taken the morning to plan out the best way to put the pieces together. Once she was familiar with the components and the process, she quickly figured out how to attack the project using a kind of assembly line approach. It took more work upfront but allowed her to complete more snowmen per hour.

The money she earned would be helpful once the baby came. Just paying for diapers was going to be a challenge.

She moved the completed snowman to the box next to her, then glanced at the clock by the bed. She had a call scheduled with Chandler in a few minutes and didn't want to be late. They only got to FaceTime a couple of times a week, so those calls were important to her.

She got up and stretched, feeling the pull in her back. She was so gross, she thought, waddling to the kitchen where she got herself another glass of water. Staying hydrated was important.

Once her glass was full, she opened the refrigerator and stared at the contents. She'd gone to the grocery store earlier to buy what she needed to fix dinner. Her dad had told her he wanted her to be responsible for dinner twice a week—not a surprise after her conversation with Wynn. She'd thought about telling him no, but it had seemed like too much energy. Plus she supposed she knew that Wynn wasn't wrong about all the things she said. Joylyn might not feel like she had it easy, but the truth was she did. The fact that she was away from her friends was her own fault. She should have stayed on base when she had the chance.

Feeling her mood spiral, she headed back to the bedroom and tried to distract herself with the snowmen construction.

Right on time, her laptop came to life, indicating an incoming call. She pushed the button to accept the call, then felt her heart jump when Chandler's face filled the screen.

"Hey, beautiful girl," her husband said with a smile. "How are you feeling?"

"I'm fine," she said, even as tears filled her eyes. "I miss you."

"I miss you, too. It's just over a month until we're together. You need to hang in there."

"I'm trying. Tell me what's happening with you."

As he told her about his days and what he was doing, she stared into his eyes and longed to feel his arms around her. Being apart was so hard and unfair.

"How are things with your dad?" he asked. "You getting along better?"

"I guess. I hate being here."

"I know you do, baby, but you and your dad used to be tight. Maybe that can happen again."

"I don't know. I just can't trust him not to leave me."

"You're the one who's going to be leaving when I come home. I hate to see you suffer."

She faked a smile. "You don't have to worry about me, Chandler."

"Sure I do. I love you."

"I love you, too."

"You heard from your mom?"

"No. Not a word." The tears returned. "I don't know what's wrong with her or why she did what she did."

"It doesn't make sense to me, either. But sometimes the things that happen aren't about us. They're about the other person."

Joylyn knew he was trying to make her feel better, and while it would be nice if her mom had sent her away because she had some issue she had to deal with, Joylyn knew the truth wasn't that convenient. Time and distance had allowed her to see that maybe she hadn't been the easiest person on the planet to get along with. That maybe her complaining and general annoyance with the world had gotten to be too much.

"I don't want to talk about her anymore," she said. "Look what I'm doing." She held up one of the snowmen. "They're for a wedding, and I'm getting paid to make them. I'm saving it all, Chandler. For us and the baby."

"That's great. How do snowmen fit in a wedding?"

She laughed. "I have no idea, but apparently it's a thing."

"If you say so." He glanced over his shoulder. "I gotta go. I love you and I'm counting the days."

She touched the screen. "I love you, too. I can't wait to see you. I miss you so much. You're everything, Chandler."

"You're everything to me, too, sweetie."

The call ended and the tears came right on cue. Joylyn brushed them away and went back to work. She might not be able to see her husband, but she could build the stupid little snowmen and save money so that when she and her husband were together again, they could buy what they needed and be happy.

The Monday before Thanksgiving, Wynn got up a half hour early and made pumpkin spice cupcakes. She showered while they were baking, then took them to the office with her. Just after eleven thirty, she drove the short distance from downtown Happily Inc out to the animal preserve where she pulled in next to her friend Silver.

"What did you bring?" the platinum blonde asked as she got out of her truck.

"I went seasonal. Pumpkin spice cupcakes."

Silver smiled. "I can always count on you to do the right thing." She held up her own container. "Potato salad. Carol texted yesterday and said she was making pulled pork sandwiches for our main course."

Their biweekly lunches were something Wynn looked forward to. They met on a Monday or Tuesday, before the craziness of the week's upcoming weddings kicked in. The location varied. When it was Carol's turn, they usually ate outside at the animal preserve. Natalie hosted at the Willow Gallery where she displayed her work, and Bethany had them out at the ranch. Pallas and Renee used the space at Weddings Out of the Box, while Wynn chose either her business conference room or her own dining table.

The meals were fun, friendly affairs. Whoever was able to come brought something. The hostess provided the main entrée and drinks. Sometimes there were five salads or five desserts, but more often than not, there was a mix of foods. The not knowing what to expect added to the fun.

They walked along the main path in the preserve, careful to close the gates behind them so no animals would escape. Last year Carol had installed a nice picnic table in a shady spot. There were supports for a canvas overhang, if the temperatures were too high. Happily Inc was a desert community, getting plenty hot in the summer. Having it be a dry heat helped, but there were a few weeks in July and August when retreating to air-conditioning was the only way to survive. But today the temperature was in the midseventies, with a bright blue sky and lots of sunshine.

"I heard there's a snowstorm expected back east, just in time for Thanksgiving," Wynn said as she double-checked that that last gate was secure.

"All those idiots traveling are going to suffer."

Wynn hid a smile. "You mean those poor people trying to get home to their families for possibly the second biggest holiday of the year?"

Silver grimaced. "Yeah, that. My sympathies and all that."

They rounded a grove of trees and saw Carol putting out stacks of plates and flatware. The table was already decorated with a brightly colored cloth. A side table held a big covered dish and a stack of buns, along with a dispenser filled with lemonade. But what really caught Wynn's attention was the—relatively—small giraffe following Carol from place to place like a very oversize and leggy dog.

"I see Bodey is still in love with you," Wynn called.

Carol looked up and laughed. "He is a curious guy." She motioned to her left where Millie stood keeping a watchful eye on her two-month-old son. "As long as Mom stays close."

Bodey was the first giraffe born in the animal preserve. He was visibly taller and stronger every time Wynn saw him.

"Hey, little guy," Silver said, slowing her approach as Bodey turned to stare at them. "We're just here to eat lunch and tell you how adorable you are. Is that okay?"

His eyes were huge—dark brown with long lashes. His nostrils flared as he studied them.

"He's cuter than he was," Wynn said softly. "How is that possible?"

Carol grinned. "I know. I keep taking pictures of him. Mathias keeps reminding me we have our own baby. I think he's jealous on Devon's behalf."

The conversation was too much, or maybe it was the sight of three humans all together. Either way, Bodey retreated on his gangly legs, circling to the far side of his mother where he could watch while protected by Millie.

"Speaking of Devon, where is she?" Silver asked, settling her potato salad next to the buns.

"She has a bit of a cold. I didn't want her exposing the other kids, so she's with her dad today." Carol's eyes were bright with amusement. "Mathias complained that he wouldn't get any work done, but the truth is they both love hanging out together. By the time I get home, she'll either be on the mend, or he'll be sick, too. I'm hoping for the former."

"It's us," a familiar voice called.

Renee, Natalie and Pallas joined them. Renee and Natalie each carried two large tote bags while Pallas had her son with her. Little Ryan squealed when he saw all his lady friends, writhing and waving his arms to be put down. Pallas obliged and the toddler took off, racing first to Wynn and then to Carol and Silver. All the women crouched down to get hugs and very wet kisses.

Just as the greetings began to calm down, Bethany walked in with her daughter Addison on her hip. Ryan clapped his hands and hurried over as fast as his chubby legs would take him.

It took several minutes to unload food and get the kids settled. Baby Bodey hovered on the edge of the picnic area, curious but cautious. Millie chewed on leaves and regarded them with bored disinterest. The only human she really loved was Carol. The rest of them were simply a part of the landscape.

"This was easier pre-kids," Wynn said as she took a seat next to Renee. "But much less fun."

Natalie sat down with Ryan in her arms. Her nephew leaned against her baby bump. "At the rate we're reproducing around here, we'll have to get a separate kids' table in another year or two."

Silver looked at Renee. "Pressure's on you, lady."

"To find a kids' table? Sure. I can do that."

Everyone laughed.

"I think she meant you should get pregnant," Wynn said.

Renee shook her head. "I will. Eventually. What about you, Silver? You and Drew aren't too old."

Silver waved her hand. "I don't know. We talk about it. Maybe. We like what we have now. Why mess with that?"

Wynn knew that Silver and Drew had a teenage daughter

together. Silver had gotten pregnant in high school and had given up the girl for adoption. Over the years, she'd stayed close with the adoptive mother and had been a part of her daughter's life. Drew had only found out about Autumn a couple of years ago, and the three of them were spending more time together. Wynn would guess Silver wasn't sure about adding a baby to the mix. She wouldn't want Autumn to feel she was being replaced.

They served themselves lunch. Conversation flowed easily between the friends as they caught each other up on what was going on.

"What's the plan for the royal holiday season?" Natalie asked Bethany.

Bethany sighed heavily. "My parents," she began, pausing when everyone laughed.

"What did the king do now?" Wynn asked. "I know the man loves royal proclamations. You should tell him to get them all printed at my shop. I'd give him the royal discount."

"Because you have so many royal customers?" Pallas asked, her voice teasing.

"Not yet, but I'm willing to explore the market. I'll be fair on the pricing. No gouging simply because he's one of the ten richest men in the world."

"I think he's only fifteenth," Bethany said.

"How tragic for you and your family," Renee teased.

"We're dealing with the ugly reality. As for the holidays, that's an ongoing discussion. El Bahar doesn't celebrate Thanksgiving—what with it being an American thing. My mom does sometimes, but she's kind of letting it go. Christmas and New Year's are more complicated."

Bethany was the adopted daughter of the King of El

Bahar. He'd married Bethany's mother nearly twenty years ago, adopting Bethany when her biological father later passed away. Bethany had three half brothers and was an actual princess, something her friends liked to kid her about.

When the king had first found out his daughter was pregnant, he'd insisted on sending over bodyguards…and a helicopter. It had followed her everywhere, ready to whisk her away to a medical facility should she have the slightest problem during her pregnancy.

"The current plan is to have Christmas here, then fly to El Bahar for New Year's." She drew in a breath. "There's going to be some kind of national celebration. You know, because of the baby."

Wynn laughed. "Poor you."

"I'll be okay. Cade's not excited."

"Who can blame him?" Pallas asked. "My brother is just a regular guy who fell in love with a princess. Now his life will never be the same."

"I'm worth it," Bethany said with a laugh.

Natalie glanced at Wynn. "Thanks for all your help with the snowman construction." She turned to the table. "Hunter is making snowmen for me, along with Joylyn."

The women exchanged glances.

"Who's Joylyn?" Carol asked.

"Garrick's daughter," Wynn and Renee said together.

"Police officer Garrick?" Carol asked. "Oh, that's right. He has a grown daughter. Is she nice?"

Wynn wasn't prepared to give an answer to that particular question. "She's having a rough time right now," she said instead. "She's eight months pregnant, and her husband's a Marine and is deployed."

"How old is she?" Silver asked.

"Twenty-one. She was staying with her mom, but Alisha has three teenage boys and that was a lot. Garrick's house is quieter, which is good, but I wonder if she's feeling isolated."

"She probably doesn't have any friends here." Pallas wrinkled her nose. "That would be hard. I mean it's great for her to be with her dad, but it's not the same as hanging out with people her own age."

"It's interesting you and Garrick both had kids when you were young," Bethany said, then turned to Silver. "And you."

"Teens will be teens," Silver pointed out. "Hormones are powerful."

So was fear, Wynn thought. She'd been so scared of losing Chas that she would have done anything to keep him with her. And he'd still left her. A pregnant girlfriend was no match for the lure of the next great ride.

She told herself that had happened a long time ago—that she was a different person and today would make different choices. While she knew all that was true, she still didn't like what she'd done. It had taken a long time to forgive herself and move on.

She thought briefly of Garrick. He was trying so hard with his daughter. The more she got to know him, the more she liked him. Their kiss had been amazing and was something she would like to repeat—this time without the potential for interruptions.

"You should bring her next time," Bethany said, pulling her daughter onto her lap. "Joylyn. I know we're not her friends, but she might like hanging out with us. Plus with all the pregnancies we've been through, we would be a great resource."

Everyone nodded as Bethany spoke.

"I'll be sure to mention it to her," Wynn said. "I think she'd like getting out of her dad's house." And some girl time just might help her attitude.

chapter seven

"This is stupid," Joylyn grumbled as she slid out of Garrick's SUV. "I don't like board games, I can't drink and the whole idea is dumb."

"Monday nights at The Boardroom are a Happily Inc tradition," he told his daughter. "You'll have fun."

She glared at him. "You can't know that."

"I can guess. Come on. Anything would be better than sitting home, alone in your room."

"I hate what you want to watch on TV."

"I've been asking you to pick the shows or movies, and you still want to stay in your room. Come on, Joylyn. Give game night a try."

She sighed heavily, then nodded, following him inside.

He'd been inspired to invite his daughter to The Boardroom after hearing a couple of guys talk about it at work. He went every couple of weeks, when he thought about it. It was always a good time, but was more fun with someone. His first instinct had been to invite Wynn. He liked her, he'd liked kissing her and he wanted to spend more time with her. But even as he reached for his phone to call and invite her, he'd realized that taking Joylyn was probably a better idea.

While his daughter was slightly less sullen than she had been when she first showed up, she still wasn't anything close to friendly. He was willing to make accommodations, but he wasn't going to beg for her smiles or good humor. He'd taken Wynn's advice and had assigned chores—something he'd assumed would lead to a fight. Instead, she'd agreed with only minor grumbling. Maybe a night out together could move them a little closer to being friends.

He held open the door for her, then followed her inside. As per usual, the place was crowded. The Boardroom always pulled in a lot of locals, but Monday night was a favorite and the tournaments were popular.

Customers were three deep at the bar and most of the tables were full. As he looked around for empty seats, several people called out greetings. His friend Jasper walked by with two beers in his hands.

"Hey, Garrick. You're welcome to sit with us, if you'd like." He smiled at Joylyn. "I'm Jasper."

"Joylyn. I'm, ah, Garrick's daughter."

Jasper smiled at her. "I figured. You're too pretty and smart to go out with an old guy like your dad." He tilted his head. "Come on. We're this way."

They reached the table. Renee was already there, casually dressed in jeans and a green shirt. She smiled at Joylyn.

"Hi," she said, holding out her hand. "I'm Renee. Wynn mentioned you were in town for a few weeks. It's so great to meet you. Natalie is so grateful for all the snowmen you're making. Without you, she would be in deep trouble."

"You know about that?" Joylyn asked, sitting across from Renee.

"I'm a wedding planner, so I'm the one handling the wedding." She passed over a drink menu. "Everything with an asterisk can be made without alcohol. They do a very nice virgin piña colada. It's not too sweet. About a billion calories, but worth it."

Joylyn looked surprised by the information. "Thank you. Most people don't know about virgin cocktails."

"I have a lot of pregnant friends, or friends who recently had babies. Our little town is in a breeding frenzy right now."

Joylyn glanced at Renee's midsection. Renee held up her beer. "Not me. Not yet."

Jasper put his arm around her. "We're thinking in a few more months we'll get serious about getting pregnant." He kissed the top of her head.

They shared a look that even Garrick understood spoke of love and intimacy and connection.

Joylyn turned away. "It's good to wait. Chandler and I didn't want to get pregnant so soon, but it happened and now we're having to deal."

Garrick hadn't known that and felt the pain of her regret. He wanted to reach out and offer comfort, but had a feeling he would be rebuffed.

A server walked by and took their drink orders. Joylyn chose the virgin piña colada. He got a beer.

Joylyn glanced at Jasper. "What do you do for a living?"

"I'm a writer."

Joylyn looked confused. "Books?"

"Thrillers."

"He's a bestselling author," Garrick added. "Very famous, but we like him anyway."

"Oh. I don't, um, read much."

Renee shivered. "Don't apologize. I can't read his books

at all. They're too terrifying. Serial killers and dismemberment."

"I don't always dismember people," Jasper said with a smile.

"No. Sometimes you shoot them or set them on fire. Your mind can be a dark place."

"How do you come up with ideas like that?" Joylyn asked.

Jasper shrugged. "I wrote a detective series for several years. Those ideas grew out of what my hero did for a living. Now I'm writing about a former soldier turned investigator. He has a different perspective."

"Were you in the military?"

"I was, for nearly ten years. Military police. When I got out, I was really messed up. I started writing as a way to clear my head, and it turned into a career."

"So you use your military experience to help you write your books?"

"Some. I do a lot of research."

"Especially when it comes to fight scenes and weapons," Renee added. "I'm forever coming home to the sound of grunting and throwing."

"I like the fighting sticks," Garrick added, then flexed his hand. "When you mess up with those, you know it."

Joylyn spun to stare at him. "You use fighting sticks?"

"Not in real life. We practice with them."

"I have a few friends who help me out," Jasper added. "They spar with me so I can get fighting scenes right. Your dad is my resource if I need information on how the police would do something. I know a few private investigators I can call on." He chuckled. "Sometimes it really does take a village."

"How did you two meet?" Joylyn asked.

Jasper raised his eyebrows. "I picked her up right here in this bar."

"You did not," Renee protested. "I picked you up."

"You wanted to, but you were scared."

Joylyn stared at them. "You really met here?"

"We'd known each other for a while, but yup, this is where the magic started."

"Being picked up in a bar does not sound romantic," Renee said with a sigh. "We need a better story."

"Who cares how it started? Look at what we have now. We've got the happy love. What else matters?"

She laughed. "You're right. The happy love is the best."

Garrick saw longing in his daughter's eyes and knew she was missing her husband. He was doing a little missing of his own, he thought regretfully, wishing Wynn was with him. Not that he wasn't having a better than expected time with Joylyn, but it wasn't anywhere near the same. With Wynn everything was easy. Plus he enjoyed looking at her. She was sexy and gorgeous and a great kisser. Yes, having her around was always a good time.

"When is the snowman wedding?" Joylyn asked.

"December 12," Renee told her. "It's our second to the last wedding of the year. I'm practically giddy. We never get the holidays off, but this year Pallas, my business partner, and I were determined to have some time at home over Christmas. So we blocked out the week between Christmas and New Year's. Then the wedding on the eighteenth got canceled, and suddenly we have a huge block of free time."

She grinned at her husband. "We're thinking of going somewhere tropical."

"You'd look good somewhere tropical."

Renee lightly kissed him, then turned back to Joylyn. "When are you due?"

"Christmas Day."

Renee's expression turned sympathetic. "Mixed feelings about that?"

"A lot. Chandler's due home on the eighteenth, so he should be here. He says he doesn't care when our son is born, as long as he's healthy."

"A good attitude."

Joylyn smiled. "He's a good guy."

The last of Garrick's tension about the evening faded. Bringing Joylyn had been the right move. She was able to get out of her head and have a little fun.

"First babies are usually late," Joylyn continued. "So I'm hoping for after the first of the year. Not that I have any control over when it happens."

"No, but if your little one waits, you can enjoy the holidays."

"Including the tree," Garrick said. "We always get a fresh one. Can't beat the smell."

Joylyn glanced at him. "Do you still have all the old ornaments? The ones we hung together?"

"Sure. They're stored in the garage, in the waterproof bins, just like always."

Her eyes widened in surprise. "I didn't think you'd keep them."

"Why wouldn't I? We always put up a tree together with all our special ornaments."

He hadn't for several years now. Not since she'd started refusing to see him. But this season was going to be different, he told himself. He would figure out what was wrong and make sure they reconnected.

The server brought their drinks along with a board game. Garrick glanced at the color cover and held in a groan.

Chutes and Ladders? He braced himself for his daughter's displeasure.

But Joylyn surprised him by taking the game and laughing. "This is great. I used to play this with my brothers." She looked at Renee and Jasper. "I have three younger half-brothers. My mom wouldn't allow any of us to be on our computers or phones on Christmas or Thanksgiving, so we had to play board games."

Jasper winked at her. "Brace yourself, kid. Sometimes the rules here aren't what you expect."

Joylyn turned to Garrick. "What does that mean?"

The bartender picked up a microphone. "Welcome to tonight's tournament. Traditional rules apply, unless the spinner lands on three or four. In that case, you lose your turn."

Joylyn's eyes widened. "But that's so arbitrary."

"Welcome to my world," Garrick said, opening the box.

Beside him, his daughter started to laugh.

Tuesday night after dinner, Wynn found herself feeling oddly restless. She knew the cause—her handsome next door neighbor. Since they'd shared that kiss, she'd thought about him a lot. If it was just the kiss, she would be okay with having him on her mind, but there were complications.

She liked him. The more she spent time with him, the more he appealed to her. Garrick was a strong, steady guy. He got involved, he cared. Even when Joylyn was throwing up roadblocks right and left, he was still trying to get close to her. He hadn't given up—not giving up was important to Wynn. The fact that she liked how he looked was also interesting, but not as important as the rest of it.

The second time she found herself standing at her front window, gazing wistfully at his house, she mentally slapped herself upside the head and told herself to grow a pair. If she wanted to see him, then she should make it happen. She was capable of doing the asking.

Before she could question herself into indecision, she pulled out her phone and sent a quick text.

Want to stop by for a quick decaf?

The answer came in seconds. Be right there.

Wynn stared at the words, telling herself not to get all fluttery. It was coffee, nothing more. But she couldn't help the quiver of anticipation that took up residence in her stomach. And when her doorbell rang less than a minute later, she found herself wanting to giggle like some teenager, which was so embarrassing, but also fun.

She pulled open the door. "Hi."

He smiled at her. "Hi, yourself." He leaned in and brushed his mouth against hers before holding out a bottle of cognac. "In case you'd rather skip the decaf."

"Interesting idea." She stepped back to let him in, trying to quiet the tingles inside. "I'll get glasses and join you in the living room. Hunter has the family room."

"Game night?"

"His favorite. But I won't complain. His grades are good, and he's keeping his sassing to a minimum."

"Hunter doesn't strike me as a kid who sasses you much."

"I know. I'm lucky."

She collected two glasses and joined him. Garrick had turned on a couple of lamps in the corner of the room but not the ones on the end table, giving the space a more intimate feel. She set down the glasses and hesitated only a second as she tried to figure out where to sit on the sofa. Not next to him—that would be weird. But not at the far end, either.

She settled about a cushion away, angling toward him as he poured cognac into each of their glasses.

"How's it going with Joylyn?" she asked, touching her glass to his.

"Better." He took a sip. "Maybe. I hope. I took her to The Boardroom last night, and she had a good time."

"What was the game?"

"Chutes and Ladders. She laughed a lot. We sat with Jasper and Renee. They were both friendly, which helped. I think Joylyn forgot to be mad at me for at least a couple of hours. It was nice to have our relationship back."

"Have you thought about asking her what happened to change things in the first place?"

"Yes."

She looked at him. "And?"

"I've asked but she won't give me a straight answer."

"Did you do anything horrible to her?"

"What?" He blinked in surprise. "No. Of course not. I would never hurt her."

"Exactly. So ask her why things are different. Maybe there's no reason, but what if there is? Maybe it can be fixed and you can be close again."

He looked doubtful. "I don't think it's going to be that easy, but I get your point." He cradled his glass. "I've been trying to remember the exact sequence of events. It was six or seven years ago, right around the time Sandy and I separated and then divorced."

He glanced at her. "I'd been starting my undercover work, so I was gone for days at a time. Sandy wasn't a fan. She'd been okay when I'd talked about joining the unit, but when she found out what was entailed, she was pissed."

"Didn't she know that would happen?"

"Sure, but I think knowing and living were different.

She wanted me to quit and go back to regular police work. I wanted to stay the year I'd committed to. She said she wasn't going to have kids with me until I was done playing at being a bad guy." He grimaced. "Those were her exact words."

Without thinking, she reached out and took his hand. "That had to be tough for you."

"It was." He squeezed her fingers before releasing her. "Plus I couldn't help thinking her complaints were all an excuse to end things. I started to wonder if she'd been looking for an out and my work gave her one."

"Was she close to Joylyn?"

"No. They got along, but it wasn't a great friendship. I don't think that's what set her off."

"It doesn't sound like it," she said. "That's when the DEA work started?"

He nodded. "The first time I went to Colombia, it was for three months. Joylyn had already started refusing to see me. I told her I had to be gone for work, and she said she didn't care."

Wynn heard the pain in his voice. "I know that was hard."

He looked past her. "It sucked. I came back and tried to get her to hang out with me, but she continued to refuse. So I took another assignment. This one lasted over a year."

"I didn't know you were gone that long."

"I didn't mean to be. Things got complicated."

She thought about the scars on his torso and wondered if they had anything to do with the "complications."

"Does Joylyn know why you were gone for so long?"

"She knows it was work. Or at least she knows that's what I told her. Based on a more recent conversation, I'm not sure she believed me."

Men, Wynn thought with a sigh. "Were you more specific with her? Does she know you were undercover, working a dangerous assignment?"

His gray gaze settled on her face. "How do you know it was dangerous?"

"Oh, please. I watch TV. Drug cartels aren't known for their philanthropy."

"I've never talked about it with her."

"Then maybe you should start there. If she knows what you were doing, she might be more forgiving of your absence. Assuming that's what she's upset about."

"I don't think it is. She was mad at me before I left." He set down his glass. "No offense, but your gender is complicated."

"Yes, we are, but we also smell nice."

He chuckled. "You do." He stretched his arm along the back of the sofa and rested his fingers on her shoulder. "Change of subject?"

She nodded, shifting closer.

"How are you doing on the Thanksgiving prep work? I'd like to help."

"Thanks, but I'm in good shape. I did my last-minute shopping this morning before I went to work, the turkey is sitting in the refrigerator and I've already put out the Thanksgiving decorations."

"You're prepared. I'm going to make Waldorf salad. I hope that's okay."

"We can always use another side."

"It's a thing. I made it every year for Joylyn and brought it over to her mom's for dinner."

And there it was. Niceness. Genuine caring. Even if she didn't think he was hot and a really great kisser, he was winning her over with stories like that.

"What did Sandy think of having Thanksgiving with her stepdaughter's mother?"

"It wasn't her favorite. She wanted her own traditions. To be fair, she was happy to include Joylyn, but I didn't want to make Joylyn have to split her time between her mom and me. Not on Thanksgiving." He drew in a breath. "I guess I wasn't always a great husband."

"Maybe not, but you were a terrific dad."

"Thanks. Tell that to Joylyn."

"I will."

Instead of smiling, he grew more pensive. "She has a doctor's appointment tomorrow. I was thinking I'd take off work and go with her." He held up a hand. "I'm not talking about going in the room or anything. I just want to be there because it's a new doctor and she's eight months pregnant."

"That's a great idea," she told him, wondering how Joylyn would react. "I'm sure she doesn't want to go by herself." But having her dad along might be too much for her. "Do you want me to go with her instead?" She shook her head. "I'm not trying to butt in, I'm just wondering if having another woman there would be easier for her."

"I hadn't thought of that, but you can't take off work."

"I can. We're not very busy right now, and it's only a couple of hours. I'm happy to do it."

"Thank you. I think it might be easier for her to have you there rather than me. If we were tight again, it would be different."

He looked so sad as he spoke that she reacted without thinking. She slid close and wrapped her arms around him.

"You two are going to figure this out."

He hugged her back. "I hope so."

"Don't give up on her. She needs to know that you can't be pushed away by her attitude."

"I'm not going anywhere."

As he spoke, he leaned close and pressed his mouth to hers. She relaxed into the kiss, liking the feel of his lips on hers.

Wanting flickered to life, but she ignored the need. With Hunter playing video games just down the hall, nothing more was going to happen, but just kissing was nice.

He moved back and forth a little, but didn't deepen the kiss, as if he, too, knew the limitations of the night. When he drew back, he smiled at her.

"I thought it was supposed to be easier when kids got older."

"I wish."

He stared into her eyes. "Me, too."

And for now, that was enough.

Joylyn sat in the backyard watching butterflies drift from one flowering bush to another. She supposed that in other parts of the country, people were bracing to deal with subfreezing temperatures and snow, but in the desert southwest, there were still flowers and butterflies.

She told herself she had to get moving, that not showing up for her doctor's appointment was a dumb move. And being scared because the doctor was new to her didn't make any sense, either. She was eight months pregnant— she needed to be seen by a medical professional.

Brushing away tears, she stood and walked into the house. She peed, then got her handbag and was halfway to the front door when the doorbell rang.

"Oh, hi," she said, surprised to see Wynn on the porch. "What's up?"

"I'm here to make an offer," Wynn told her. "Feel free to say no. Your dad told me about your doctor's appointment this morning. I would imagine you're not excited about seeing someone new when you're so far along. If you think it would help, I'm happy to go with you. Not into the room or anything, but just on the drive and in the waiting room. For moral support."

The unexpected act of kindness brought the ever-present tears back to the surface. Joylyn blinked them away.

"That would be really nice," she said, her throat tightening. "I was a little nervous about going, so a friendly face would help."

"Then let's go. Want me to drive?"

"Do you know where my appointment is?"

"Yes. I use the same practice. All the doctors there are great."

Joylyn got into Wynn's car and fastened her seat belt. Some of her tension eased.

"How are you feeling?" Wynn asked as she backed out of the driveway.

"Good. The baby is very active, which I like."

"Do you talk to your husband much?"

"We FaceTime a few days a week, but I still miss him."

"You're down to less than a month until he comes home, right?"

"I'm counting the days. I keep telling myself I should have stayed on base rather than moving in with my mom. I miss my friends there."

"When will you go back?"

"Once Chandler's home and his leave is done, we'll get a new assignment and new housing."

"It must be hard to feel settled when you don't know where you're going to end up."

"It is."

Wynn drove through the streets of town. Joylyn had a

vague idea of where the doctor's office was and appreciated that she didn't have to worry about finding it.

"Are you going to stay with your dad until then?"

Joylyn glanced at her. "What do you mean?"

"I just wondered if you were going to stay in town here, rather than moving back with your mom. There will be three of you and from what I understand, the house is already full." Wynn smiled. "I think your dad would be happy to have you stick around."

Stay here? Joylyn had never considered that. She'd assumed they would leave the second Chandler got back, which was a week before the baby was due. Wynn's point was a good one though—there wasn't all that much room at her mom's place. But staying here?

"He doesn't want me here."

"Your dad?" Wynn shook her head. "You're wrong about that. He's excited you're staying." She smiled. "He's lived next door to me for about a year, but we never really said much more than hi until he found out you were going to be moving in. He came over and asked me to help get the house ready so you'd be comfortable. He had the bedroom set, but not any of the linens, and his empty kitchen was a total disaster."

Joylyn didn't know what to say to that. While she wanted to believe her dad was glad she was around, she just couldn't.

"I used to be important to him," she admitted. "Just not anymore."

"Why would you say that? Your dad loves you, Joylyn. He's so proud of you. I don't know what happened before, but I would suggest you at least talk about it. Ask questions. The answers may surprise you."

Joylyn didn't want to fight, so she nodded, as if she

would take Wynn's advice to heart. The truth was, she didn't care about questions or answers. Not when it came to her dad.

She put her hand on her stomach. "I've been thinking about what you said about being alone when you were pregnant. How did you handle that?"

"I didn't have a choice. There wasn't anyone else. I tried to save as much as I could so I could take off for three weeks after the birth, but I had no idea how much everything cost. Have you priced diapers? They're really expensive."

"I know, and babies need a lot."

"More than you think—that's for sure." Wynn made a left turn. "I had a small inheritance from an old lady in our building. Ms. James. She'd never married and she didn't have much when she died, but she left it all to me. She used to tell me I could make something of myself if only I'd put in the effort. It broke my heart to use that money to pay for food and rent. She'd wanted better for me."

Joylyn glanced at her. "Like going to college?"

"Something like that. Certainly more than me getting pregnant the way I did." Something flashed in Wynn's eyes. "She would have been very disappointed with me."

"What happened? How did you end up here?"

"Hunter's father died. I didn't know until a lawyer showed up at my front door to tell me there was a life insurance policy. I was three weeks away from being evicted, and when the man told me about the money, I couldn't stop crying."

"What did you do with it?"

"Paid my rent." She glanced at Joylyn and grinned. "Bought diapers." Her smile faded. "I got myself into a two-year graphics program at a local community college, and I worked my butt off to be the best student I could. After I graduated I got a job in the business and continued to learn the industry. When I found out about a business for sale in some little town I'd never heard of, I came to check it out. That was ten years ago."

"You're really brave."

"No. I was scared every second, but I recognized the chance I'd been given. I was determined not to blow it. I wanted more than I had, and I was going to make it happen."

Joylyn was pretty sure that was the definition of being brave. That if you weren't scared, then there was no courage in the act. She wondered if she'd been in the same circumstances if she would have acted the same or if she would have crumbled and given up. She couldn't think of a single time in her life when she'd been the least bit brave. Or even determined. If she were honest with herself, she had a feeling she would have to admit that when the going got tough, she found a place to hide until all the bad stuff went away.

chapter eight

Thanksgiving morning Garrick got up early to make the Waldorf salad. He'd gone to the grocery store the day before, shocked at the crowds and the long lines to check out. But he'd wanted to have all their traditions in place. He had ingredients for the salad and the blueberry pancakes he always made on the special morning. He'd also bought yellow roses—Joylyn's favorite—for the kitchen table. He knew her plans were to return to Phoenix as soon as Chandler was home, so the week before Christmas she would be leaving. This was the only holiday he was going to get to spend with his little girl.

By seven the salad was assembled and in the refrigerator, ready to take over to Wynn's later that afternoon. He had batter ready for the pancakes and coffee brewing. As he wasn't sure what time Joylyn would get up, he busied himself going online to study patterns for bassinets.

The idea had come to him a couple of days ago. He wanted to give his daughter something special for her baby. Joylyn and Chandler had a gift registry and he'd looked over that. There were a lot of great items, but rather than buy any of them, he was going to give the new parents money to use as they liked. But he also wanted to give them something personal. He'd always enjoyed woodworking and had made a few pieces of furniture. From what he'd learned online, a simple wooden bassinet wouldn't be too difficult a project. If he got started this weekend, he should have it finished in plenty of time.

A little before eight, Joylyn wandered into the kitchen.

"Morning," he said cheerfully. "Happy Thanksgiving."

"Happy Thanksgiving," she said, her expression neutral.

He tried to find comfort in the fact that she wasn't glaring at him. Progress. Of course it was still early—there was plenty of time for her to get pissed at him for no reason.

He poured her juice. "Do you want bacon with your blueberry pancakes?"

"Yes, please."

"How are you feeling?" he asked as she took a seat at the table.

"Awful, but regular awful. Nothing worse."

"Counting the days?" he asked sympathetically.

She rubbed her belly. "Being pregnant is harder than I thought it would be."

He knew her doctor's appointment the previous day had gone well, so there were no physical concerns about the baby, but just looking at her belly and the way her back bowed when she walked made him uncomfortable. He couldn't imagine having to live it.

He was just about to pour the batter on the griddle when her phone chimed. Joylyn glanced at the screen before smiling at him.

"It's Chandler. Can we hold off on breakfast?"

"Sure," he said, even though he was already talking to

her retreating back. She ran down the hall and disappeared into her room.

He stood at the counter, not sure if he should make his own breakfast or wait for her to come back. He figured there was a fifty-fifty chance of him picking wrong regardless, but he erred on the side of waiting. It seemed more polite.

As Joylyn took her call, Garrick carried his coffee out to the living room and stared out the big front window. He supposed he should be happy that things weren't worse between them, but he sure wished they were better. He missed his little girl.

Okay, Joylyn wasn't a child anymore, but it wasn't about her being small. It was about them being close. He loved her and wanted the best for her, but he also wanted them to be friends. He wanted to know what she was thinking and feeling. He wanted to be a part of her life—only they'd been apart for so long, he didn't know how to get them connected again.

About fifteen minutes later, she came out of the bedroom. Her eyes were red and swollen and her face was wet with tears.

"I hate this," she said, her voice thick with emotion. "Being apart from him like this. He's so far away. I miss him and I can't do this without him."

He instinctively reached for her. She jerked free of his touch.

"You can't make this better," she screamed. "You can't. Just leave me alone. I don't want to see you or talk to you. I don't want to have Thanksgiving with you. Leave me alone. Just leave me alone!"

She returned to her bedroom and slammed her door shut. Even from the living room he could hear the sound of her sobs. He stood where he was and had absolutely no idea what to do next. Finally he walked into the kitchen and dumped the batter into the trash before changing into sweatpants and a T-shirt and heading out for a run.

Wynn looked around the kitchen, double-checking that she had everything handled. The turkey was in the oven and three pies were cooling on a rack. She had the casserole dish with dressing ready to go in the oven when the turkey came out. She and Hunter had already watched the Macy's Thanksgiving Day Parade, and now her son was curled up in the family room, watching the football game and reading comic books.

She crossed to the dining room to make sure that was ready to go, as well. She'd set the table earlier that morning, using her good china and the seasonal table linens. Instead of flowers as a centerpiece, she had small gourds running down the center of the table, along with red and orange leaves, a few pinecones and several beautiful seashells she added for texture. The largest shell she placed in the center was red, but the rest were cream and brown and pink, blending with the autumn colors of the linens.

The side table was set up to serve as the buffet. Wynn had all her serving pieces out to make sure there was room for everything. Renee and Jasper were bringing a sweet potato casserole and Drew, Silver and their daughter Autumn had offered to provide green beans and fresh rolls that Silver and Autumn were making fresh this morning. Garrick, of course, had his Waldorf salad.

She liked the idea of a full table at the holidays. Friends that were her family. It gave her a sense of belonging and showed Hunter the importance of community.

She heard her front door open.

"It's me," Garrick called.

Her body reacted with a bit of a tingle and a happy lift to her heart. She smiled as she met him in the living room.

"Hi," she said, stepping into his arms for a hug and a kiss. "Happy Thanksgiving."

"Happy Thanksgiving." He held out a foil-covered bowl. "I bought some wine," he added. "I left it on the porch. Let me go grab it."

She took the salad into the kitchen and found space for it in the crowded refrigerator. Holiday meals were always a challenge. She had a countertop convection oven she'd bought at a garage sale a few years back. It was plugged in and sitting on the kitchen table, ready to heat any extra sides that showed up.

Garrick joined her, a bottle of white wine in each hand. "They're already chilled."

She looked at him, noting the tension in his jaw. "What happened?" As Joylyn wasn't with him, she could make a couple of guesses but figured she should hear the whole story from him.

"She's not coming."

"Why?"

"I have no idea." He put the wine on the counter. "She was okay when she got up this morning. Not superfriendly, but not hostile. Then she got a call from Chandler. After that she was crying and screaming and didn't want anything to do with me. She wouldn't eat breakfast or talk to me. When I asked her to come over just for a few minutes, she screamed at me to go away."

"I'm sorry."

"Me, too. I don't know what's wrong, and I don't know how to get through to her."

"You need to talk to her."

"I've tried."

She looked at him without speaking.

"You're saying try harder?" he asked.

"I am." She stepped close and rested her hands on his waist. He pulled her close and hugged her.

"Kids are difficult," he murmured. "Even when they're grown up."

"Yes, they are. But you love her, Garrick. You've got to keep pushing until she lets you in."

"I know. I'm the parent and all that, but I have to tell you, the rejection is tough. Sometimes she looks at me with such loathing, I wonder if she wishes I was dead."

"She doesn't. You're her dad."

The doorbell rang and they stepped apart. Wynn let in Jasper and Renee, along with their dog Koda. The old guy sat politely until Hunter came running.

"Koda! Happy Thanksgiving."

The dog's tail wagged as Hunter collapsed to the floor and wrapped his arms around the dog. Then Hunter glanced up at Jasper and Renee.

"Happy Thanksgiving," he told them. "Thanks for bringing your dog."

Renee glanced between them. "You really should think about getting—"

Wynn shook her head. "Don't even say it. I don't need one more thing right now."

Jasper shook hands with Garrick, then kissed Wynn's cheek and handed her a ceramic frog container filled with a leafy plant. "Not for the table. I know you do your own thing for that. Maybe for the windowsill." He started for the family room in the back. "Got the game on, Hunter?"

"Uh-huh. It's tied at seven."

"Come on, Garrick. Football."

Garrick glanced at Wynn. "The age-old division of the sexes. Let me know when you want me to pull the turkey out of the oven."

"I will," she murmured, carrying the plant into the kitchen.

Renee trailed after her, then put the sweet potato casserole on the counter. "He does know this isn't your first Thanksgiving, right? That you managed to wash, season and stuff the turkey, not to mention get it in the oven, all by yourself."

"He's trying to be helpful."

"I know, but they're so unaware of what we do in a day."

Wynn pulled a pitcher of orange juice and a bottle of champagne out of the refrigerator. While the guys had a few beers as they watched the game, she and her girlfriends would sip on mimosas. Hunter had the thrill of soda pop *in the house*. It was a holiday tradition that he looked forward to.

Wynn had just opened the champagne when the doorbell rang again. She and Renee greeted Silver, Drew and Autumn. Drew made his way to the family room while Silver and Autumn walked into the kitchen.

"There's soda," Wynn told Autumn.

Autumn laughed. "Hunter must be excited."

"He is," Wynn said with a smile. "How's school?"

"Good. I'm doing really well in my math and science classes."

Silver put her arm around her daughter. "She got into a STEM school. They have a fairly rigorous application process, so we've all been crossing our fingers."

Renee sat on one of the stools by the island. "What's a STEM school?"

"The academic focus is science, technology, engineer-

ing and math," Autumn said. "I want to be a chemical en-
gineer."

Silver grinned proudly. "I know. Where did she get
that?" she asked with a laugh.

"Oh, Silver. You're smart, too. And Drew. I get it from
you guys."

With that, she left to go hang out with Hunter. Silver
watched her go.

"She's amazing."

"You and Drew should have more kids," Renee offered.

Silver sighed. "Maybe. We're talking about it. At first he
just wanted to focus on getting to know Autumn, but now
he's mentioned having more kids." She looked at Wynn.
"What do you think?"

Wynn handed her a mimosa. "Why are you asking me?"

"You have a child almost the same age. Would you start
over again? Have more kids?"

"I don't know. It's never come up." Wynn passed a drink
to Renee. "When I moved here, I was terrified of failing
so all I thought about was raising Hunter and making my
business successful. I didn't date for years or think about
having more kids."

"But that's all different now," Renee said. "You're successful, you have a network of friends. Were you waiting
to fall in love? Did you want a partner this time? Because
while you make being a single mom look easy, I doubt
that it was."

Wynn sipped her own drink. "Having a partner would
make a difference." But she'd never let herself go there. She
hadn't dated—not in the conventional sense of the word.
She'd had relationships that were kept separate from her
life with Hunter. The guys never met him and weren't to
let him know they even knew his mom. Jasper had violated

those rules when they'd been together, and she'd ended things without a backward glance.

It was the guilt, she told herself. Because of her past and what she'd done. After all these years, she was finally ready to let it go, but did that mean she was open to having more children?

"I want to say I'm too old," she said slowly. "But I'm not."

"You're what? Thirty-four?" Renee waved her glass. "Lots of women have kids in their thirties. Some don't even start until their forties. You two should both have more kids."

"You're very free with the advice," Silver teased.

"I know. My turn is coming. I just want a little more time with Jasper."

Hunter walked into the kitchen, Koda at his heels. "Mom, where's Joylyn? I thought she was going to be here."

"Her dad said she didn't want to come."

Hunter shook his head. "That's not right. It's Thanksgiving. She shouldn't be alone. I'm going to talk to her."

He started for the front door. Koda watched him go, then hurried over to Renee and lay down at her feet.

Wynn hoped her son wasn't setting himself up for disappointment. She knew his heart was in the right place, but Joylyn didn't make things easy on anyone around her.

Joylyn sat at the kitchen table, her paper supplies spread out around her. Even as she brushed away tears, she folded and glued the paper to make snowmen. So what if her life was falling apart—at least when Chandler got home she would have money in her savings account for them and the baby.

On the tablet screen, she saw Chandler holding out his

hand to her, then pulling her close for their first dance together. Everything about the image was perfect—Chandler
so tall and handsome, how her dress swayed, the happiness
on both their faces.

She missed him so much. Missed them. She was lonely
and scared and uncomfortable. Thoughts swirled and
crashed together, making her more miserable by the second.
Tears fell faster as emotions overwhelmed her. She crushed
the small snowman in her hand and threw it onto the floor.

"I hate this!"

There was no one to respond because she was by herself. No one to—

The front door opened.

"Joylyn? It's Hunter."

She quickly brushed the moisture from her face. "In
here," she called.

He walked into the kitchen. "Whatcha doing?"

"Just making snowmen."

"But it's Thanksgiving. Why would you want to stay
here by yourself instead of being with us?"

A very good question, and one she could no longer answer. "I just do."

He sat across from her. "I don't believe you. Why are
you crying?"

"I'm not."

"You were."

She sniffed. "It's just everything. My mom called for
maybe two seconds. She's so busy with her dinner and
stuff. I talked to Chandler, but he's far away and I miss
him. Everything is awful."

Hunter's mouth twitched. "You mean awesome."

She rolled her eyes. "That's not funny. My life is horrible, and I hate that it's the holidays."

Hunter stared at her for a long time. "I don't get it," he said at last. "Why do you always look at the bad side of stuff? You never see what's good."

"That's not true." Only she knew it was.

"You miss Chandler, but he's not in a war zone and he'll be home in less than a month. You have a lot of family. You have your mom and your dad. I never had a dad. He died and I never knew him. Mom's shown me some pictures, but they don't mean anything. We don't have any other family. It's just the two of us. I'd never want to be mad at her the way you're mad at your dad. I'd never want to hurt her feelings or make her sad. I don't know how you can stand it."

His unexpected confession and his very accurate assessment of her life made her feel ashamed. "It's different for me. You're too young to understand."

"You're hiding because you're scared. That never works out." He stood. "Come to dinner. You know you want to. Being by yourself only makes you feel worse. Jasper and Renee brought their dog. Koda's a great guy. Someone abandoned him at an RV park in Texas. Jasper found him and brought him home. Now he's happy. There's a lesson there."

Joylyn looked at the teen and saw the man he would be one day. He had a solid character and a caring soul. Somewhere out there was a teenage girl who was going to marry a great guy.

She looked at the snowmen she'd made that morning and the stacks of paper waiting to be put together. While she wanted to earn the money, maybe the snowmen could wait.

She stood. "I probably won't like it," she grumbled.

Hunter only laughed.

Wynn was shocked when Hunter reappeared, Joylyn at his side. Later she would ask him what happened, but for now she did her best to act casual as she introduced Silver and Autumn.

"It gets hectic in an hour," she told them, then turned to Joylyn. "The men are watching football in the family room. You're welcome to join them or hang out with us."

Autumn walked over to join Hunter. "There's too much adult talk here," she said. "I'd rather watch football."

Joylyn elected to join the kitchen conversation. Wynn poured her juice, and they all gathered around the kitchen table.

"What weddings do you have this weekend?" Wynn asked.

"It's busy after today," Renee said. "A traditional wedding tomorrow night, a full-on princess wedding on Saturday, then a small bird wedding on Sunday."

Joylyn stared at her. "Birds getting married?"

"Shades of the big dog wedding from last year," Silver said with a laugh. "Not birds. People getting married and their theme is birds. Bird everything."

"She's right," Renee said brightly. "The invitations, the decorations, the cookies. The centerpieces are a play on a bird nest. It's beautiful and still kind of weird."

"So are they having chicken for dinner?" Wynn asked.

Renee glared at her. "Of course not. They're vegetarian."

"Egg drop soup?" Joylyn asked with a grin.

"Stop. They are not eating any bird products." Renee frowned. "Although now that I think about it, I'm pretty sure the bride's train has feathers in it."

"Why birds?" Wynn asked.

"I didn't ask." Renee sighed. "I am so looking forward to our three weeks off. No birds, no snowmen, no action figure–costumed grooms."

Silver turned to Joylyn. "What was your wedding like?"

"It was very traditional. No birds." She smiled. "Chandler and I got married in a church, and the reception was in my mom's backyard." Her tone turned wistful. "I was just watching a video of the wedding. Everything turned out perfectly."

"That's nice," Renee said. "Do you have a lot of family?"

"Not as much as Chandler. He's one of six kids, and there are tons of aunts and uncles and cousins. My dad and my stepdad walked me down the aisle, so that was nice. And all our friends were there."

"This will be your mom's first grandchild, won't it?" Wynn asked.

Joylyn nodded. "My mother-in-law has three already. But this is the first boy, so she's really excited. She offered to let me stay with her when Chandler was deployed. I would have gone, but she lives all the way in North Carolina. That seemed so far."

"I can see why you'd want to stay close," Silver said. "Is she going to come be with you when the baby's born?"

"Uh-huh. She said she'll come out the second month and stay for a few weeks. My mom says she'll be around for the first couple of weeks." Her mouth twisted. "At least I hope she will." She dropped her gaze. "She's really busy with stuff."

"Having family around will be a big help," Wynn said, hoping to deflect her from potentially difficult subjects. "Babies are a challenge."

"I couldn't have done it," Silver said. "I had Autumn right out of high school. I hadn't been pregnant very long when I realized I was in no way prepared to be a mom."

Joylyn stared at her. "You gave her up for adoption?"

"I did. I found the family and they were great. I ended up living with them for a while. Autumn and I have always been close." She smiled. "It's complicated, but we're all a family and it's pretty wonderful."

Wynn stood. "All right, ladies. We've left the men alone for too long. Why don't we join them until it's close to dinnertime?"

Everyone stood and headed for the living room. Wynn was pleased to see Renee link arms with Joylyn, making sure she stayed with the group. Wynn checked the turkey and did a quick time calculation in her head, mentally figuring out how long it would take to get everything ready once the main oven was free.

Once she confirmed her calculations, she made a quick review of the dining room, then turned to go to the family room, only to nearly run into Garrick.

"You joining us?" he asked.

"On my way. Did you see Joylyn?"

"I did." His gray eyes met hers. "Hunter's doing?"

She nodded. "He said she shouldn't be alone on the holiday and went to get her. I'm not sure what he said, but it worked."

"Your kid is impressive."

"Thank you. I like to think so." She smiled. "I'll remember his actions so the next time he gets into trouble, he gets some bonus points for previous excellent behavior."

"You're very fair," he said.

"I try to be."

They stared at each other. She felt a yummy kind of tension flare and knew there was absolutely nothing they could do about it.

As if reading her mind, he murmured, "We have got to work on our timing."

"Maybe it's because we're out of practice."

"Something we should change."

She smiled. "I'm game. Just maybe not with a houseful of people."

"I'd say we could pretend it's just part of the entertainment, but your son and my daughter being here adds an element I'm not comfortable with." He leaned in and lightly kissed her. "Soon?"

"Yes."

He put his arm around her and they walked toward the family room. Wynn enjoyed the feel of him next to her and told herself the anticipation was nice...even if she would much rather have the real thing.

chapter nine

Garrick sorted through the tools he had on hand, putting some of them in drawers under the workbench and hanging others from hooks on the pegboard. Once he got the workshop area of the garage cleaned up, he would swing by the hardware store and pick up his order.

He'd researched the best wood to use to make the bassinet for Joylyn and the baby. He wanted something strong but with a beautiful grain. With the simple design of the piece, the wood would be the star. He would use an organic stain, avoiding anything toxic, which meant no varnish. The directions were fairly easy, and he'd made furniture before. Most of the time would be spent sanding the wood to a silky finish—something he would enjoy.

He picked up a box of roofing nails and put them in a drawer, then grabbed three more screwdrivers and put them in loops on the pegboard.

At some point he really needed to sort through his tools and get rid of duplicates. It was one thing to have a spare, but at last count, his screwdriver collection had topped twenty. He doubted he needed even half that many.

When the bench was clean, he gave the garage a quick sweep. The Saturday morning weather was perfect. Bright and sunny, with a hint of coolness in the air. With a little luck, he would have a quiet couple of days off and no emergency calls. He would have time to work on the bassinet and get out Christmas decorations. He and Joylyn wouldn't get a tree for another week or so, but they could do the other decorating. He had wreaths for the door and a Nativity, along with little holiday odds and ends they'd bought together. Maybe he'd show her everything later this afternoon.

If all went well, maybe tonight or tomorrow he could figure out a way to sneak off with Wynn for a few hours. They both seemed ready to take things to the next level, but for that to happen, he wanted more than fifteen minutes up against a wall somewhere. He wanted time and privacy so he could give life to all his Wynn-based fantasies. He wanted to learn what she liked and then do it better than anyone ever had. Sure, a quickie was fun, but not for their first time.

And probably not today, he thought as he put the broom in the corner and grabbed his list for the hardware store.

He was halfway to his SUV when a red 1965 Mustang convertible pulled up in front of the house. The car was beautiful—with new wheels and a glossy coat of paint.

Three young women stepped out, but he barely noticed them. He could see the upholstery was original and he was itching to look under the hood and see what the engine looked like.

One of the women, a pretty brunette in a crop top and shorts, walked up to him.

"Hi," she said with a wide smile. "I'm Yolanda."

He looked past her to the car. "That is a beautiful Mustang."

"Thanks. It's my brother's. He lost a bet and now it's mine for the weekend."

Garrick glanced at her. "Is he at home crying?"

She laughed. "He is." She pointed to the other two women. "That's Joni and Enya. We're here to see Joylyn. We thought we'd surprise her with a girl party."

That got Garrick's attention. He turned to the young women and realized they looked college-age and somewhat familiar. He might have met them at the wedding, he thought.

"I'm glad you made the trip," he said. "She's inside."

The other two turned toward the house, but Yolanda lingered.

"You're her dad, right?"

"I am." He held out his hand. "I'm Garrick."

She shook hands with him, then looked him up and down. "I remember you."

There was something in her tone that warned him this conversation could go places he didn't want to go. He deliberately took a step back and pointed to the house.

"She's that way."

"Want to get a drink later?"

The direct question surprised him. "No, thanks."

She seemed more surprised than upset. "You sure?"

"I'm otherwise engaged."

"Lucky her." With that Yolanda sauntered to the house, her hips swaying with each step.

Garrick returned his attention to the car, giving it a once-over before retreating to the safety of his SUV. He'd liked it better when all Joylyn's friends had talked about were horses and their dolls. Not that it was much of a problem for him. He would be happy to spend the afternoon safely in his garage, working on the bassinet and hiding out from the likes of Yolanda. As for any holiday decorating—that could wait until his daughter's friends were gone.

Joylyn sat at the table by the pool while her friends relaxed in the chaises. As the afternoon wore on, the three of them got more and more drunk, leaving her feeling like the odd girl out. The initial excitement at having them drop by had faded about two hours ago. Now she was tired, crabby and wishing they would leave.

Enya jumped into the shallow end of the pool, her drink in her hand. "Come on, Joylyn. The water's fantastic."

Joylyn shook her head. All three of her friends had great bodies, and while she'd been careful not to put on extra weight, she was still nearly nine months pregnant. No way she was putting on a bathing suit for them to judge her.

Joni, a tall leggy blonde, joined her at the table. She smiled and rattled her vodka-filled glass. "What's going on with you? You don't want to swim, you won't drink. It's like you're not one of us anymore."

Joylyn stared at her. "I'm pregnant. I can't drink. It's bad for the baby."

Joni waved away the statement. "Sure, now they say it's bad, but thirty years ago, our moms were drinking all the time. I bet in ten years they decide a little alcohol makes everything better for the kid. You can't take life so seriously."

Joni leaned close and lowered her voice. "You seeing anyone?"

"What?" Joylyn's voice was a yelp. "I'm married. And pregnant."

"I know, but Chandler's gone. Why not have fun?" Her

gaze dropped to Joylyn's distended belly. "Okay, maybe some guys would be put off by all that, but I'll bet there are some who think pregnant women are hot. You could look for one of them."

"Not interested."

The idea was disgusting. She didn't want some random guy—she wanted her husband back home.

Joni stretched. "This is nice. The pool and the house. You've got a good setup here. Better than at your mom's. All those kids running around. It was loud, plus your mom never let us drink in front of them. You and Chandler could just move in here. I'll bet your dad wouldn't mind. Mooch off him for a while."

Joni's phone buzzed. She glanced down and smiled. "It's this guy I met last week when we went up to LA. He's an actor and so cute."

"Are you going to class at all?"

"Ugh. Don't sound like my mother. I go." She grinned. "Sometimes." She shook her glass again. "Sure you don't want a sip?"

"No, thanks."

Joni got up and joined Enya in the pool. Yolanda drained her glass, took off her bikini top and jumped into the pool with them. They started splashing each other and shrieking.

Joylyn watched for a few minutes, then got up and went inside. She saw the large bottle of vodka they'd brought with them was nearly empty. How much had they been drinking? And why had she ever thought those women were her friends?

For the thousandth time she wished she'd stayed on base in San Diego. At least the other wives would have understood what she was going through and have given her support. She would have had more things to do than hang out at her dad's and spend her day making snowmen for a wedding.

"It's all about the money," she reminded herself, walking into the family room where she'd set up a card table with her supplies. In the corner was a growing stack of boxes filled with paper snowmen.

She got out everything she would need and prepared to work. Before she started, she sent a quick text to her friend Holly, mentioning Joni, Yolanda and Enya had stopped by, not that she expected a reply anytime soon. It was a Saturday morning. Holly and Rex would probably be doing something together. But eventually Holly would answer and be sympathetic. She'd never much liked Joylyn's college friends.

She ignored the shrieks from the backyard. In some ways ignoring the noise reminded her of how it had been back when she'd lived with her mom. Her brothers were insanely loud and always getting into something. It was much easier being at her dad's, she thought. There was always food in the refrigerator and the house was quiet. Plus they were getting along better now. He didn't act like he resented having her around. Sometimes he even made her feel he was glad she was here. So why hadn't he been like that before?

As if he'd sensed she was thinking about him, her dad walked into the family room.

"What are you doing?" he asked, coming to a stop when he saw her. "Your friends are out by the pool."

She wrinkled her nose. "They're drunk and talking about people I don't know and places I haven't been."

He pulled up a chair. "You're just in different places right now. You're pregnant and married and they're—" He hesitated.

"Swimming topless in your pool?" she offered.

He winced. "Tell me that's not true."

"Sorry, but it is."

"Damn, and I was going to go sit outside and enjoy the day."

"You don't want to see their boobs?"

Her dad grimaced. "They belong to your friends, so no."

"But other random twentysomething boobs would be okay?"

He chuckled. "Sure. As long as they're random."

"Da-ad."

"I'm a guy. Many of us like boobs. It's a thing." He picked up one of the snowmen. "You're making progress."

"I know. Hunter made about ten, then decided he didn't need the money that much. I don't mind the work. I text Natalie every couple of days and update her on my count."

"I'm sure she appreciates that."

A loud burst of laughter had them both turning toward the back of the house.

"How long are they staying?" he asked.

"I don't know. They'll want to go out soon enough. When that happens, I'll tell them not to come back."

Garrick looked concerned. "You don't have to do that, Joylyn. They can stick around if you want."

"It's not fun for me. I wish I'd stayed on base."

"You could go visit those friends."

"It's too long a drive."

"What if I took you?" he asked. "You could stretch out in the back of the SUV. We'd stop every hour for you to walk around."

"Thanks, but no."

"Then let's decorate the house later. It's the Saturday after Thanksgiving, so we need to put up wreaths and stuff."

He sounded sincere, like he would really do that with

her, she thought. This was the father she remembered—the one who took care of her.

She put down the half-finished snowman. "Dad, why did you stop seeing me? Before, I mean. When I was a teenager."

He stared at her, his confusion almost comical. "We've talked about this, honey. I didn't stop seeing *you*. You're the one who told me to go away. You said our weekends were boring and that you had better things to do. You refused to see me for weeks and weeks."

He was right, she thought reluctantly. That *was* what had happened. She'd been angry and she'd lashed out. Her mother had talked about forcing her to see her dad, but she never had. Joylyn had been left to make the choice herself, and once she'd turned her back on him, she hadn't known how to change things.

"You should have tried harder," she whispered, staring at the table. "You should have made me."

"Is that what you wanted?"

"I don't know. Maybe." She looked at him. "Then you were gone. I talked to mom about calling you, but you were just gone. You abandoned me."

"Joylyn, you weren't abandoned. I was working."

"Doing what? Why would you disappear for months?"

"The first time was only a few weeks, and I was on assignment." He hesitated. "I was in a joint task force with the DEA."

She stared at him, not sure what to think. DEA? As in Drug Enforcement Administration? "Why would you work with them?"

"They were doing some things in the Phoenix area, and I had a little undercover experience. They'd offered me a couple of assignments, but I never took them because I didn't want to be away from you. When you refused to see me for all those weeks, I finally accepted the job."

"You worked for the DEA?" she demanded. "Was it dangerous?"

His gaze slid from hers. "I was perfectly safe."

"You're lying. You weren't safe. You weren't safe at all. You were working for the DEA and you didn't tell me. That's wrong, Dad. It's really wrong."

"Joylyn," he began, but she cut him off with a shake of her head.

"No. I don't want to talk about this anymore. I don't want to know any of it. You should have told me back then and you didn't, so I don't want to know now." She pointed toward the front of the house. "I have work to do. You need to leave me alone to get it done."

"I want to talk about this."

"No. We're not talking." She felt the familiar tears fill her eyes. "No talking."

"Joylyn, please."

She closed her eyes, willing him to leave. It took nearly a minute, but finally she heard him get up and walk out of the room. When he was gone, she opened her eyes.

More laughter erupted from the backyard. The sound made her feel empty inside. They weren't her friends, not anymore. She placed a hand on her belly and willed her love to flow to her son.

"We'll get through this," she told him. "I'm never going to leave you or let you feel scared. I'm going to take care of you. Your dad will, too. You'll see, little one. You'll see."

After church, Wynn changed into old jeans and a T-shirt. She wanted to go through her decorations and figure out what would last another holiday season and what needed to be tossed. While she believed in the magic of a glue gun, sometimes an item was beyond repair and had to be released to find a new life elsewhere.

She walked into the garage and pushed the button to open the big door to give her light and a breeze. At the far end were several shelving units filled with clear bins. All her decorations were stored there, by holiday. The Christmas ones took up two entire shelving units.

She ignored the bins with wreaths and lights. She always checked both at the end of the season, so she knew they were fine. The same with the ornaments. It was everything else that needed to be examined.

She moved her car outside to give herself extra room. As she walked back into the garage, she couldn't help glancing toward Garrick's house and smiling. They'd talked the previous evening. He'd phoned close to nine, and they'd stayed up talking until nearly midnight.

Their conversation had started out being about Joylyn's horrible friends who had finally left around five in the afternoon, but then they'd ended up discussing everything from their favorite subjects in school to how he'd met his first wife. They'd only hung up when both their cell batteries had started flashing warnings about being seconds from dying.

She supposed given that they lived next door and the late hour, she could have suggested he come over. As long as they were relatively quiet, Hunter wouldn't know—once he was asleep, he was out for the night. But she hadn't. Some because she didn't want their first time to be like that and some because the anticipation was really nice.

She pulled out the first bin and opened it. Inside were decorations she put around the house. There were several stuffed Santas in all shapes, sizes and species. She had a cow, a giraffe and a space alien, all in Santa suits. She checked each item to make sure it was still in good condition, then moved on to a bin filled with Jim Shore holiday pieces. There was a small jewelry box tucked in the corner. Inside was a pinecone charm on a chain—something she wore every year at the holidays.

She fastened the chain around her neck, then smoothed the charm with her fingers.

"I'm ready for Christmas now," she said with a laugh.

Another bin held a half dozen throws in Christmas patterns. At the bottom of the bin was a blanket she'd crocheted. It wasn't especially fancy or even square, but she'd made it herself after Hunter had been born and she'd wrapped him in it over their first Christmas.

That had been a hard time—she'd been so scared. Not just about him but about how she was going to keep him in diapers and herself in food. She'd been too young, too poor and too alone to manage, but she had. How would it be different now?

The question surprised her. Why did it matter? She wasn't having more children. She was done with that. Hunter was fourteen and she…

She was only thirty-four, she reminded herself. A lot of women hadn't even started having kids at that age. She was healthy—there was no reason to think she couldn't get pregnant and have a baby. She certainly had financial resources and a support network beyond what she could have dreamed about the first time around.

Funny how she'd made all kinds of rules for herself when it came to romantic relationships, but she'd never thought about having more kids. Not seriously. But as she turned the idea over in her head, she realized that it wasn't totally crazy. She liked children. She liked being a mother. She would prefer to have a man in her life, but even if she didn't she would be fine.

The unexpected line of thought had her shaking her head. She decided to let the idea sit for a while. Later, she would take it out and see how she felt, but for now she still had decorations to get through.

Over the next hour she examined the tree skirt, the silk poinsettias she used to make a display in a fireplace and did a battery count for her flameless candles. She was just putting the last bin back on the shelf when Joylyn wandered into the garage and waved a greeting.

"Hi," Wynn said. "I'm getting ready for holiday decorating. I like to go through everything to make sure it's all in good condition, then Hunter and I will start putting things out tonight. What's going on with you?"

"Not much." She sighed as she spoke.

Wynn started toward the door to the house. "Come on," she said. "I made lemonade yesterday, and there's some coffee cake from breakfast. We'll be more comfortable in the kitchen."

Joylyn followed her. Wynn pushed the button to close the garage door, then collected glasses and dessert plates. When everything was prepared, she sat across from Joylyn.

"You feeling all right?" she asked.

The young mother-to-be nodded. "Physically it's all what it's been. My back hurts, I can't see my feet. You know—normal."

"Considering how pregnant you are, yes."

Joylyn picked at her piece of coffee cake. "It's just everything is different. My friends stopped by yesterday."

"Were they the ones driving that great old Mustang? It was a sweet ride."

Joylyn pressed her lips together. "They drank all day and

hung out by the pool. It's like we have nothing in common. They're interested in having fun and getting laid, and I'm just not into that. Not anymore."

"You chose a different path."

"Was it the right one?" Joylyn looked at her, tears trembling on her lower lashes. "Did I make a mistake?"

Wynn had a feeling the question was a lot more about feeling lonely than any serious introspection.

"Are you sorry you married Chandler?"

"What? No! Of course not. I love him. I'm not sorry we're married." She put a hand on her belly. "I wish I hadn't gotten pregnant when I did, but we were always going to have kids. It's just everyone's having fun but me."

"You do have more responsibility than your friends. But you're also more settled. While they're still trying to figure out their lives, you know where you're going."

"You're right." Joylyn sipped her lemonade. "I wouldn't want to be dating. I'm glad I found Chandler when I did. We're right together. I guess I'm lonely."

"That makes sense. Your husband is deployed, your friends are all somewhere else. You have your dad, but no real girlfriend support system."

Joylyn nodded glumly. "I should have stayed on base. If Chandler gets deployed again, I'm staying close to the other Marine wives."

"So you have a plan."

Joylyn looked at her. "How did you handle having Hunter on your own? I think about my son being born and it terrifies me. I have no idea what to do or how to take care of him. I mean I have younger brothers and I remember when they were babies, but that's different. My mom was there. This time I'll be the mom."

"You do what you have to do. It is terrifying. The first

fever, the first time he gets a cold. It's a nightmare, but you learn and you get through it."

"My mom was really young when I was born. Like seventeen. So was my dad. That's four years younger than me. I mean they both had their parents, but still." Joylyn paused. "My dad worked with the DEA."

"On a joint task force."

"You knew? Did everyone know but me?"

Wynn picked her drink. "He told me a few weeks ago."

"I just found out yesterday." Her tone was bitter. "He just left me to be some hero."

"I wasn't there, but my understanding is that you refused to see him. He showed up every weekend for nearly two months, and every time you sent him away. Then he accepted the assignment. Or am I wrong?"

Joylyn shifted on her seat. "Okay, that's how it happened, but it's not how it felt."

"How did it feel?"

"Like he didn't care about me."

"Have you told him that?"

"He wouldn't get it if I tried."

Wynn sensed that Joylyn was telling the truth—from her perspective, her father hadn't cared. What she didn't know was why Joylyn would go there. Garrick had shown up faithfully, begging his daughter to spend time with him. She'd been the one to refuse. So why would that leave her feeling rejected?

There was something she didn't know, Wynn told herself. Some piece to the puzzle she couldn't see.

"Did you and your dad have any Christmas traditions?" she asked.

Joylyn picked up her fork and took a bite of the coffee cake.

"Sure. Lots of them. We always had a tree—a real one. My mom insisted on an artificial one because she didn't want to deal with the needles and stuff, but Dad got us a real one. He always insisted we get a tree from Wishing Tree, Washington, because he said those are the best. We had our own ornaments, and we always decorated it together."

She smiled. "Every year I was into something different. One year the tree was all done in fairies and princess ornaments. It was so girlie—even the lights were pink—but he never complained. He always got me an Advent calendar. One year it was like a jewelry kit. I could make string bracelets and necklaces, adding beads every day."

"That sounds like fun."

"It was. He mentioned decorating yesterday, but we started talking about other stuff and it never happened. I miss how it used to be."

"It's not going to be exactly that, but you two could still have fun together."

Joylyn paused, as if considering the suggestion. "Maybe. I spent Christmas Eve with him every year, and we would get up at five to see what Santa had left at his place. Then we went out for breakfast and got to my mom's at about seven. He stayed all day. Even when he was married to Sandy, he did that with me."

She finished the coffee cake. "He always took off the week between Christmas and New Year's, and we always went up in the mountains to play in the snow. One year there just wasn't any in the mountains outside of Phoenix so he drove us all the way to Utah so we could have our day."

"Those are great memories."

"They are."

"You should talk to him."

Joylyn stiffened. "What about?"

"The real reason you stopped seeing him. You're angry because he hasn't guessed what it is. Here's my life secret—no one can read your mind, and if you're waiting for that to happen, you're going to be disappointed for the rest of your life. You love your dad and you miss him. The only way to fix the problem is to tell him what's wrong."

She thought Joylyn might burst into tears or start screaming or even run out of the room. Instead, she sucked in a breath and nodded.

"You're right. I should do that. I don't know if I can, but I need to try."

chapter ten

Garrick was weary to the bone. His morning had started at three with an Amber Alert. The missing kid was a four-year-old boy who had been taken by his noncustodial father. While Happily Inc didn't have a lot of crime, bad stuff happened everywhere. His officers had issued the alert and started patrolling the area, looking for the man's car. The father's violent past had added urgency to the search.

The department had been contacted by a concerned citizen who had heard screaming while on a morning run. Garrick had joined his officers on the edge of the desert and had found the boy and his dad, setting up camp. The father had defied the police order to put up his hands. Instead, he'd gone for his gun. When the shooting had stopped, two officers were injured, the man was dead, but the boy was safe. Traumatized, but safe.

Garrick had spent the rest of the day dealing with the paperwork that followed a situation like that. The boy had been bruised from a beating, but otherwise physically all right. Back in town, the mother had a black eye and a broken arm. Garrick had insisted that in addition to a medical checkup that they both got counseling to deal with the aftermath of what they'd been through. He didn't believe killing a suspect was ever a positive outcome, but sometimes there wasn't a choice and every now and then, he thought maybe the world was better off because of it. This was one of those days.

He'd spoken with all the officers involved in the shooting, visited the two injured officers at the hospital, been reassured they would be released in the morning and had given an accounting to the local TV station. Garrick told himself the kid and the mother were safe and that was what mattered, but he didn't like the reminder that the world could be a dark place, even in Happily Inc.

By the time he got home, he wanted nothing more than a shower, a beer and a couple of hours of watching his favorite football team kick someone's ass. Instead, he found his daughter pacing in the living room.

"I heard," she said, staring at him wide-eyed. "About that man kidnapping his son. There was a shoot-out. Are you all right?"

She sounded worried, which felt kind of nice. Without thinking, he held open his arms, before remembering that for some reason, Joylyn didn't want anything to do with him anymore. Only instead of rejecting him, she raced into his embrace and hung on tight.

"I was so scared," she said.

"I'm fine. I wasn't in any danger."

He held her, aware of the differences in her body. Her huge belly got between them, reminding him that his little girl was a grown woman and soon to be a mother herself. He thought about how scared the boy's mom had been and knew if something like that ever happened to Joylyn, he would move heaven and earth to keep her safe.

She stepped back. "Did you go to the shoot-out?" she asked.

"It wasn't a shoot-out. It's not like in the movies."

She glared at him. "Did the suspect have a gun and did he fire at officers?"

"Yes."

"Were any of them injured?"

Damn. "A couple."

"So you were in danger."

"I was coordinating the action. I wasn't in the direct line of fire."

"But you still could have been shot."

"I suppose, but I wasn't. I'm fine."

He thought she might continue to grill him, but instead she nodded. "Okay, Dad. I know you want to take a shower. We'll talk after that."

Twenty minutes later, he joined her in the kitchen. When she saw him, she got a beer from the refrigerator and opened the bottle, then poured herself some water. She put out chips and dip, along with a plate of cut-up vegetables.

"Thanks," he said, both surprised by and wary of her thoughtfulness.

She picked up a slice of red bell pepper but didn't take a bite. He waited, wanting her to tell him what was on her mind. He assumed she would want to know more about the morning's events, but she surprised him by asking, "Were you working for the DEA when you were gone that one year?"

He groaned silently. Not a topic he wanted to discuss with her. He didn't like talking about that time in his life. So much had happened that still haunted him. His capture and torture, Raine's death, the realization that someone he'd trusted had betrayed him.

He nodded slowly. "Yes, I was on assignment in Colombia, working undercover. I wasn't supposed to be gone that long, but the cartel found out who I was and took me prisoner."

Her eyes widened. "Wh-what?"

He raised one shoulder. "It was a long time ago and I'm fine."

"It wasn't a long time ago. You came home less than four years ago." She brushed away tears. "I thought you were just living your life. No one told me."

"I'm sure your mother didn't want to upset you."

"Upset me? She didn't tell me my own father was held captive by some drug cartel? How did they even know who you were?"

"Someone on the inside told them."

The tears stopped. "Do you know who did that?"

He nodded. "He's dead."

"Did you kill him?"

He managed a slight smile. "No. I don't do revenge killings. The cartel did it. While they appreciated the information, they knew he could never be trusted, so they killed him." He didn't mention they'd slit open his belly and left him to bleed out and be eaten in the jungle.

"Did they hurt you?"

He thought about the scars on his torso, reminders of the knife fights he'd been forced into. He thought of the beatings and the starvation, of how they'd poisoned him just enough to make him wish he would die, but not enough to actually kill him.

"Joylyn, I'm fine. Why do you want to talk about this?"

"Because I should know what happened to you. What

if you'd died? What if the last thing I ever said to you was that I didn't want to see you anymore? I thought you were just ignoring me, and now I find out you were in Colombia and kidnapped and I never knew."

"Maybe if you'd bothered to talk to me, this wouldn't be such a surprise. I showed up every damned weekend for months before taking the first assignment. When I got back, I kept showing up. Every weekend, Joylyn. Until you graduated from high school. What the hell?"

She stared at him, wide-eyed. "You've never sworn at me before."

"You've never poked at the open wound before." He sighed. "I'm sorry. I won't swear at you again."

"It's okay. I probably deserve it."

He leaned toward her. "Tell me what happened. Please. I want to know. Why did you turn your back on me? I want to say it was just some teenage thing, but I know it wasn't. I can't think of a single thing I did that was worthy of that kind of rejection. Just tell me."

She lowered her gaze before looking at him again. "It was Sandy."

"My ex-wife? What does she have to do with anything?"

Sandy had never been thrilled to have a stepdaughter, he thought, then reminded himself it wasn't the stepdaughter she'd objected to as much as Garrick's devotion to Joylyn. That was what had pissed off Sandy.

"When you two split up, she came to see me." She bit her lower lip. "She said you'd thrown her out because you'd gotten tired of her. She said you'd never really loved me and that she wanted me to prepare myself because I was next. She said you couldn't wait for me to grow up so you could be done with me."

"What?" he roared, coming to his feet.

Joylyn stared at him without speaking. Probably for the best, he thought, pacing the length of the kitchen, looking for something to throw through the window.

How could she? That bitch. Only the word wasn't strong enough and he couldn't think of one bad enough. How could she have done that? *Who* would have done that to an impressionable kid?

He returned to the table and sank back in his chair, then stretched out his arms and took Joylyn's hands in his.

"I love you," he said, doing his best to keep his voice calm. "Joylyn, I have always loved you. Do you believe me?"

She hesitated before nodding.

"Good. Now look into my eyes so you can see I'm telling the truth. I did not dump Sandy. She left me because she hated everything about our life. She made that very clear. She was angry that I wouldn't move to a different city or find another job. She wanted me to sell insurance or some such nonsense."

"You'd be really bad at that."

"I probably would. Salespeople have skills I don't begin to understand. Anyway, I came home one day and she was moving out. She had a whole list of reasons."

"Was I one of them?"

Now it was his turn to pause. He weighed the consequences of lying, only to realize he had to be completely honest. "Yes."

"She never liked me."

"I think the person she didn't like was me, kid."

One corner of Joylyn's mouth turned up. "That might be true."

He squeezed her hands. "I never wanted to stop seeing

you. I didn't look forward to you growing up and moving on. If it were up to me, I would have kept you nine forever."

"Why nine?"

"It was a good age."

She smiled. "Dad, I couldn't be nine my whole life."

"You didn't even try."

She laughed, then started to cry. She pulled her hands free and wiped her cheeks. "Sorry. I'm one blubbering emotion these days."

"It's okay. I want you to believe me. I'll give you the phone number of some of my friends back in Phoenix. You can text them and get all this confirmed. I didn't dump Sandy, and I would never abandon you."

"I know."

Some of the tension left his body. "You believe me?"

She nodded. "I do."

"Was that really why you refused to see me? You were leaving me first?"

"It wasn't a very formed plan. Part of it was that and part of it was me testing you, I think. I wanted you to push back. I wanted you to get mad and demand I see you."

"I would have, only I was giving you space." Completely the wrong thing to do, he thought grimly. "The whole time you assumed my actions proved what you already believed."

She nodded.

"I wish you could have talked to me," he said.

"Me, too. And I wish you would have told me more about the divorce."

"I didn't want you to worry." He ran his hand through his hair. "We are terrible communicators."

She smiled. "Mom's at fault, too. She should have made me see you."

"I'll be sure to mention that the next time we talk. She always enjoys being told she's wrong."

Joylyn laughed.

He reached for her hand again. "Can we start over? Can you believe that I'm so happy you're here and that no matter what, you're never getting rid of me?"

"I'll try."

"I love you, Joylyn."

She swallowed. "I love you, too, Dad."

He let the words wash over him. For this moment, things were good. He wasn't dumb enough to believe one conversation could fix five or six years of problems, but it was a start.

"You want to go out to dinner?" he asked. "You can pick where. We can even go to that horrible barbecue place you like."

"Why don't you like it? You like barbecue."

"It's too cute. They're trying too hard."

"You just don't like the dancing pigs. I think they're the best part."

He rose. "That's where you want to go, isn't it?"

She grinned. "You know it. And when we get home, we're going to decorate the house."

"As long as it's not with dancing pigs, I'm in."

Got a second?

Wynn stared at the text, ignoring the sense of excitement that bubbled up inside her at the message. Garrick wasn't texting her about sex—it was after eight on a school night. There was no way they could do anything. Not that it being a school night mattered for them, but it meant Hunter was home.

Maybe she should hint to Hunter to have a sleepover with one of his friends, then figure out a way to subtly tell Garrick that she was going to have the house to herself, she thought with a smile as she texted him back.

Yes and you can even have more than just the one second.

Very funny. I'll be right over.

She stood and looked at her son. Hunter was stretched out on the family room sectional, his gaze glued on the television where one of his favorite sitcoms played.

"Garrick's going to stop by to talk about something," she said. "We'll be in the living room."

"Okay, Mom." His attention never left the screen.

"Later we're going to hunt parrots and sell them on eBay."

This time Hunter turned to face her. "Just because I don't look at you doesn't mean I'm not listening."

She laughed. "Just checking."

"Where would you hunt parrots? Aren't they from South America? That's a long way to go."

"Yes, it is, although I believe there is a flock of parrots living somewhere in Los Angeles. And it's not really a flock. A group of parrots is called a pandemonium."

"You're making that up."

"Not even a little."

Hunter sighed. "Parents are weird."

"And yet you love me anyway."

She headed for the front door and pulled it open just as Garrick stepped onto her porch.

He looked good. Tall and lean, with a hard edge to his

expression. She thought about the events that had dominated the local news.

"Hi," she said, stepping into his embrace and hugging
him tight. "You okay after today?"

For a second he looked confused. "You mean the shooting." He swore. "That's not even what I wanted to talk
about. Damn, it was a day."

She led him into the living room where they sat on the
sofa, facing each other. She tucked her feet under her.

"What happened?"

"With the shooting? From what I heard, the local news
got all the details right. My guys are going to be okay.
They'll both be released in the morning. The suspect is
dead, and based on what I saw he did to his own kid, I'm
okay with that." He held up a hand. "That makes me a bad
person, I know. I'll live with it. Should he have been shot
in cold blood? No. But he drew first and injured two of my
men. He could have killed them and more, so he got what
he deserved."

It was a lot to take in. She stayed quiet so he would keep
talking. She didn't know much about what it took to work
in law enforcement, but she was clear on the fact that even
in Happily Inc, Garrick saw things she couldn't imagine.
When she added in his time in Phoenix and the DEA, he
was dealing with more than most.

He gave her a few more details about what had happened
at work, then sucked in a breath.

"I talked to Joylyn."

"Good talk or bad talk?"

"Good. Tough, but good." He looked at her. "I found out
why she stopped wanting to see me."

Wynn leaned toward him. "Tell me."

"It was my ex-wife. She lied. She said I'd dumped her

and that I couldn't wait to get Joylyn out of my life. She said my own daughter was a burden and that I didn't really want to spend time with her." Pain filled his eyes. "It wasn't like that. Sandy left because she didn't want to be married to me anymore. She'd always resented how close I was to Joylyn and how I made her a priority. At the time I knew I was probably pushing things in my marriage. I made sure all the holidays revolved around Joylyn without letting Sandy have input. But to lie to my daughter, to make her feel I didn't care about her."

His jaw clenched. "I want to do something, but I don't know what. Finding her and confronting her all these years later probably isn't a good idea."

"No, it isn't. Especially when you're angry."

"I'd never hurt her."

"No, but you might scare her and that doesn't help anyone. What did you tell Joylyn?"

"That I loved her and always wanted to see her. I reminded her I showed up every weekend, hoping she would see me."

He leaned forward and took Wynn's hand in his. "I missed her so much. Being with her was the best, and one day it was just gone. I didn't know how to deal with that."

"Which you also told her, right?"

"I did. I offered to give her the phone numbers of my friends back in Phoenix so she could confirm the story with them. I wanted her to know I was telling the truth."

Which was just like him, Wynn thought. No one could question his affection for Joylyn.

"I'm sorry Sandy did that. She must have been really upset to lash out the way she did, which is an observation, not an excuse. Even if she felt justified to hate you, hurting Joylyn like that crossed a line."

He shifted so he was leaning back against the sofa, but kept hold of her hand. "When we got married, we talked about having kids, but we wanted to wait. After a couple of years, I started bringing it up, but she always had a reason why now wasn't a good time. Eventually we started fighting about it. I accused her of changing her mind."

He looked at Wynn. "I wonder if my relationship with Joylyn had something to do with that. I wonder if she thought I wouldn't love our child the way I loved Joylyn."

"Did she ever say that?"

"No. I would have denied it. Of course I would have loved our kid just as much. It's not like I have a limited amount of parental love and Joylyn got it all."

"That's the rational argument."

He nodded. "You're right. I really was unreasonable with Sandy. She begged me to make changes in some of the holiday rituals Joylyn and I had. So the three of us could do them together. But I said what we did was important and I wanted everything to stay the same."

"Like?"

"Like we spent every Christmas Day at Alisha's house."

"That's very modern of you."

"Yeah, well, Sandy had family in the area. She said we should at least alternate so she could sometimes see her family on Christmas."

"She's not wrong."

"I know. I just…" He looked at her again. "I wanted to spend every second with my daughter. I wanted her to feel safe and loved." He shifted his gaze to the front window. "When I got a job on the Phoenix police force, I talked to Alisha about joint custody. She didn't want to do that. I even went so far as to talk to a lawyer. She said I had a good case—that I'd agreed to the parenting plan when I'd been a minor and my situation had completely changed. She thought I could get more time with Joylyn."

"Why didn't you pursue it?"

"How do you know I didn't?"

"Because your lawyer said you had a good case, so if you had, the parenting plan would have changed. If it changed, Joylyn wouldn't have been a position to refuse to see you. So why didn't you?"

"Joylyn didn't want me to do it," he said. "I talked to her about it. She would be testifying in court. She got upset and said she didn't want to hurt her mom. That it would be hard for everyone. She liked how things were."

"Which must have hurt to hear."

"Some," he admitted. "In my head, I got her point. Joylyn had a routine she liked. She had brothers and a stepdad. Mitch is a good guy. Why upset everything? So I didn't move forward, and then I met Sandy and you know the rest."

"You're a good dad. I'm sorry you lost so much time with Joylyn."

"Me, too. I told her about Colombia. She was asking questions and it came out."

"She's twenty-one, married and pregnant. I think she's mature enough to handle the information."

He turned to her. "I told her I'd been captured because somebody who knew who I really was betrayed me, but I didn't tell her the rest of it."

Questions bubbled up, but she held them inside. She had a feeling Garrick needed to talk about what had happened, but that would go better if he went at his own pace, and not hers.

He rubbed his thumb against the back of her hand. "I was sent into Colombia as an American with a drug distribution connection. I had a good identity and a partner. Raine. She was a DEA agent—one of their best. We were supposed to be newly married and very happy together. Everywhere I went, she went. She played dumb, so eventually the men started ignoring her."

Wynn felt a knot form in her stomach. Whoever Raine was, Wynn hated her. Pretend married? So they'd slept together.

"Was she beautiful?" she asked before she could stop herself.

He chuckled. "Yes, but that's not the point."

"Still, it's interesting information." She cleared her throat. "Go on."

"We gathered information and sent it back home. It was a dangerous lifestyle."

She thought of the scars on his torso. "I've, ah, seen you mowing the lawn without a shirt." She made a vague motion with her hands.

His humor faded. "The guys in the cartel liked to prove themselves with knife fights. I trained before I went on assignment, but it took me a while to get good."

She winced. "They could have killed you."

He nodded. "But they didn't. Once they trusted me, we started to set up the distribution chain. We were about to put it all in play when someone told them who I was, and Raine and I were taken prisoner."

"That must have been hard."

He didn't meet her gaze. "It was. Harder on Raine, in some ways. We both knew we were on assignment and that our being married was just an act, but there were things we had to do and eventually it got real for her." He looked at her. "She fell in love with me."

The knot in her stomach tightened. "You didn't share her feelings?"

He shook his head. "I knew it was a problem, but there was nothing I could do about it. Breaking up with her wasn't an option, and neither of us wanted to end the assignment because her feelings had changed. We agreed to move forward and deal with it when we got back to the States."

"She was hoping you would fall in love with her," Wynn said.

"Yeah. That was the plan. I knew it wasn't going to happen, but like I said, there wasn't anything I could do about it. Then we were ratted out and stuck in a cage." He drew in a breath. "Some of the scars I have are from that time. Like I said, they enjoyed playing with knives. I could handle it, but when they went after Raine, I nearly lost it."

Wynn knew he wouldn't tell her any details, which was fine with her. She could make up her own, and they were awful enough without her knowing the truth.

"How did she die?"

"I didn't say she was dead."

"But she is."

He nodded. "Yes." Darkness filled his eyes. "We came up with an escape plan. It was risky, but we knew it was just a matter of time until we were killed. The cartel wanted ransom, but even if the DEA paid it, there was no guarantee we would be released."

He leaned back his head and closed his eyes. "During the escape, someone came after us with a gun. Raine threw herself in front of me, taking the bullets. She died and I got away."

Wynn couldn't process all her feelings, and she hadn't even been there. What must Garrick be going through?

Instinctively she closed the distance between them and

wrapped her arms around him. He shifted, pulling her close and hanging on so tightly, she could barely breathe.

"I'm sorry," she whispered.

"Me, too. Everything happened so fast. One second we were running and the next that guy was there."

She felt the tension in his body. Even as she tried not to imagine the scene, she could see it clearly in her head. He didn't say what had happened to the man who tried to stop them, and she didn't ask. She didn't have to—she already knew. Garrick would have killed him, then escaped.

"I carried her out," he said quietly. "I wanted to get her body back to her family. It was the least I could do."

"It's not your fault. You didn't ask her to do it."

"She loved me and I didn't love her back. She died knowing that."

"She died saving the man she loved. She would do it again."

"You don't know that."

She drew back enough to stare into his eyes. "Yes, I do. I've been in love. I know what it feels like. A woman in love will do almost anything for her man."

Wynn had. She'd made incredibly stupid decisions in the name of love and had lived with the consequences. Fourteen years later, she was only just beginning to forgive herself.

"I didn't put it in the report," Garrick said. "Or mention it in the debrief. I figured no one had to know how she felt. It wasn't their business."

"You were right to do that."

He loosened his hold on her but kept his arms around her. She felt him relax, as if in the telling, he was able to let the past go a little.

They sat in silence for a minute or so, then he said, "When I got home, I went to see Joylyn. I needed to see her and know that she was okay, but she refused to have anything to do with me. She was close to heading off to college. I was restless and didn't know what to do next."

"Did you go back to the Phoenix Police Department?"

"Sure, but my heart wasn't in it. Then I got offered a job here."

"So you moved back."

"I went to see Joylyn, to tell her what was happening. She said she didn't care and shut the door in my face."

She put her head on his shoulder. "Does knowing why she acted like that help?"

"Some, but it doesn't make up for everything we missed together."

"The road ahead is going to be a little bumpy at times, but you two have made progress. Give her some time to let it all sink in. You're going to be a grandpa. You can start new rituals together."

He stared at her. "Holy crap. I'm going to be a grandfather. That makes me feel old."

"If it helps, you still look good."

"I'm thirty-eight and I'm going to be a grandfather. How could I not have figured that out before?"

"It is surprising. The big belly bump should have been a clue."

"Smart-ass."

She grinned. "Uh-huh. Pretty much all the time."

"I'm not complaining. I like it. I have a list of things I like about you."

Before she could do much more than get all tingly from the compliment, he leaned in and kissed her. The feel of his mouth—warm and just the tiniest bit demanding—made her melt into him. He put his hands on her hips and shifted her so she was straddling his lap. He broke the kiss and stared into her eyes.

"I'm very clear on the fact that your son is just down the hall and that he could walk in on us at any moment."

He pushed down on her hips, settling the very center of her against his crotch. She was pleased to feel the hard ridge of an erection through his jeans.

"But," he added, "a few minutes of making out might be nice."

"I agree," she said, rocking slightly against him.

Instantly his eyes dilated and his breath caught. "That could be dangerous."

"It could."

She bent her head and brushed her mouth against his. At the same time, she pulled his hands to her breasts. His fingers immediately found her tight nipples and rubbed them.

Heat flared everywhere before settling between her legs. She couldn't help rubbing against him again, a little more frantically this time. He inhaled sharply and claimed her with a hot, deep kiss that stole her breath.

She wanted to strip off her clothes and have him touch her everywhere. She wanted him parting her legs and filling her until she had no option but to lose herself in a powerful orgasm that made her scream. She wanted touching and kissing and claiming and—

He drew back and swore. "We have to stop."

He was right, of course, but still she wanted to protest.

"I want you," she whispered.

His jaw clenched. "Tell me about it. I want you, too."

"I'll talk to Hunter about spending the night with a friend. Maybe this weekend."

"That would be great. Better than great."

She smiled and shifted off him. He rose.

"I should be going."

She stood as well, then glanced at his crotch.

"You're, um, going to want to walk around a while before going home."

He looked down at himself, then back at her. "Technically that's your fault. At least it's dark out. I wouldn't want to scare the neighbors."

"I don't think they'd be scared. I think they'd be impressed."

He chuckled, kissed her briefly and walked to the door. "Thanks, Wynn. For all of it."

"Anytime."

He left. She locked the front door, then leaned against it and smiled, thinking she felt like a teenager—counting the minutes until the weekend.

chapter eleven

Wynn had to admit she was having a good morning. Her sexy make-out session with Garrick had left her smiling, and Hunter had already made plans to spend Saturday night with a friend. She and Garrick would have the house to themselves and plenty of time to take things to the next level. All in all, a happy chain of events.

Her nine o'clock meeting had been successful, with the bride and groom narrowing down her invitation choices to just three. Wynn had ordered the samples, and they'd set up a second meeting to talk about the various options. A local business had ordered postcards for a mailing along with several sets of business cards, and more of Natalie's special-order paper had arrived.

Wynn did her best to keep her happiness to herself. Being cheerful was one thing, but giddy tended to confuse her employees and frighten the customers. During a brief lull, she busied herself putting up seasonal decorations, including a beautiful menorah, a tabletop Christmas tree, a Kwanzaa flag and her silly plastic *Snow White and the Seven Dwarfs* set. The latter had been a gift from Ms. James, Wynn's neighbor when she'd been a kid. Ms. James had always believed in Wynn. Later, when Wynn was a scared and struggling single mom, she would think of Ms. James and vow to make her proud. She brought out the set every holiday season, mostly to try to show her friend that somehow she'd managed to pull it all together.

Wynn got herself a cup of coffee and retreated to her office. She had several orders to proof, then payroll information to send over to her accounting person. She picked up the first flyer and studied the design. After measuring the borders, she carefully read each word to make sure it was spelled correctly. She'd just initialed the sticky note attached to indicate she'd reviewed the design when her cell phone rang.

"Hello?"

"Is this Wynn Beauchene?"

"Yes."

"Hi, I'm Camilla Henderson. We're in the process of reviewing Hunter's Junior ROTC application, and I have a few questions."

Wynn stared unseeingly at the work on her desk. The caller was unfamiliar, as was the topic. Hunter's what?

"I'm sorry, but who are you again?"

"I'm Camilla Henderson. I work for the local JROTC director. There are a few items missing from the application. I could get the answers now from you, if it's a good time."

"His application to Junior ROTC?"

"Yes."

What on earth? Hunter hadn't applied to Junior ROTC. Wynn didn't even know what that was. They'd never discussed anything like it, and Wynn had never signed any kind of application.

Even as she mentally tried to make sense of it all, a bigger, uglier problem sat down in front of her. There was no way Hunter could have applied to any kind of program without getting a parent's signature. And if Camilla had an application in her hands, one Wynn didn't know about, then someone had faked the parental approval. And that someone was most likely Hunter.

Disappointment joined confusion. She still wasn't sure what was going on, but she was going to have to figure it out.

"Sorry for sounding so distracted," she said, doing her best to fake a casual tone. "I'm in a meeting. May I call you back later?"

"Of course." Camilla gave her a direct number and hung up.

Wynn turned to her computer and typed Junior ROTC into the search engine. Seconds later she was on the website and learning that JROTC was, in fact, a real thing. From what she could tell, it was a leadership program that was very successful. She'd heard of ROTC at the college level but not anything in junior high or high school. But when she checked the local area, his school was listed as having a program. All of which was interesting, but didn't change the fact that Hunter had gone behind her back to apply. He hadn't bothered talking to her at all—he'd just done it.

What had he been thinking? Did he really believe he could get into an ROTC program without her knowing? Even more to the point, why hadn't he said anything to her? They talked about everything—or she had thought they did. Now she wasn't sure about anything where he was concerned.

She got to her feet and circled her desk. Her stomach hurt, and her head was spinning with questions and

thoughts. This wasn't her kid. Hunter didn't act like this.
When he wanted to do something, he asked and they talked
about it. She wasn't unreasonable. Why had he done this
and what was she supposed to do now?

She picked up her phone to text one of her friends, only
she didn't know if any of them would have the kind of advice she needed. After hesitating a few seconds, she texted
Garrick.

I have a kid problem I need to talk about. You have any
free time today?

It took only a minute for him to answer. I could grab a
coffee right now if that works.

It does. Thanks.

They settled on a place. Wynn took her handbag from
the drawer in her desk, told her office manager she would
be gone for about an hour, then drove into the center of town
where she parked and walked to the coffee shop by the river.

She ordered two lattes and carried them to a table in the
corner. For once the view of the Rio de los Suenos didn't
make her happy, nor did she appreciate the beauty of the
day or the little Santa on the table.

Two minutes later Garrick walked in. He spotted her
and headed for the table. Under normal circumstances, she
would have appreciated seeing him looking all manly in
his uniform, but even that wasn't enough to distract her.

"I got you a latte," she said. "I hope that's okay. Or do
you only drink black coffee?"

He sat across from her and picked up the drink. "I enjoy

a latte from time to time. Thanks for getting it for me. What's going on?"

"It's Hunter."

One corner of his mouth turned up. "I kind of assumed that, with him being your only child."

She tried to smile back at him, but couldn't, then explained about the unexpected phone call.

"I went online," she said. "Junior ROTC really exists."

"Sure. They're at the high school. Ninth graders in junior high can also join the last semester before they graduate."

"How do you know that?"

"I know about all the extracurricular activities going on at both the high school and junior high. I know which ones make my day easier and which ones don't."

Interesting, but Garrick being good at his job wasn't something she could care about right now.

"He lied to me," she said, doing her best to stay in her head. If she gave in to her emotions, she would end up losing control. Later, when she'd figured out what to do, she would cry and scream and throw things, just not now.

"He lied to me," she repeated. "He doesn't do that." She held up a hand. "I'm not saying he never lies—of course he does. He messes up. He can be lazy and forgetful. He's a normal person. But this is different. It's out of character for him, and I don't know why he did it. Why didn't he talk to me in the first place?"

She looked at Garrick. "He never mentioned the JROTC thing at all. I had no idea he was thinking about it. I didn't even know it existed. I don't get it. Why wouldn't he bring it up in conversation? Why wouldn't he ask? He went behind my back and faked my signature. How can I ever trust him again?"

Garrick put his hand over hers. "Breathe."

"I'm breathing." Sort of. She pressed her free hand against her chest and consciously tried to relax. "Where did this come from and why didn't he talk to me? I know I keep saying that, but it's a real question. Why not discuss it the way we talk about everything else?"

"Do you have any opinions on the military? Anyone in your family a former sailor, Marine, whatever?"

"What? I don't know. It was just my mom and me. I never knew any extended family, so I have no idea if anyone ever served." She paused, trying to formulate an answer to the question. "I support the military. I appreciate those who serve. We need a strong defense."

His gaze was steady. "'But not my kid?'"

The question was a kick in the gut. She withdrew her hand. "I never said that."

"I know. I'm asking if you think it. Do you make it clear to Hunter that's not an option? Not overtly but in subtle ways? JROTC isn't a direct line to joining one of the branches, but it would expose him to the idea of it. Would you be okay with that?" He shook his head. "No, would *he* think you're okay with it?"

She wanted to say she'd never even hinted that he shouldn't consider the military, but stopped herself. Was that true? While she knew she'd never said anything directly, she wondered if somehow she'd had a bias.

"I don't know," she admitted. "I might have said something. I wouldn't have meant it in a bad way. I'd be worried about his safety, and I have no real experience with the concept. It's just not part of my world. It's not like we're near a military base or anything." She clutched her coffee. "Does it matter? At the end of the day, he went behind my back and he was dishonest."

"I agree that's the bigger issue. I was just trying to find out if there was an obvious reason."

"Not one I can see. I'm going to have to talk to him," she said. "He is going to be in such trouble. I don't even know where to begin with the punishment. And when we—"

She stared at Garrick as an awful truth popped into her head. "Oh, no. He lied on his application. He wanted to join and by lying, he's violated the honor code or whatever it is." She dropped her head to her hands, then straightened. "Great, now it's on me. I either keep quiet about the lie so he can be a part of JROTC, or I tell the truth and he doesn't get in. If I don't say anything, then I'm teaching him the wrong lesson, and if I rat him out, I'm the bad guy."

"You wouldn't be ratting him out."

"You're objecting to the word choice, but not the reality. This puts me in a horrible situation." She slapped her hands on the table. "Why did he have to do this?"

"I don't know. I'm sorry you have to deal with it."

"Me, too. I don't want to be the grown-up. I'm not the right person to be doing this. I can't do this."

He leaned toward her. "Wynn, you're the strongest person I know. You'll figure it out. Trust your instincts."

"I can't. I have crappy instincts sometimes. I've done horrible things in my life. Maybe this is a payback for that."

"Life isn't that tidy. Besides, I don't believe you've done terrible things."

"You're wrong. I have."

"Shoplifting when you were seven?" he asked, his voice teasing.

"No. I never did anything like that."

"You're a good person. This is not some karmic justice. Hunter messed up. That's all."

She knew in her head he was right, but in her gut she was less certain. She looked at him.

"When I was nineteen, I fell wildly in love with a guy named Chas." Despite everything, she smiled. "Not short for Charles or anything so mundane. Just Chas. He was blond and gorgeous and everything I'd ever wanted."

Garrick's gaze narrowed. "Are we talking about Hunter's father?"

"We are. He was a professional surfer, waiting for the season to start up. Our meeting was so random, it shouldn't have happened, but it did and I fell for him. I knew he was going to leave and I didn't want him to go."

She remembered the pain of realizing Chas was going to leave her forever. She didn't think she could physically survive—without Chas in her life, she thought she would cease to exist.

"I begged him to take me with him. I told him I would pay my own way, carry his gear, anything." She dropped her gaze to the table. "He said he wouldn't take me along because he needed to focus. I would only be a distraction. I gave him my heart and he said I was a distraction. My heart broke."

"What did you do?"

She reached for her coffee again, sucked in a breath and looked at Garrick. "I got pregnant. I did it on purpose. It wasn't a mistake or an accident. I knew exactly what I was doing because I believed once he knew about the baby, everything would change. I knew it was wrong and manipulative, but still I did it."

Garrick's eyes widened slightly. She sensed he was trying to hide his shock, but she saw the tension in his body. "What happened?"

"I told him I was pregnant, and he said it didn't change

the fact that he didn't want me with him. He was sorry that I'd made the decision to try to trap him, but he was leaving. I could have the kid or not. That was on me. Then he left and I never saw him again."

Garrick swore under his breath. "That was pretty cold-hearted."

"I don't know. Part of me agrees with you and part of me says I got what I deserved. I knew I was doing the wrong thing when I did it, and that didn't stop me. I can make excuses, but the truth is I made an awful decision. You can't force someone to be with you. The situation was never going to end well."

It had taken her a long time to come to terms with that. To accept that the blame was all hers. Chas had been clear about what he did and didn't want—she'd been the one who wouldn't listen.

"You could have had an abortion," he told her.

"Legally, yes, I could have, but I wasn't going to do that. Once I accepted I was on my own, I came up with a plan and hoped for the best. But having a child by myself was so much harder than I'd imagined. Everything was so expensive. I worked three jobs as long as I could, but once I had Hunter, I couldn't make enough to afford day care. Just paying for the diapers about killed me." She shook her head. "They're expensive. I was out of money and about to be evicted when Chas's lawyer showed up to tell me Chas had died and left me the proceeds of his life insurance policy."

"He hadn't forgotten you or the baby."

"I guess not. I was shocked and ashamed and grateful. I vowed to make the most of what he'd left me. If he was still alive, I would want to apologize for what I did. I can't regret Hunter, but my actions were unforgivable."

"You were just a kid," he told her. "You made a dumb

choice and you dealt with the consequences. Look what you've done with your life. I hope you haven't been beating yourself up about this for the past fourteen years."

"Some," she admitted. "It's hard to let go, but I'm finally in the place where I think I can move on. Then Hunter does what he did and it makes me question everything."

"What you did has nothing to do with his actions."

"Are you sure? Maybe I somehow made it all happen."

"No," he said firmly. "How would that be possible? Did you do some kind of mind-meld where you secretly convinced him to join JROTC and not tell you? If so, you have amazing powers and you should use them for good."

Wynn smiled. "When you say it like that," she began.

"It's true."

She supposed he was right. The two wrongs had nothing in common. "I wish I knew what to do."

"You'll figure it out. You're the most amazing parent I know. If I had half your skills, I wouldn't have lost all those years with Joylyn."

"That's not true. You're not to blame. It was your ex-wife."

"And Hunter made his own choices. That's not on you."

A sensible point of view, she thought. Even though she knew Garrick was right, she couldn't help wondering if somehow she was the one to blame.

"Thanks for listening to me rant," she said.

"Anytime. You ready to go back to your office?"

She nodded. "I'm going to try not to think about what I'm going to have to do later when he and I talk. I thought parenting would get easier with time, but it doesn't. Just when I figure something out, it all changes."

"You're going to do great."

He rose and pulled her to her feet, then hugged her. The

feel of his strong embrace helped as did the knowledge that he was someone she could talk to.

"I'll let you know what happens," she said.

"Good. And I'm right next door if you need anything." He looked into her eyes. "Trust your gut. You're a great mom."

"Thanks."

As she walked back to her car, she thought about what he'd said. How her screw-ups had nothing to do with Hunter's mistakes. While she knew he was right, she couldn't help thinking that maybe there was just the tiniest bit of karmic payback in what she was going to have to wrestle with. If God wanted to teach her a lesson, He'd picked a doozy of a way.

Joylyn took the shoebox-size package from the mail carrier and thanked her. The familiar loopy writing on the mailing label made her smile. She had no idea what Holly was sending her, but knew it would be great. Holly was a good friend.

Joylyn put the rest of the mail on her dad's desk, found a pair of scissors in the top drawer and quickly opened her box. Inside was a stuffed blue bunny—the kind you would win at a carnival or arcade game. The note tucked inside explained that Holly and Rex had won the bunny at the pier and wanted her to have it for her baby.

The ever-present tears appeared, but this time Joylyn didn't care. Happy tears were never a problem. She put the box in the recycling, then set the blue bunny on her dresser.

"Look what Auntie Holly got you," she told her baby as she rested a hand on her belly. "You're going to love him."

She picked up her phone and took a picture, then texted it and several heart emojis to her friend.

Seconds later her phone rang. Joylyn laughed when she saw Holly's picture.

"I would have called, but I didn't know when you were on break," she said, stretching out on the bed. "Thank you so much for the cute bunny. I love it."

"The second we saw it, Rex and I knew we had to win it for you."

There was something in her friend's voice—a level of excitement that seemed bigger than just an arcade bunny. "Are you all right?"

"Yes. You'll never believe it. It's so insane and yet, it's happening. I'm floating."

"Holly, what are you talking about?"

"Rex proposed! We're getting married."

"What?" Joylyn sat upright. "That's so great. When did it happen? What did he say? Were you shocked? Have you set a date? Tell me everything!"

"He proposed last night. We had dinner and then walked on the beach and before I knew what was happening, he went down on one knee. It was so beautiful and I said yes and we both cried. I love him so much."

"I know you do." Joylyn thought about Chandler's proposal and how happy she'd been. "You're going to have a wonderful life together."

"I know we are, but first we want to get married." She hesitated. "And really fast. We're both up for new assignments, and if we're married, we can request something where we're together."

Joylyn's mind started working through possibilities. "Then we have to put together a wedding as quickly as we can."

"Oh, we don't have time for a wedding. We need to be

married before the end of the year. We're just going to city hall or something."

Joylyn knew that Holly didn't have any family, so there was no dad to walk her down the aisle or siblings to help out. But she had friends.

"You have to want a wedding," she said.

"Sure, but it's not practical. I want to be married to Rex more than I want to wait and plan something fancy."

"You need a wedding. It will be something you'll remember forever. I'm living in a destination wedding town right now. My next door neighbor knows people who put on weddings for a living. I'm making a thousand little snowmen for a wedding that's coming up soon. Let me talk to Wynn and get her advice. Even if all I learn is just ways to have a fun reception, it will be good information."

"Thanks. I would like something more than a civil ceremony, but there isn't much time."

"Let me go talk to Wynn and I'll get back to you later today. Then you can decide."

"You're a good friend."

"I love you and I'm super happy for you. He proposed! Yay!"

They talked for a few more minutes, then Joylyn got in her car and drove to Wynn's business. She and her mother had taken nearly a year to plan her wedding. She had no idea how to throw something together in a couple of weeks. It might not even be possible, but Joylyn wanted to find out for sure.

She walked into the printing and graphics company. There was a long counter on one side and several complicated-looking machines available for the public to use. Signs advertised different kinds of services: printing, shipping, design work, wedding invitations.

There were about six employees, all working away. Joylyn was about to ask one of them where Wynn was when she spotted the other woman in her office.

Joylyn walked over and knocked on the open door.

"Hi. Do you have a second?"

Wynn stared at her as if she'd never seen her before. Joylyn was about to take a step back when Wynn shook her head and smiled.

"Sorry. I was lost in thought. It's been one of those mornings with a lot of unexpected disasters, but I'm good now. Come on in."

Joylyn sat on the chair across from Wynn's. "I need your advice. A girlfriend of mine just got engaged. She and her fiancé are both Marines. It's really great—they're perfect for each other."

"That's wonderful. Congratulations."

"Thanks. Anyway, they want to get married before the end of the year. It's a whole thing so they can be assigned together. She was talking about going to city hall, but I know they would both hate that. I wondered if I could get some advice about pulling a wedding together in a couple of weeks. How do you do that? I want to help, but I don't even know where to start. I met Renee when my dad took me to The Boardroom a couple of weeks ago and again at your place on Thanksgiving. Do you think it would be all right for me to get in touch with her and ask her thoughts?"

Wynn picked up her phone. "I'm sure it would be, but let's find out."

She pushed a couple of buttons, then waited.

"Hi, Renee. It's Wynn. Joylyn, Garrick's daughter, is here with me. She needs some advice on putting together a wedding. Do you have some time to talk to us today?"

She paused, nodding as she listened. "We can come right now," she said, looking at Joylyn.

"I'm free."

Wynn smiled and returned her attention to the phone. "We are on our way. See you in a few."

She hung up. "Let's go see what the miracle workers at Weddings Out of the Box have to say about all this." She grabbed a pad of paper and a pen, passing both to Joylyn.

They walked to Wynn's car and drove the short distance to Weddings Out of the Box. The large location had different facades on each side, ample parking and a big outdoor area. Wynn led the way inside.

Renee was waiting for them in the large foyer.

"A wedding," she said, hugging them both. "I love a wedding. Tell me everything."

Joylyn explained about the proposal and the quick time line.

Renee, perfectly dressed in a tailored navy suit, with her long red hair pulled back in a ponytail, pressed her hands to her chest.

"So romantic. I think we can work something out for two soldiers in love."

"Oh, they're not soldiers," Joylyn said quickly. "They're Marines. A Marine is a Marine."

Renee laughed. "Lesson learned. Come on to the conference room and we'll talk."

Renee motioned for them to sit on either side of the table. She sat next to Joylyn and set a tablet in front of her. After she touched a few buttons, the screen on the wall lit up and a chart appeared.

"Weddings are all variations on a theme," Renee said. "You have the wedding couple, the person marrying them and guests. There is a ceremony and a reception. What you do with those elements determines the personality and expense of the wedding."

She pushed a button and another chart popped up. "Usually we like about a year to plan everything, but we can work a quicker time line."

The chart was replaced by a calendar of the month of December. "No pressure, but we have a cancellation for the eighteenth of December."

Joylyn looked from the screen to Renee. "I don't understand. You're saying Holly and Rex could get married here?"

"If they wanted to. Unless it's too far."

"They're in San Diego. They could make the drive. What would be involved and what would it cost?" She hesitated. "Neither of them have any family or money. Just what they make from their jobs."

"So here's the thing," Renee told her. "The wedding that was scheduled for that day didn't cancel very long ago. That means some items are already purchased and paid for. If Holly doesn't mind not having a lot of choices, we can use what's been arranged. I can pull together some numbers, if you'd like."

"Yes, please."

"What's the theme?" Wynn asked.

"Theme?"

Renee smiled. "We do theme weddings here. Luckily for your friend, this one isn't space aliens or apples. It was going to be a Christmas wedding. Very traditional. I have all the decorations and linens already. Tables and chairs are no problem. I'll ask the caterer what's been ordered and get her costs to move forward. Oh, I'll need the number of guests."

"It won't be very many. Like I said, they don't have family. But I'll ask her."

"Great, and I'll get you my information by this time tomorrow."

Joylyn felt the familiar burn of tears. "You're being so nice. Thank you. This could be amazing for her and Rex."

"I hope so. We don't get many military weddings. This would be really fun for all of us to give them the wedding of their dreams." She smiled. "In three weeks or less."

"I'll text her as soon as I get home." She turned to Wynn. "Thank you so much for helping me."

"I'm happy to be a part of it."

chapter twelve

After work Garrick drove up the mountain to Jasper's house. About once a month the guys liked to get together to watch a game. They'd stolen the idea from the women in town who had biweekly girlfriend lunches. They rotated locations, and the host provided food. While the women had fancy things like dips and salads, the guys preferred an easier menu, often with a barbecue or smoker involved.

Garrick parked next to Drew's SUV and walked inside. Koda was on guard duty, watching as each person entered, carefully sniffing fingers to make sure he really knew who they were. Garrick crouched and petted the old dog before heading into the family room to join his friends.

He was still thinking about what Wynn had told him that morning. Knowing how she'd come to be pregnant with Hunter didn't make him think less of her. He could understand why she'd done what she'd done. He supposed if he had to explain why it was on his mind it would be because he was so impressed with the person she'd become.

She'd taken herself from a struggling single mother to a

successful businesswoman. She was strong, compassion-
ate, caring. He knew she gave generously to local chari-
ties and had a feeling those gifts were her attempts to pay
forward some part of what Chas had done by leaving her
his insurance money.

"Garrick, you made it," Mathias Mitchell called, waving a beer. "Drinks are in the kitchen and Jasper's out back
working the smoker."

Garrick greeted everyone else, then made his way to the
kitchen. He grabbed a beer from the refrigerator, pausing
to talk with Nick Mitchell, Mathias's older brother, before
heading outside where Jasper stood in front of the smoker,
talking to Cade Saunders.

As Garrick joined his friends, he inhaled the scent of
meat, barbecue seasonings and wood chips.

"What are you smoking?" he asked. "It smells great."

"I'm starving," Cade admitted. "Being out here isn't
helping."

"Only a few more minutes," Jasper told them. "I have
ribs. Pounds of ribs. The sides are waiting inside."

Cade laughed. "Trying to show us all up?"

"Renee got me the smoker for my birthday. It's fun to
get to use it like this." Jasper picked up his beer. "Planning
to stay through the whole game?" he asked Cade.

"Get off me." Cade's tone was good-natured. "She's only
eight months old. It's hard to be gone."

"Bethany is more than capable of taking care of your
daughter for a single evening."

"She's more capable than me, but I like to be around."

Cade and his wife had had their first child earlier that
year. Their circle of friends was in something of a baby
boom right now.

"I'd be careful if I were you," Garrick told Jasper. "Your

time is coming, and Cade is going to be the one teasing you about how you can't leave your kid for five minutes."

Jasper grinned. "Yeah, I know it's coming and I don't mind. For so long I never thought I'd have kids, but since marrying Renee, it's been on my mind. We're currently dealing with logistics. Renee loves her work too much to want to give it up, and I feel the same about what I do." He shrugged. "We're talking about getting in some full-time help. We have enough land where we can build a good-sized cabin right here on the property."

The plan made sense, Garrick thought, looking around at the surrounding forest. He wasn't sure how big Jasper's lot was, but it was at least a dozen or so acres. Adding a cabin wouldn't be a problem. As for paying for it all—the new building, the full-time nanny—that wouldn't be an issue, either. Jasper was a successful author whose books sold around the world. When combined with what Renee made at Weddings Out of the Box, he would guess they weren't ever going to have money problems.

A different situation from when Joylyn was born, he thought. Back then his mom and Alisha's mom had pitched in to cover a lot of the baby duty, and both families had taken care of the expenses. He and Alisha had still been in high school. Even when they'd graduated and gone to college, Alisha's mother had been a big part of the caretaking.

"Verity, Renee's mom, has told us she wants to come stay for at least the first month," Jasper added.

"You're the only one holding up the program," Cade teased.

"Renee's not quite there, either," Jasper said. "But in the next few months we'll be ready." He looked at Garrick. "What about you?"

"Me? I have my kid, and she's about to give me my first grandchild."

"Sure, but you're still in your thirties. Don't you think about having another family?"

"I haven't been." It had been on his mind when he'd been married to Sandy, but not since then. He would want to find the right woman—someone who had the same set of values he did. Someone he loved and who could be a great mom.

"We want more children," Cade said. "I just wish they could all be girls."

"Afraid what the king will do when he has a grandson?" Jasper asked with a chuckle.

"You have no idea how intense that man can be."

Bethany had grown up with American sensibilities and royal protocol. Despite living on a ranch in Happily Inc, she and Cade still had to deal with royal trappings, including very involved and excited grandparents to their daughter.

"Didn't the king declare a national holiday when your daughter was born?" Garrick asked.

"There was a parade, not a holiday."

"So he's saving that for the boy?" Jasper asked.

"Don't even joke about it."

Garrick and Jasper exchanged a high five.

"Laugh all you want," Cade told them. "But one day the two of you will have more kids, and you'll know it's never easy. Even if your father-in-law isn't royal."

Wynn sat on her front porch. It was nearly ten in the evening. She was tired, but wasn't sure she was going to be able to sleep—not with everything on her mind.

A familiar SUV pulled in next door. Garrick got out and walked over to sit next to her.

"How was the man-fest?" she asked.

"Good. The Seahawks won and Jasper made ribs with his new smoker."

"He's cooking? Good for Renee. She's training him well."

He looked at her. "How are you holding together?"

"By strings that are fraying as we speak." She pulled her knees to her chest. "I haven't said anything to Hunter yet. I just can't figure out how to start the conversation. Once I get my thoughts together, I'll talk to him. In the meantime I called back the lady at Junior ROTC and answered the rest of her questions."

He put his arm around her. "Do you know what you're going to do?"

She shook her head. "I feel trapped. It's what I said before. If I tell them what he did, which is the right thing to do, he'll be thrown out of the program. If I don't tell them, he can stay in but I'm teaching him a lousy life lesson."

She looked at him. "I spent some time online, reading about the program. It's really great. The main focus is leadership. They emphasize helping young women and minority students. He would be exposed to excellent ideals and learn a lot. There are Facebook groups for parents. It's a wonderful program."

"So why didn't he just talk to you in the first place?"

"I have no idea." She sighed, feeling the weight of her responsibilities. "I know what I'm supposed to do, but I don't want to do it. I don't want him to lose the chance before he even starts. I wish he'd talked to me."

"Would you have said yes?"

A question she'd been asking herself all day. "I don't know. I like to think I would have done my research and then I would have said yes, but I'll never know."

"I'm sorry." He held her close.

"Thanks. I'll get through this." She straightened. "On

the bright side, Joylyn's friend Holly got engaged. Do you know her?"

"Yes. I met her at the wedding. How do you know about the engagement?"

Wynn told him about Joylyn coming by and asking for help with the wedding. "There was a recent cancellation at Weddings Out of the Box. The thinking is Holly and Rex can take that spot. Some things are already paid for. Renee's putting together some numbers."

"How far would a couple of thousand dollars go?" he asked.

She shifted so she could look at him. "What do you mean?"

"I'm happy to kick in the money to help pay for the wedding. If I'm remembering who Holly is, she doesn't have any family to help. They're both Marines, getting by on their salary. I doubt they have money put away for a wedding. I'd like to help."

The sadness in her heart eased a little. "That's really nice and a great idea. I'll talk to Renee about it. I'm sure that kind of money would go a long way. I can donate some, too."

"You don't have to. You're doing enough helping my daughter."

"It would make me feel better about my life."

He leaned close and pressed his forehead to hers. "I'm sorry about Hunter."

"Me, too. This is going to mess up our weekend plans." Whatever happened with her son, there was no way she was going to let him spend the night with a friend.

"I figured as much. I was looking forward to our plans, but this is more important."

"Thanks for understanding."

"Hey, I have a kid, too. I know what it's like."

She appreciated the information and the understanding. "You could have been mad."

He lightly kissed her. "Not my style. Besides—" He grinned. "I'm looking pretty good right about now."

Despite everything, she managed a laugh. "You know what? You really are."

Garrick glanced at the clock on the kitchen wall and was pleased to see there was time for a second cup of coffee before he had to head to work. He'd just finishing pouring when Joylyn walked in.

"I hate it here," she announced, her face blotchy and her eyes swollen. "Everything about this stupid town is awful. I wish I was anywhere but here."

What the hell? "But things were great yesterday," he said before he could stop himself. "You were happy. You're making your snowmen, and you and Holly are planning her wedding. You said you were feeling good. What went wrong?"

She glared at him. "I don't want to talk about it."

He was proud of himself for holding in the instinctive response of, "Well, I don't care. You're going to talk about it." Instead, he forced himself to relax then said, "Joylyn, I can see you're upset. I'd like to help. Please tell me what's going on."

She slumped down at the table. "You can't help me. It's awful. I hate my life."

Despite a need to bolt for safety, he sat across from her and prepared to wait her out.

The glare sharpened. "You're not going to make me talk. I have nothing to say to you."

He sipped his coffee.

She threw up her hands. "Fine. Get off me. I'll tell you." Tears rolled down her cheeks. "I have to go to my birthing classes by myself. I don't have anyone to go with me."

Was that all? "I'll go with you."

"Oh, please. That's ridiculous. You can't go to a birthing class."

"Why not?"

"You're my father."

"I'm someone who loves you. I know you'll be back in Phoenix when the baby's born, so it's not like you have to worry about me being there. Chandler will be the one taking care of you. It's just the classes, right? I can do it." He smiled at her. "I want to do it, sweetie. Besides, I'm sure all the information will completely freak me out and you'll like that."

She smiled. "There are videos of childbirth."

What? Why would anyone want to see that? He held in a shudder. "See? You're proving my point. I'll be your birthing class partner. We'll have fun like we used to. Remember when we did everything together? This can be like that."

She looked skeptical. "It's a bunch of hours."

"I'm in. Totally and completely in. Just say when and where and I'll be there." He held up a hand. "I'll come home first and pick you up, but then I'll be in."

"It's two evenings this week and next."

"Done." He smiled. "So it's a date?"

"Fine. Don't be late."

"I won't be." He winked. "Should I bring popcorn for the videos?"

"Dad!"

"So that's a no?"

"You're impossible," she muttered, but she was smiling when she spoke, and that was all he needed.

* * *

Wynn nodded as she held her cell phone to her ear. "Uh-huh. I'm putting in five hundred and Garrick wants to put in two thousand. Joylyn says there will be about fifty guests."

On the other end of the phone, Renee said, "That's a manageable number. Nick and Pallas have also offered two thousand, and Jasper and I will make up whatever the difference is. We'll use white linens and add color everywhere else. Obviously the venue is already paid for. I'm talking to the florist right after you and I are done. Silver is holding the spot open, so that's the bar service. I rebooked the caterer. I'll let her know the number of guests, and then she'll send me some menu options. Do we know if Holly has a dress?"

"I have no idea."

"Okay. I'll text Joylyn. The cake is going to be an issue. We're really limited on choices because of the short time frame. The baker the previous bride used will make the cake for us, but says the decorations have to be simple. I'm working on some ideas."

Renee paused. "Okay, I think that's all my notes. I'll let you know when we get our video conference set up. It will be in a day or so. I don't want to wait any longer than we have to. Time is ticking."

"I'll be there."

"This is fun. I know I plan weddings all the time, but this one is different. I want Holly and Rex to have the wedding of their dreams." She laughed. "And I look forward to meeting them."

Wynn smiled. "Talk to you soon."

"Bye."

They hung up. Wynn tucked her phone in her drawer, then tried a few deep breaths. She'd asked Hunter to stop by after school, and he was due any second. She still wasn't sure what she wanted to say to him—obviously she would be expressing her disappointment, but there was a lot more involved in what he'd done.

Right on time her son walked into her office. He was getting taller by the day, she thought. He was still lanky, but he was a good-looking kid. Affable, well-liked, athletic. A few days ago, she would have said she was so lucky that he never did anything really wrong. How she wished that was still true.

"Hey, Mom. What's up?"

She motioned to the chair opposite hers. He slipped off his backpack and took the seat, then looked at her expectantly.

"Camilla Henderson called me a couple of days ago," she said.

Hunter's eyes widened, then he flushed and dropped his gaze to the floor. "Ah, what did she want?"

"You'd left some information off your JROTC application. She wanted me to fill in the blanks." She put her hands on the desk and laced her fingers together. "You can imagine my surprise to hear what you'd been planning. Joining something like that is a big deal. But that wasn't the worst of it, was it? Because I quickly realized you hadn't just applied. You'd faked my signature on the forms."

He swallowed hard, then looked at her. "You're mad, huh?"

"Yes, I'm angry and I'm disappointed. In a funny way, I'm also hurt and a little surprised. I never thought you'd do something like this, Hunter. I never thought you were dishonest. Not in that way. You didn't talk to me, you lied to them and you lied to me by not telling me. The entire purpose of the program is to teach leadership and personal responsibility and this is how you start?"

"Mom, don't." He blinked back tears. "I didn't know what to do. I really wanted to join the program, but I knew you'd say no."

"How could you know? You never asked. I refuse you very little."

"You wouldn't want me learning to shoot and stuff. You'd think it was wrong."

"I don't know what I would think because I never got the chance to figure it out."

"I wanted to join so I could show you how good it was." He wiped away tears. "It's a really great program, and I wanted it so much. I thought you would be proud of me when you found out later."

She tried to remember the last time he'd cried. It had been at least a year, maybe longer. The tears were genuine—Hunter had never been a faker—but they didn't move her.

"I'm really sad," she said quietly.

"Mom, don't say that!" He looked at her. "A lot of moms said no, so I got scared. I really wanted this. I know I was wrong and I'm sorry, but you have to understand."

"You betrayed my trust in you. I thought we were a team. I thought we had a special relationship where we understood we would always take care of each other. But you didn't trust me to want what was best for you. You didn't trust me to listen and be reasonable. You didn't trust me at all."

The tears spilled down his cheeks. "Don't say that," he said, his voice cracking. "Don't say that."

"Have you ever faked my signature on a form before?"

He stared at her. "No. I'd never do that."

"But you did this time, and I don't know if I can believe you about anything."

"That's not fair. It was one time. Just one time. Mom, don't be like this. Don't say we're broken. We're not. I'm still who I was. I wanted it so much. You have to understand." He wiped his face again. "You're right. I should have asked. I was wrong not to ask. You should punish me really bad. Like a horrible punishment so I'll never do it again. I'll earn your trust back, I swear. I'll do anything."

His mouth twisted. "I'm sorry. I didn't mean to hurt you or disappoint you. I wouldn't do that. I wouldn't!"

"But you did."

The tears fell faster. "Mom, please. I'm sorry. I'm so sorry."

She believed he was but wasn't sure that was enough. And she was still in an impossible situation.

"What am I supposed to do now?" she asked.

Hunter looked at her. "What do you mean?"

"What should I do? Tell them what you did?"

His eyes widened. "If you do that, they won't let me be in the program. Mom, you can't."

"You want me to lie, too? You want me to lie for you?"

He shifted on his seat. "Not exactly."

She waited. He hunched over in his seat.

"If you don't tell them," he said, his voice low and full of pain, "then you're teaching me the wrong lesson. You're teaching me that it's okay to lie. If you don't tell them the truth, then we're betraying everything ROTC stands for."

"Yes, we are."

He stared at her. "What are you going to do?"

Until this second, she honestly hadn't known. She didn't like either option. Because of what he'd done, he'd put her in an impossible situation—unless she believed she'd raised a good kid who, despite recent events, understood the difference between right and wrong.

"That's up to you."

His eyes widened. "What do you mean?"

"What I said. It's up to you. You created this problem, so you're going to figure out how we deal with it." She paused. "Regardless of what you choose, you're going to have to be punished, but that's a separate matter. You tell me how you want to handle this. You can let me know in the morning."

"You'll do whatever I say?"

Her stomach flipped over a couple of times as she thought about changing her mind.

She nodded. "It's on you, Hunter. I'll go along with whatever you decide."

chapter thirteen

Garrick thought he knew everything about Happily Inc, but he was wrong. He never would have guessed the hospital offered birthing classes to expectant mothers.

"Welcome," a fifty-something woman said when he and Joylyn entered. "I'm Serenity, your instructor."

Serenity? he mouthed, looking at his daughter.

She rolled her eyes, then looked at Serenity. "Hi. I'm Joylyn Kaberline."

He held out his hand. "I'm Garrick."

"Joylyn and Garrick Kaberline," Serenity said, checking her clipboard.

"Not Kaberline," Joylyn said quickly. "I mean that's my last name, but it's not his." She sighed. "He's not my husband. Chandler's still deployed. He should be back before the baby's born. This is my dad."

Garrick did his best not to chuckle. "I'm standing in for Chandler."

Serenity offered him a glowing smile. "What a wonderfully supportive thing to do for your daughter." She patted Joylyn's arm. "You're a lucky girl to have such a caring father."

"Thank you," she muttered.

Serenity pointed to a few empty chairs. "Have a seat. We'll get started in a few minutes."

"Did you hear that?" Garrick asked as they walked into the room. "I'm wonderfully supportive."

"Be quiet."

"You're a lucky girl."

"Stop it."

But she was laughing as she spoke.

They sat next to a couple in their thirties. The very pregnant woman smiled at them. "Hi. I'm Jill and this is my husband Jack." She held up a hand. "Please don't say anything. We've heard it all before."

"I won't say anything," Joylyn promised. "I'm Joylyn and this is my dad. My husband is deployed so he's filling in."

Jill looked at him. "Are you? That's so nice. My dad would never do that. You're really lucky to have him."

Joylyn groaned. "So I've been told."

Garrick winked at her. This had been a great idea. While he was always happy to help out his daughter, he hadn't expected so much praise. To be honest, he was feeling pretty damned good about his parenting skills right about now.

The glow lasted nearly thirty minutes, which was about the time it took Serenity to get the meeting started and everyone to introduce themselves. Less than two minutes into the actual instruction part of the evening his stomach was in knots, and he had a very strong need to wait for Joylyn in the safety of the parking lot.

He'd been fine with the course outline at first. The birthing process was a given, and dealing with pain, while not pleasant, wasn't a surprise. But "Common Complications"? That was wrong. Complications shouldn't be common, and while he knew that wasn't what the title meant, he didn't want to think about any complications when it came to Joylyn and his soon-to-be grandson.

"Finally, we'll tour the maternity ward and, if you're having your baby here, get you preregistered." Serenity smiled. "One less thing for you to deal with while you're in labor."

Joylyn leaned close. "Dad, are you okay? You've gone white."

"I'm fine. Just paying attention."

She didn't look convinced. "If you're this tense now, how are you going to get through the videos?"

"I have no idea."

An hour into the evening, they took a fifteen-minute break. When Joylyn returned from her bathroom visit, she waddled back to her seat.

"I'm feeling so much better," she said. "Having this information makes me feel like I know what I'm doing. Or I will. I should have signed up for a class a long time ago."

He stared at her. "Are you insane? You'd want to know sooner? Why?"

She smiled. "I just told you. Dad, are you going to make it through this? We have three more nights."

"I'm fine," he said automatically.

He was doing his best to take in all he'd learned. The entire process was iffy at best, and they hadn't even touched on "complications."

"What was God thinking?" he demanded. "You can't do this. There's no way something that big can pass through any part of your body. There are major design flaws. And how does the baby tell your body it's time? It's a baby. It can't communicate."

Joylyn grinned. "Dad, there's no talking. It's a chemical thing, not an email."

"Still. The whole process is beyond comprehension." He looked at her. "You are the bravest person I know. I mean that. You, especially, but all women. Why would you do this? If it were up to me, the human race would be done. I'd refuse. There is no way I would go through any part of having a baby."

She patted his arm. "I know. It's okay. I've got this."

"I'm glad someone has, because it sure isn't me."

Wynn walked into the kitchen the next morning to find Hunter already up. He was sitting at the kitchen table, still in his pajamas. His face was blotchy, and he looked like he hadn't slept.

Her first instinct was to rush over and check if he had a fever, but she knew that wasn't the problem. He'd been thinking about what he did and wrestling with the consequences. Now she was going to find out if she'd been right to trust him with the decision about what to do.

She sat across from him and waited. He drew in a breath, then looked at her.

"Can you meet me at the JROTC office after school?" he asked.

She nodded.

"I'm going to tell them what I did." He swallowed. "I don't think they're going to let me into the program after they find out about how I lied and stuff, but telling them is the right thing to do."

Relief was instant. She did her best not to show her feelings, nor did she rush over to hug him. He had to manage this on his own.

"All right," she said. "You'll make an appointment and text me the time?"

He nodded.

"Okay, then. Want some breakfast?"

"I'm not hungry."

He rose and walked out of the kitchen. She stared after him, her heart aching. Nothing about this was easy, but she knew it was the right decision. Hunter would learn from what he'd done—at least that was the plan. As much as she didn't like the idea, she was also going to have to punish him herself. She wanted to say not getting into the program was enough, but she knew there had to be more. He'd in essence lied to her—and he'd betrayed her trust. That had to be dealt with.

She turned on the coffeepot and thought how life had been so much easier when he'd been little and most of his transgressions could be solved with a time-out.

Major Orin Rumsey was a stern looking man, with graying hair and glasses. Wynn would guess he was in his late fifties—still fit and strong, and plenty intimidating. His desk was neat. The only seemingly out-of-place object was a small ceramic cat wearing a red bow tie and glasses, sitting next to his computer. The incongruous item added a touch of whimsy to an otherwise plain space.

As promised, Wynn met Hunter at the JROTC office just after three. Hunter was pale and she suspected he was shaking, but she didn't try to comfort him. She was there as a witness and possibly to answer any questions, but this was her son's meeting.

Major Rumsey smiled at them as he indicated chairs in front of his desk.

"What can I do for you, Hunter?" the older man asked.

"I need to withdraw my application."

The major raised his eyebrows. "All right. Want to tell me why?"

Hunter looked at her, then at the floor, before raising his gaze to the instructor. "I lied on my application."

Wynn gave the other man credit. His expression didn't change at all.

"In what way?" he asked.

"I faked my mom's signature."

"I see." Major Rumsey looked at her. "So you didn't know Hunter had applied."

"Not until I got a call from Camilla, asking a few questions."

The major's expression turned thoughtful. "I'm sorry to hear that, Hunter. Why didn't you talk to your mother about the program?"

His shoulders hunched. "I don't know. I really wanted to do it, and I was afraid she'd say no. A couple of my friends wanted to apply and their moms said they couldn't."

Major Rumsey kept his gaze on the teen. "But you never discussed the program with your mother?"

"No. I thought..." He sighed. "I was wrong. I should have had the conversation with her. She's not unreasonable. I just kind of reacted and that was dumb. Then I signed her name." His shoulders hunched more. "I don't know why I thought that was a good idea. It wasn't."

He straightened. "It's all on me. She didn't know any of it. Once she found out, she said she was in an impossible situation. If she ratted me out, I'd get kicked out of the program. If she didn't, she was teaching me the wrong lesson."

"I see. So how did you come to be in my office today?"

"She said it was up to me. That she would do whatever I decided."

Major Rumsey looked at Wynn. "You took a chance."

She managed a slight smile. "I hoped for the best."

"And it happened." He glanced between them. "I assume that your presence here today means you're not opposed to JROTC."

"No. I'm not sure what I would have thought before, but from what I've read about the program, I'm impressed. I think Hunter would have done well here."

Major Rumsey turned his attention back to Hunter. "How old are you, son?"

"Fourteen."

One corner of his mouth turned up. "I made a lot of mistakes when I was fourteen, and they all had consequences. What have you learned from this?"

Hunter shifted in his seat. "That I need to tell the truth. That there's a price for screwing up and it's really high." He stared at Major Rumsey. "I really wanted to do this. I think I would have been good at it. I like the training and the guys already in the program. I wish…" He hung his head. "I'm sorry."

"How are you going to punish him?" Major Rumsey asked her. "Take away his phone?"

"That's an ordinary punishment. This isn't an ordinary infraction." She glanced at Hunter. "I'd planned to talk you about this later, but as it came up, I'm thinking you can pressure wash and paint the deck in the backyard over your holiday break and do twenty hours of community service between now and the end of January."

Hunter's eyes widened, but he didn't speak.

Major Rumsey nodded. "That sounds fair. It will give

Hunter a lot of time to think about what he did wrong." He steepled his fingers. "Junior ROTC is different from the college program. There's no commitment of military service, and we are working with young people who are still developing. I have a fair amount of discretion when it comes to admissions. Our goal isn't to exclude anyone interested in our program. Society as a whole is better when people understand commitment, leadership and service."

He dropped his hands back to the desk. "If you complete your punishment at home and the community service and stay out of trouble, you can reapply for next fall." He looked at Wynn. "Assuming you agree."

"I do."

"Then we have a plan." He stood and held out his hand to Hunter. "I hope you take this opportunity to learn an important lesson."

"I will," Hunter promised. "You'll see."

Wynn thanked him and they walked out. Once in the hallway, Hunter leaned against the wall.

"It's not over. I have a second chance."

"Yes, you do."

He flung himself at her, holding her tight. "I'm sorry, Mom. I won't ever screw up again, I swear."

She chuckled as she hugged him back. "If only that were true."

Joylyn stared at her phone as it rang. The picture and accompanying *Mom* made it clear who was calling. She'd spent the past week or so only dealing with her mother by text, where it was easy to pretend everything was all right. A phone call was different.

She debated not picking up but knew that was an immature response to what was going on, so told herself to suck it up before pushing the speaker button.

"Hey, Mom."

"Hi, sweetie. How are you doing?"

A simple enough question, Joylyn thought. And yet she wasn't sure how to answer.

"I'm good. Dad and I went to the first birthing class last night."

"Your father went with you?"

"Someone had to. I can't go alone—I need a partner." Something her mother should know.

On the heels of that thought came an uncomfortable combination of resentment and hurt. After all, her mother had been the one to kick her out of her own home and force her to go live with her dad. Something Joylyn had resented. Only now that she was here, she found herself enjoying her time with her father more than she would have thought.

"Did it go all right?" her mother asked.

"Yes. Dad's pretty freaked about it, but I'm happy to have the information."

"So things are good between the two of you?"

There was a tentative quality to the question, as if her mother wasn't sure she wanted the answer.

"They're better now." Joylyn put down the paper snowman she'd been assembling. "Mom, why did you let me not see Dad when I was a teenager? Why didn't you force me to go with him on the weekends? I was a kid. I shouldn't have been making that kind of decision myself."

"You were determined not to see him anymore. You said you'd run away if I made you."

"And you believed me?"

"I don't know. Maybe I should have pushed the issue. There was a lot going on in my life, Joylyn. You were a moody teenager, and I had three boys under the age of ten. As you'll find out when you have children of your own, knowing the right thing to do isn't exactly intuitive, okay?"

"You sound really defensive."

"I feel defensive. All you do is complain. It's not pleasant."

Joylyn stared at the phone in surprise. "I'm not complaining. I'm asking why you let me stop seeing my father when I was fifteen years old. The parenting plan gave him every other weekend. But you didn't enforce that."

Her mom was quiet for nearly a minute. "I don't know why. It was easier to give in and not fight you on that. Maybe a part of me was jealous that you always had such a good relationship with your father when all you and I did was fight."

Joylyn felt her mouth drop open. "Why would you be jealous? You're my mom."

"I know, but I had the day-to-day slog, and then you'd go off and have fabulous weekends with him. When you got home, you couldn't stop talking about how great a time you had. You always had secrets with him and things you did together." Her mother sighed. "I'm sorry. That's on me, not on you. There's no one reason I didn't push you to be with him. I guess I should have tried harder to make you. I'm sorry."

"It's okay," she said softly. "I did what I did because Sandy said he'd dumped her because he didn't care about her and I was next. I got scared that she was telling the truth, so I stopped seeing him before he could tell me he didn't want to spend time with me anymore."

"What? No! That bitch. I never liked her. What a horrible thing to say. You know it's not true, don't you? Honey, your dad adores you. He always has. If anything, I'm sure Sandy was jealous because you were so important to him."

Pretty much what her dad had told her, which was nice to get confirmed.

"What a mess," her mother said. "This makes me feel awful. I really should have made you keep seeing him. I'm sorry."

"It's okay, Mom. It's not your fault."

"It feels like it is. Then I sent you away. Do you want to come home?"

Even two weeks ago that question would have had her throwing her things into her suitcases and heading west. But since then, a lot had changed. She and her dad were doing better. Plus she had a meeting at Weddings Out of the Box to talk about Holly's wedding.

"I'm good here," she said. "It's easier for everyone."

"Are you sure?"

"I'm fine, Mom. Really. I'll be back when Chandler gets home."

"I miss you so much."

"I miss you, too, Mom."

They hung up.

Joylyn stared at the phone, then picked up the snowman she'd been working on. Funny how a little information could change so many things, she thought. What was that saying? Perception was reality, or something like that? Whatever the saying was, she never would have guessed it was true.

Hunter was quiet the rest of the afternoon and evening. Wynn decided rather than press him to talk, she would let him work out whatever he was feeling on his own. A little after seven, he said he was going to read in his room—confusing, but again, she let him be. About twenty minutes later, there was a knock on her front door.

She opened it to find Garrick on her front porch. The sight of his handsome face and strong, broad shoulders had her flinging herself at him. He caught her and pulled her close, then eased them both in the house and closed the door behind him.

"Bad day?" he asked, lightly kissing her.

"No, just stressful. You smell like wood shavings. It's nice."

"I was working on the bassinet. Now that all the wood is cut and sanded, it's coming together quickly."

"Joylyn is going to be excited when she sees it. She still doesn't know?"

"No."

They walked to the sofa. He sat first, then pulled her down next to him. She leaned her head on his shoulder and rested her arm across his chest.

"Tell me what happened today," he said, fingering one of her curls.

She told him about visiting Major Rumsey and how Hunter had come clean.

"I didn't know what he was going to do until he asked me to meet him at the JROTC office and told me he was going to tell the truth." She looked up at Garrick. "I wanted him to do the right thing and I hoped he would, but until that moment, I wasn't sure."

"You should have been. You've raised a great kid. He's going to be a good man."

"I hope so. Parenting is hard."

"And yet people do it again and again."

They did, she thought. They had multiple kids and raised them and were happy.

"I should have had more kids," she said impulsively.

"I agree, but that was one of the ways you were punishing yourself."

She grimaced. "You figured that out?"

"Once I knew your history, it wasn't hard. Don't give me any credit for being insightful. You believed you'd done a bad thing, so you stayed away from relationships—at least the guy-girl kind. Without that, it's tough to get pregnant."

He was right. She hadn't thought she was worthy. She'd carefully chased away anyone who had tried to get close. Something she was fairly sure she was over, which made her relationship with Garrick intriguing. She wondered how he felt about having more kids—not that she was going to ask. They hadn't even slept together. Asking about children would send him screaming into the night.

"Hunter's upset," she said, returning to the original subject. "He was quiet all afternoon. I know it's a lot to take in."

"He'll work through it and next fall he can apply again."

"I hope he does. I think the program would be good for him. Rules and discipline as he enters high school. It's a mother's dream." She looked at him again and smiled. "And in your world?"

"I went to my first birthing class."

She laughed. "How was it?"

"Horrifying. I'm not sure how I'm going to get through the videos. The whole process is insane and unnatural."

"It's actually very natural."

"For you." He shuddered. "The cliché is true. If it were up to men to have babies, the human race would be dead in a generation. Can we talk about something else?"

"Is this where I point out you were the one who brought up the birthing class?"

"Sure, but I take it back. I was wrong."

"Ah, the *W* word. That's exciting to hear. All right—a new topic. We're having the meeting about Holly's wedding tomorrow. I'm really excited to see what Renee's pulled together. With what we've all pitched in, Holly and Rex are going to have a great wedding."

"Something they can remember always," he said.

"That's what a wedding should be. Especially because they're still young."

"And you're old?" His voice was teasing.

"No, but I'm less idealistic than I was." She sighed. "I had to cancel Hunter's sleepover."

"I figured."

"So we won't have the house to ourselves."

He put his hand under her chin, pressing gently until she looked at him.

"I want nothing more than to make love with you," he said gently. "But our lives are complicated. I'm not going anywhere, Wynn. When the time is right, we'll take that step, but until then, it's okay."

Which was exactly the right thing to say, she thought happily. "That's what I think, too."

"Good."

"Why aren't you married?"

He chuckled. "There's a question."

"What's the answer?"

"I was married and it didn't work out."

"So you won't do that again?"

"No." He paused. "After Sandy and I split up, there was the whole Colombia thing. That messed with my head. When I got home, I was restless. I heard about the job here and moved back. Since then, I've been busy settling."

"It doesn't take three years to get settled."

His gaze was steady. "I'm not opposed to marriage. Are you?"

She fought against the urge to put a little distance between them. Somehow the conversation had gone in a direction she hadn't expected.

"I'm not," she said softly.

"Good to know. Now I'm going to suggest we go watch some TV before we both feel this has gotten too awkward."

She laughed and stood up. "Any suggestions on what kind of show?"

"Maybe a medical drama."

"Not a reality show about fashion?"

He smiled. "I hear chunky heels are making a comeback."

"Do you even know what a chunky heel is?"

"No, but it sounded good, didn't it?"

chapter fourteen

Joylyn didn't know what to expect from the wedding consultation. She knew time was tight, and Holly would have to take what could be put together in days rather than weeks or months. When she and Chandler had planned their wedding, they'd taken almost a year. She and her mother had gone over every detail, and the day had been exactly as she'd dreamed it would be.

She arrived at Weddings Out of the Box right on time. Wynn arrived seconds later and parked next to her. They walked in together, passing several decorated Christmas trees and a dozen or so freestanding, six-foot-tall candy canes.

"I'm looking forward to this," Wynn said. "All my friends are in the wedding business, but I rarely get involved in the actual planning. Maybe one or two weddings a year. This is going to be fun."

"I know Holly's excited," Joylyn said. "I hope we're able to make the day special for her. It's really last minute."

Wynn smiled. "Renee knows how to work a miracle.

I think you're going to be pleased with what she's pulled together."

They walked into the conference room. It was plain, with a long table and a large video screen at one end. Renee was already there, looking pulled-together in a beautiful dark green suit. Her thick, long, red hair was pulled back in a ponytail. She smiled when she saw them.

"Hi. I think I have everything ready. It's been a whirlwind, that's for sure." She waved to the empty chairs. "Have a seat and we'll get started."

Joylyn and Wynn sat across from her. Renee typed on her laptop and the screen lit up, showing the same view as her computer. She dialed a number and they connected with Holly. The screen on the wall split, showing Holly on one half and the display from Renee's computer on the other.

Joylyn waved at her friend. "Hi! I can't believe we're doing this. Are you excited?"

"I am." Holly smiled. "Rex and I are so happy we're going to have a real wedding."

"You are," Renee said with a laugh. "I'm Renee by the way. Nice to see you in person, Holly."

"Nice to see you, too."

"This is Wynn," Joylyn said, pointing to her. "She's my dad's neighbor. She's the one who suggested checking with Renee about putting on the wedding."

Wynn waved. "Nice to meet you."

"Now that everyone has met," Renee said, opening her tablet, "let's get busy with planning. Holly, are we still at fifty guests?"

"Yes. That number is firm. Joylyn is going to be my attendant. It's more complicated for Rex." Holly grinned. "He has five Marines who are going to be co–best men. So we'll need room for them there."

Joylyn looked at Wynn and Renee. "They all served together and they're like brothers. Ben S, John, Ben Z, Peter
and Will."

"We will make that happen." Renee typed on her tablet.
"So let's talk about the overall structure of the day. We have
a large room that we can easily partition. We'll use part of
it for the ceremony and part for the reception. For the ceremony with fifty guests, we'll do a center aisle, with say
seven rows of ten chairs. I know that gives us more seat-
ing than you'll need, but sometimes people like to leave a
seat empty."

She put a picture of chairs up on the screen. Large lanterns sat on the floor, along the aisle.

"We have these in our warehouse," she said. "They're
about eighteen inches high, so substantial but they don't
get in the way. We also have flameless candles that go inside. The only cost is for new batteries."

"They're lovely," Holly said.

"Good. Now I'm thinking we'll do a cluster of deep red
dahlias on the backs of the chairs along the aisle. Probably
every other chair, so it's not too busy. The florist will add
ribbons and some greens to make them pretty."

"I like the look," Holly said, her tone hesitant, "but
there's a cost factor."

Renee glanced at Wynn, then back at the screen. "Let
me explain all my suggestions and we'll talk money at the
end. For now you can simply enjoy the show."

Holly nodded. "Okay. Sure."

Joylyn thought the slide with the lanterns and flowers
was beautiful, but she was with Holly. No way could they
afford that.

"We've reserved a local minister to perform the ceremony," Renee said. "Now about your bouquet—what are you doing for a dress?"

"I don't know," Holly admitted. "I found a dress at David's Bridal I really like. It's on sale, but it's still three hundred dollars. I think that money might be better spent on the wedding itself."

"Do you have a picture?" Renee asked.

Holly reached to her left and came back with a printout of a strapless dress. The style was simple—fitted to the waist, then gently flaring out to the floor. Joylyn leaned closer to study the sweetheart neckline and the pleating at the bodice.

"It's beautiful," she said. "You'll look amazing in that."

Holly smiled. "It's taffeta and looks great on. I don't need much in the way of alterations, but the cost…"

Renee typed on her tablet. "It's lovely and very classic. I think a teardrop bouquet with cascading flowers would be best. Red roses." She smiled. "They'll look fantastic against the simplicity of the dress."

Joylyn met Holly's gaze on the screen. A bouquet like that was going to be expensive. Roses? Really? Maybe Renee didn't understand Holly didn't have a lot of money. But before she could figure out what to say, Renee had moved on to the reception.

"We'll do rectangular tables forming a loose square," she said, putting another picture on the screen. "More dahlias down the center with votives floating in glasses. The long-stemmed glasses will give height and interest, but won't get in the way of conversation across the table."

Holly nodded. "The centerpieces are beautiful."

"For the dinner, I've spoken with the caterer. Are there any vegans?"

Holly smiled. "No. All our friends eat meat."

"Good. We'll have a vegetarian option, just in case. Risotto is always good. For the first course, given the time of year, we're thinking soup. A butternut squash soup with an Asiago truffle mac and cheese muffin is very popular."

"It sounds delicious," Holly said. "But expensive."

"No thoughts of money just yet. Don't forget, our previous bride has paid for a lot of this."

"Okay. I'll just listen."

Renee went through the rest of the menu, including filet mignon and a potato gratin.

"I was thinking simple for the dessert," Renee said, putting another slide on the screen. "Chocolate dipped strawberry towers. They look incredible, they're light and delicious. Plus it's fruit. The serving plates are tiered, so the stacked strawberries take the shape of a Christmas tree."

"They're beautiful," Holly murmured.

"Great." Renee made more notes. "The cake is problematic. We are stuck with what the previous bride ordered. It's a four layer cake. There's no time to get anything fancy, so what I suggest is a simple white frosting and then we cascade red roses down the side. It's elegant, it's easy and it meets our time constraint."

Holly nodded without saying anything.

Joylyn could see her confusion and worry. Even with the deposit money waived, there was no way Holly and Rex could afford even a portion of this.

"On to the drinks," Renee said. "We're thinking traditional. A champagne toast after the ceremony, then an assortment of champagne cocktails to start, with red wine at dinner. Is that all right?"

"It all sounds wonderful."

"Good," Renee said quickly. "Now, last but not least, the wedding favor." She put up another slide. This showed a round red ornament personalized with Holly's and Rex's names, along with the date.

"I have someone who can do the fancy writing," Wynn said. "We'll use a gold marker and tie a gold bow on the top. We can put them in big bowls by the door and people can take one as they leave."

Holly pressed her lips together. "We can't afford this. I'm sorry you put all this work into the presentation, but our budget is—"

"There's no cost," Renee told her. "Everything's already paid for."

Holly's expression of surprise was nearly comical, although Joylyn had a feeling she didn't look any different.

"What? No. That's not possible." Holly's eyes were wide. "Rex and I can't let some poor bride who had to cancel her wedding pay for ours."

"She's not." Renee smiled. "I told a few people about you and Rex, and they offered to chip in. Word spread and even more people wanted to help out. The bride who had to cancel is getting all her money back, and you're getting the wedding I described. You might want to head to David's Bridal and buy your dress."

Tears filled Joylyn's eyes. Holly had a bit more control, but she still looked shaken.

"I don't understand," she whispered. "Joylyn, did you know about this?"

"Do I look like I knew about it?" She turned to Wynn. "What happened?"

"What Renee said. People wanted to be a part of this."

Renee nodded. "I'm serious, Holly. It's all being taken care of. You and Rex just have to show up. Oh, and his five co–best men, too."

The rest of the meeting was a blur. When they were

done, Joylyn drove to the Happily Inc police station and asked to see her dad. She was shown back to his office. When he saw her, he immediately came to his feet.

"Are you all right? What's going on? Do you need to go to the hospital? Is it Chandler?"

The tears returned and she couldn't speak, so she held open her arms. Her father came around his desk and hugged her.

"Talk to me, Joylyn. I'm freaking out here."

"We're all f-fine," she managed to say, then gave into the sobs.

He held her against him, angled so there was room for her belly. She cried until she was empty, then took the tissues he offered her.

"I'm fine," she repeated. "It's just I was at a meeting for Holly's wedding and everything is paid for."

"Oh, that." He looked relieved. "Why is that a problem?"

"It's not. It's wonderful. Her wedding is going to be perfect. But I don't understand. Why would people who've never met her give money to her?"

"Why not? She and Rex don't have much financially, so we're helping them out. Come on. They're Marines and it's Christmas. What else would we do?"

She stared at him. "You gave money?"

He shrugged. "Some. I helped."

"Why didn't you tell me?"

"I knew you'd find out at the meeting. I thought that was more fun."

Which was just like him, she thought. He'd always done nice things for her and her friends. He was generous and kind and she couldn't believe how stupid she'd been as a teenager.

"I'm sorry I wouldn't see you all those times," she said, brushing away more tears.

"Water under the bridge."

She leaned against him again. "I love you, Daddy."

"I love you, too."

The temperature might be close to seventy, but the scent of pine in the Christmas tree lot made it feel like the holiday season. Wynn inhaled deeply, enjoying the familiar smell. Yes, an artificial tree was more practical, but she didn't care. The real ones were a tradition.

She stood next to Joylyn while Hunter and Garrick debated the merits of each tree. Wynn had already reminded them twice that they only had eight-foot ceilings in their respective houses and anything taller than that was going to have to be topped off, but the guys seemed determined to go with the biggest tree they could.

Joylyn shook her head. "He was always like this when I was a kid. He bought some huge tree, then was shocked when it didn't fit into his place." She yawned and covered her mouth. "Sorry. The baby was active last night and kept me up."

"You're going to have to get him on a schedule."

Joylyn smiled. "I know."

"Speaking of him, where are you and Chandler on names? I feel funny just saying 'him' every time I mention him."

Joylyn laughed. "I know. We talk about that, too. But we want to wait until he's born. It feels weird to name someone before you've met them. We have a list, but we'll decide on the day."

Hunter walked over to her. "Mom, do you want a taller tree or a fatter tree?"

"Probably best not to call the tree fat. You might hurt its feelings."

Her son rolled his eyes. "Fine. Wider or taller?"

"Wider. These trees all have good shapes. It's silly to have to cut off the top two feet because it's too tall for the room."

He turned to Garrick. "See? We want a fat—ah, wider tree."

"But tall is majestic," Garrick insisted.

Joylyn sighed. "Dad, you do this every year."

He grinned. "I know. I can't help myself."

"Then it's decided," Wynn told him. "You can be weird and get the too-tall tree. Hunter and I will get one that can hold more ornaments."

"It's not a competition," Garrick muttered. "Although your point about the ornaments is a good one. We do have a lot."

He walked around the four trees that had made the finals. Wynn tried to be subtle as she checked out his butt. The man was good-looking, and their regular make-out sessions kept her girl parts humming. As Hunter was scheduled to do deck work and community service over his holiday break, she was starting to think there was no reason not to let him have a sleepover the next time he asked.

She forced her attention back to the trees. "I like the one on the far right. Hunter, what do you think?"

He nodded. "It'll look good in the front window."

"I agree. Okay, we've picked ours." She patted Joylyn on the arm. "Good luck with your dad."

Joylyn laughed. "You can't just leave me here. What if he takes another hour to make up his mind?"

"I won't take an hour," Garrick grumbled. "Ten minutes, tops."

"Let's go to the front of the lot," Wynn told her. "We'll pay for our tree, and you can find somewhere to sit."

Once the tree was purchased, one of the guys on the lot tied it to the top of her car. She and Hunter waved at Joylyn as they pulled out. When they got home, they managed to wrestle the tree off the car and into the house.

"I got this, Mom," Hunter said. "Get the stand in place, and I'll handle the tree."

"You're so strong," she said, remembering when he'd been younger and smaller. "This growing thing is starting to freak me out."

It didn't take long to get the tree secured and in front of the window. They left it a few feet out from the wall so they could move around it to decorate, then push it in when they were finished.

"I'll go get the ornaments, Mom," Hunter said.

She followed him onto the front porch and saw Garrick and Joylyn pulling in next door, a tree sticking out of the back of his SUV.

"Which one did you get?" she asked, crossing her driveway.

Joylyn smiled. "The wider one so more ornaments will fit."

Wynn looked at Garrick. "You were sensible."

"Don't sound surprised. I saw the value of your point and agreed with you."

"Still, a man who can be reasoned with. Impressive."

He winked at her, then picked up the tree as if it weighed nothing and carried it inside. Wynn sent Hunter to help him get the tree into the stand before heading to the garage and carrying in the last of the bins. Joylyn followed her.

"I'm not going to be much help," she said, patting her

belly. "I'm not sure I can get close enough to hang anything."

Wynn pointed to the sofa. "Why don't you keep me company while I decorate?"

"I wouldn't want to get in the way of your traditions with Hunter."

Wynn shook her head. "You won't. He likes putting on the lights, but after about five minutes of hanging ornaments, he wanders away."

"Oh, okay, then sure. I'd like to stay."

She settled on the sofa. Wynn had just pulled out the various strings of lights when Garrick and Hunter walked in.

"Our tree is in its stand," Garrick said. "We're here for light duty."

"Because putting on the lights is man work?"

"Of course. Decorating is more a woman thing."

She put her hands on her hips. "It's Saturday. There's no professional football on today."

Hunter shifted his feet. "There's a great college game on, Mom. It's the end of the season so who wins is important."

Wynn glanced at Joylyn. "Too bad you're having a boy."

Joylyn laughed. "I can see that it might be a problem."

The guys made quick work of the lights. Garrick plugged in each string to make sure it was working, then he and Hunter wound them around the tree. They all squinted at the finished product and declared the lights were even, then the two of them disappeared next door to do the same to Garrick's tree.

Wynn turned on Christmas music, made hot chocolate for herself and Joylyn, then put out a plate of cookies before opening the bins and studying the contents.

"I still have all the ornaments Hunter made for me in school," she said. "Some of them are pretty fragile. Last year I freshened all the glue so they would last a few more years."

Joylyn picked up a star made of popsicle sticks and glitter. "You must love these."

"I do. They're silly, but so special."

She sat on the floor and started pulling out other ornaments. "I have a few from my mom." She held up a wishing well ornament. "She said as long as we could make wishes, it was going to be a good Christmas."

"When did she pass away?"

"While I was pregnant with Hunter."

Joylyn's eyes widened. "You were young."

"I was. She was living in Alaska at the time." Wynn remembered her mother telling her she was moving. "She believed she needed a man in her life to be happy. When I was little, she told me I had to be pretty in order to win my handsome prince."

"Shouldn't the message be more about studying hard and making something of yourself?"

Wynn smiled at her. "You'd think, but no. While I was growing up we had a neighbor, Ms. James. She was a schoolteacher who had never married. She always talked to me about going to college and being successful. My mom said Ms. James hadn't amounted to anything because she never had a man in her life. It was confusing."

She unwrapped several ornaments before finding the one she was looking for. She put the sparrow in its nest ornament on the palm of her hand.

"Ms. James gave me this one year. It's supposed to remind me that if I want to get anywhere, I need to spread my wings."

"I love it when ornaments tell a story," Joylyn said. "My dad and I had a different themed tree every year. I wonder if he kept the ornaments we collected together. He said he did." Her tone was wistful.

"When we're done here, we'll go over to your place and find out."

"You don't have to decorate our tree as well as yours."

Wynn stood. "It's not difficult work."

With carols playing in the background, she and Joylyn chatted about Holly's wedding and Joylyn's upcoming birthing class. Wynn decorated the tree, filling up the branches with happy Santas and red and gold stars. She hung two boxes of ornaments that looked like icicles before finishing with the decorations Hunter had made for her. When she was done, she stood back and admired her work.

"I like it," she said. "When Hunter gets back, I'll have him push the tree closer to the window." She grinned at Joylyn. "Teenage boys don't mind grubbing around on the ground, so that's a plus."

"I'll look forward to that."

She struggled to her feet, then rubbed her back. "I am counting the days until this baby is born."

"I'll bet. The last month is the most difficult. It's hard to get comfortable anywhere."

Wynn carried the mugs and the plate into the kitchen before opening the front door. She and Joylyn walked over to Garrick's place. Sure enough, the giant TV was tuned to a college football game.

"Hey," Garrick said, not taking his gaze from the screen. "How did it go?"

"It's beautiful," Joylyn told him. "You should go take a look."

"I will. At halftime."

Joylyn shook her head. "Dad, it's just football."

"I'm going to pretend I didn't hear that."

The game went to a commercial. Hunter sprang to his feet.

"Come on, Garrick. We should go to my place to watch the rest of the game."

"Why?"

Hunter sighed heavily. "Mom's going to talk the whole time she's decorating the tree. She's going to ask Joylyn about every ornament and tell her stories about when I was a kid."

Garrick looked at her. "You do that?"

"Every year."

He and Hunter headed for the front door. "You girls have a good time."

"Women," she called after him. "We're women."

The door closed behind them.

Wynn walked over to the tree in the corner. It was tall, but stopped a few inches short of the ceiling. The lights were on and a stack of three boxes stood beside it, along with a small gift bag.

She handed the gift bag to Joylyn. "This is for you. I brought it over a few days ago."

The younger woman looked confused. "Thank you." She opened the bag, then pressed her free hand to her mouth. "Oh, Wynn."

She pulled out a small silver ornament. A little bear was sleeping on a quarter moon.

"Baby's first Christmas," Wynn told her. "I would have had your son's name engraved on it, but seeing as you and Chandler haven't decided, that can be done later. I bought the ornament at a local jewelry store in town. Just have your dad take it in and they'll engrave it for you."

Joylyn's eyes filled with tears. "It's lovely. Thank you so much."

She reached for Wynn and held her tight, her belly

jammed between them. Wynn felt a strong kick against her midsection and jumped.

"I'd forgotten what that was like," she said with a laugh. "No wonder you're tired all the time."

"He's very athletic." She sniffed and looked at the ornament. "Thank you again. This is wonderful."

"You're welcome. Now relax on the sofa and I'll get to work."

She knelt in front of the boxes, doing her best to appear normal, which was unexpectedly difficult. Equally confusing was the sharp pang of longing that had shot through her when she'd felt Joylyn's baby move. A longing for more children.

She'd punished herself for so long—for some reason deciding she didn't deserve a happy relationship or a bigger family. Yes, she'd messed up with Chas, but she'd been wrong to think she should be punished forever. She'd missed out on so much.

Which was not something she should be thinking about right now, she told herself. She opened the first box.

"All right," she said. "Let's see what we've got here."

She unwrapped nearly a dozen Barbie ornaments. "Someone had a favorite doll."

Joylyn laughed. "I know. My poor Dad. We did the tree in Barbie ornaments accented with pink and purple balls." She leaned back against the sofa. "We even found pink tinsel. I thought it was the most beautiful tree I'd ever seen. I can't believe he kept those all this time. Oh, one year it was just animal ornaments. Does he still have those?"

Wynn didn't find any in that box, so she opened the second one.

"I'm seeing really cute animals," she said, holding up a cow ornament. "Does this look familiar?"

"It does."

Wynn pulled out an elephant ornament and a little baby lamb with a pink bow. Joylyn clapped her hands.

"He kept them! I can't believe it. Although I guess I shouldn't be surprised at all."

Wynn privately agreed with her. From everything she'd seen, Garrick had been a wonderful father, taking care of his daughter and understanding what was important to her. Despite their time apart, they were reconnecting and it was wonderful to see.

Her hunky neighbor was turning out to be one of the good guys. Wouldn't it be ironic if the very thing she'd been looking for had been right next door all along?

chapter fifteen

Joylyn waited impatiently at the desk in her bedroom. Right on time, her computer beeped to let her know she had an incoming call. Immediately after, Chandler's face filled her screen.

"Joylyn! How are you feeling? I miss you so much."

She smiled and fought tears. "I'm good. I miss you, too. I'm counting the days until you're back. On Monday, I'm going to do the math and start counting hours."

Chandler laughed. "That's more than I can do. So you feel okay?"

"Uh-huh. Huge, but that's a given. My dad and I went to another birthing class." She grinned as she remembered the evening. "They showed a couple of videos. I thought he was going to pass out."

"That bad, huh?"

"It was what I'd been expecting, but he kept telling me there were too many fluids and it was all terrifying."

"So you're getting along?"

She thought about how great things had been since she'd

learned the truth about their past. "We are. I was wrong to pull back from him the way I did." She sighed. "I talked to my mom about it a little. I asked her why she didn't make me see my dad. I mean come on. I was a kid."

"What did she say?"

"That she had made a mistake. She basically told me she was jealous of my relationship with my dad. I don't get that at all. She's my mom. But I believe her."

"I'm glad you're happier than you were."

"I am. We put up a tree yesterday. My dad kept all my old ornaments. I couldn't believe it." She held up the silver quarter moon with the sleeping bear ornament. "Look what Wynn got us. When we pick a name for the baby, the store where she bought it will engrave it. Isn't that adorable?"

He smiled. "It is. Of course if our little guy is late, it won't be his first Christmas until next year."

"You're right. I hadn't thought about that. I was so upset to have a Christmas baby, but now I think it would be amazing."

"I'm ready whenever he is. I just want you to be okay."

"I am." She touched the screen. "I promise. Oh, I finished all the snowmen. I made one thousand of them. I put the check in our account. It's going to really help with all the baby stuff and when we move into our next place."

"I can't believe you did that many."

"My hands got sore, but it was worth it."

"Open your bottom desk drawer."

The change of subject confused her. "What?"

He grinned. "Just do it."

She pulled open the drawer and was surprised to find a five-by-seven-inch envelope there. It was addressed to Wynn in Chandler's handwriting.

"This is very strange," she said. "You sent something to Wynn and it's in my desk drawer?"

"I wanted to send you a surprise. Open it."

She did and found a postcard from Hawaii. It was a view of their honeymoon hotel with a stunning sunset as the backdrop. The familiar tears returned as she turned it over and read the message.

You're the best thing to ever happen to me. I'll love you always.

"Oh, Chandler," she said. "How did you get this?"

"I bought a few of them when we were on our honeymoon."

"I didn't know that."

"Which was the point. You'll be getting them every now and then, over the years. Just to let you know how much you mean to me."

"You're the most wonderful man ever. I love you, Chandler."

"I love you, too, Joylyn."

The night Garrick and Joylyn came over for dinner, Wynn made tacos and served Christmas cookies for dessert. Joylyn kept yawning through the meal. When they were done, she excused herself.

"I just want to go to bed," she said, carrying her plate over to the sink.

"Take some cookies home with you," Wynn said, getting out a small reusable container. "For later."

Joylyn thanked her and left. While Hunter cleared the rest of the table, Garrick glanced toward the front door.

"She's tired a lot. I know they said in the class to expect that, but I'm worried."

"She's fine," Wynn assured him. "She's seeing her doctor regularly, and everything is progressing as it should. At this point in her pregnancy, she's uncomfortable all the time. It's hard to sleep."

Hunter finished his kitchen duty and excused himself to go hang out in his room. Wynn and Garrick moved to the living room and took their usual places on the sofa.

Funny how so much of what they did together had become familiar, she thought. Hanging out like this, having dinner with their kids. She and Garrick texted regularly, made out when they could.

"What's so funny?" he asked.

"I was thinking we're very couple-like."

"We are. I like it. Do you?"

"Very much, but you've never once taken me on a date."

His look of surprise made her laugh.

"It's okay," she added. "We've had a lot going on."

"You're right. I haven't asked you out even once. I'm a terrible boyfriend. I'm sorry." He reached for her hand. "Wynn, I'd very much like to take you out. How about The Boardroom?"

She was still processing the use of the word "boyfriend." Was that what they were? Boyfriend and girlfriend? They were in a relationship—it hadn't been planned, but it was where they'd ended up. But boyfriend and girlfriend?

"Are you making me wait to punish me?" he asked, his voice teasing.

"What? No. Sorry. I was somewhere else. I would very much like to go out with you, and The Boardroom sounds fun."

"It'll make things public," he said. "You all right with that?"

He had a point—if they went together, all their friends

would know. Of course her friends kind of knew already. "I am."

"Good. Me, too."

He leaned in and kissed her. The feel of his mouth against hers was instantly arousing. She rested her hands on his shoulders and parted her lips. His tongue had just touched hers when she heard Hunter's door open. She and Garrick immediately drew back.

"Mom," Hunter said, walking into the living room. "I was texting with Jackson and he asked me to spend the night." He held up a hand. "I know it's not allowed on school nights, but it's not really a school night because we have a late start tomorrow. I don't have my first class until ten thirty. What do you think?"

Wynn did her best not to look at Garrick. She had a feeling she knew what his vote would be—an opinion she shared. But was it the right thing to do?

She thought of how hard Hunter had worked to show her he understood what he'd done wrong. Honestly, if she wasn't seeing Garrick, she would have no problem saying yes.

"You can," she told him. "But try to be asleep before midnight."

Hunter grinned. "That's what his mom said, too. I'll go get my stuff."

He ran out of the room. Wynn glanced at Garrick, who was studying her.

"Joylyn sure seemed tired," he said carefully.

"She did."

"She's probably in bed already."

"I'm sure that's true."

"Would you like some company after Hunter leaves?"

Their gazes locked. "I would like that very much."

His slow sexy smile made her stomach lurch and her thighs tremble.

"Good. I'll walk out with Hunter," he said. "And be back in a few minutes."

"You don't have to leave."

He glanced toward the hallway, then spoke with a lowered voice. "I do unless you have condoms."

"Oh. I, ah, don't, actually."

Hunter appeared in the living room, a backpack over his shoulder.

"I have my school stuff, Mom. Jackson's mom will take us tomorrow when it's time."

She got up and hugged him. "Be good."

"I will."

"I should be going, too," Garrick said, standing.

He and Hunter headed out together. Wynn watched her son go down three houses, then cross the street and enter Jackson's house. When the door closed behind him, she turned around, wondering what she should do to get ready. Brush her teeth, but then what? Should she put on something sexy? Did she own anything sexy?

She went into the master bath and brushed her teeth, then turned on the lamps on the nightstands and folded down the comforter. Not sure what else to do, she returned to the living room just as Garrick knocked on the front door.

She let him in.

"You're not holding anything," she said.

He pulled several condoms out of his front pocket. "I didn't think you wanted the world to know what I'd brought over."

She smiled. "An excellent point. Hunter's at Jackson's house."

"I saw."

She hesitated, not sure what to do now. Did they talk some more? Just get to it? And if it was the latter, did she initiate things?

Thankfully Garrick didn't seem to have the same concerns. He raised his hand to touch her cheek. "You are so beautiful."

He kissed her lightly, then took her hand and started toward the bedroom.

Once inside, Wynn made sure the door was locked before turning to Garrick. In that brief second before he reached for her, she wondered if things were going to turn awkward or if he would start to have second thoughts about wanting to make love with her.

But before she could ask or really get her worry going, he was pulling her hard against him.

"I have been dreaming about this," he said right before he kissed her. At the same time, he dropped his hands to her butt and squeezed the curves. She wrapped her arms around his neck and pressed her body against his, delighted to feel his arousal.

He swept his tongue against her bottom lip, and she parted for him. At the same time, he unfastened her jeans and slid down the zipper. She had no idea what he was going to do, but as long as he was touching her, she was happy.

Once her jeans were loose, he returned his attention to her butt, this time slipping in under her jeans and panties, his fingers squeezing bare skin.

"I love your ass," he murmured against her mouth. "There's just something about it. If you're moving around a room, I'm always looking."

"Why didn't I ever notice?"

"You're too busy admiring my dick."

She laughed. "I'm not."

"I know. But you do check out my chest."

She stared into his eyes and smiled. "It's very manly."

"Want to touch it?"

"Yes, please."

He unfastened the buttons at his wrists then pulled off his shirt in one easy movement.

She studied the wide shoulders and strong muscles. There were dozens of scars everywhere. Small, flat scars and larger, raised ones.

"They don't hurt," he told her. "You can touch them."

"I'm more interested in touching you."

"Nice."

He put her hands on his skin. He was warm, and she liked how he felt against her fingers. After a couple of seconds, she decided it was only fair if she gave him the same opportunity. She pulled off her T-shirt, then unfastened her bra. Before the garment hit the floor, Garrick's hands were on her breasts and his fingers were playing with her nipples.

"Tell me you're already wet," he said, staring into her eyes.

"I'm wet."

"Good."

He bent his head and took her left nipple into his mouth. Without removing her jeans, he moved his hand down her belly and between her legs.

The combination of him sucking on her breast and rubbing against her clit had her breathing hard in seconds. She didn't know where to focus her attention—everything he was doing felt so good.

He moved to her other breast and shifted so he could slide two fingers inside her. She tightened her muscles around him, wanting him to go deeper.

Instead of obliging, he stepped back and grabbed her

wrist, pulling her along with him. They made it to the bed where they both kicked off their shoes. Garrick grabbed her jeans and gave one strong tug, pulling them and her panties to her ankles. He dropped to his knees and removed them, along with her socks, then urged her to sit on the edge of the bed.

As soon as she did, he told her to lie back and moved between her parted legs.

She knew where this was going, and the thought of his mouth on her made her shudder with anticipation.

"It would help if you talked," he said.

She half sat up and stared at him. "Excuse me?"

"Tell me if it feels good. Harder, softer, now. I want to get it right."

She appreciated his attention to detail. "I'll do my best."

She stretched out on the bed. For a second he did nothing, then she felt his warm breath followed by the feel of an openmouthed kiss on the very center of her. She relaxed into the sensations he created, letting the heat spread through her body.

He moved slowly at first, his tongue more teasing than serious, circling her clit, then dipping inside her. She was sensitive and swollen, and whatever he did aroused her more. When he returned to the heart of her and began to move his tongue with a more steady rhythm, she knew it wasn't going to take long—not with the need pulsing through her.

With every flick, every stroke, her muscles tensed. He moved a little faster, carrying her along with him. She couldn't quite seem to catch her breath.

"Just like that," she whispered, remembering he wanted instructions. "It's perfect."

Or so she'd thought because even as she spoke, he slipped two fingers inside her, filling her. She gasped at the sensation of him moving in and out of her. All the while he stroked her with his tongue.

The delicious friction stole her ability to think or do anything but feel what was happening to her body. She was getting closer and closer, her orgasm as inevitable as the earth's rotation.

"Oh, Garrick," she breathed, pulsing her hips in time with what he was doing. She was close, so close. Almost there…

He opened his mouth around her clit and sucked the swollen knot of nerves. It was just enough to send her over the edge. She cried out as she fell into the pleasure that rippled through her. Her release went on and on, easing slowly until the last whisper of it faded and she could only lie there like the puddle she was.

"How did you do that?" she asked, barely able to open her eyes.

"I've been thinking about it," he said. "Planning my attack."

"You give a great attack."

He grinned, then stood and quickly pulled off the rest of his clothes.

The sight of him naked—and very aroused—was enough to pique her interest. She slid onto the mattress while he opened a condom and put it on, then settled between her thighs.

"I want this," he said, staring into her eyes.

She shuddered in anticipation. "Me, too."

She reached between them and guided him in. He moved slowly, filling her until her nerve endings all cooed in delight. When he was all the way in, he groaned.

"Better than I imagined," he told her, his eyes dilating.

She smiled. "I agree, but it seems to me you're an orgasm behind. Let's catch you up."

"Let's."

He withdrew only to push in again. She wrapped her legs around his hips, tilting her pelvis so he could go in deeper. They both gasped.

They moved together in the age-old dance of lovemaking. With every stroke, she was more and more aroused, her body aching for another release.

"You're close," he said, his gaze locking with hers. "I can feel it."

"I am. You feel good."

"Touch yourself."

The request was thrilling. Still staring into his eyes, she moved her hand between their bodies and pressed her fingers to her swollen center. Garrick eased back, more on his haunches as he thrust inside her. They both looked at where her fingers circled and his penis moved in and out.

The visual was the most erotic thing she'd seen, and she felt herself getting closer and closer to another release.

"I'm going to come," she gasped.

"Good. Tell me when."

She moved hard and faster, his thrusts matching her movements. Her body tensed as she got closer and closer.

"Now!"

She felt her muscles tighten around him as she lost herself in the glorious waves of pleasure. Seconds later, Garrick called out her name as he pushed in deeply, then stilled. She consciously clamped around him, wanting to make it as good as possible. Their eyes opened and they stared at each other, body to body, soul to soul.

Garrick found himself whistling on his short drive home from work. He'd spent the day in a better than usual mood. He'd smiled so much, a couple of the officers had asked him what was going on. Nothing like a great night with an amazing woman to change a man's outlook on life, he thought as he parked in the driveway.

His time with Wynn had been even better than he'd imagined. She was sexy and responsive and just plain fun. They'd made love twice before he'd had to head back to his place. He wanted to be with her again and again. Once had definitely not been enough.

But between her kid and his, life was a little complicated, so intimacy would have to wait. On the bright side, he had a date with her to look forward to.

He walked into the house and called out a greeting. Joylyn waddled out of her bedroom, smiling when she saw him.

"Hi, Dad. How was your day?"

"Pretty good. You look more rested. Did you get some sleep?"

She nodded. "I've been lying down every couple of hours. Even if I only sleep for a little bit, eventually it adds up, right?"

She pointed toward his office. "A package came for you. I put it on your desk."

He smiled. "Good. I've been waiting for that. Give me a second to change my clothes, then we'll open it together."

"Now I'm intrigued," she said with a laugh.

"Good."

He went into the master and put on jeans and a short-sleeved shirt. After carrying the box to the kitchen table, he cut the tape before stepping back and motioning for her to do the honors.

She gave him a quizzical look as she opened the flaps and pulled out a smaller box. She opened that, then stared at the contents.

"Oh, Dad."

Her voice was thick with emotion, but the happy kind. She removed a small round handprint ornament she'd made when she was five or six.

"I don't understand," she whispered, touching the smooth clay.

"I called your mom and asked if she could send along your old Christmas decorations. She was going to give them to you when the baby was born, so she had them packed up. I thought you might like to have them on the tree here—you know, to make you feel it was more like Christmas. When you go back to Phoenix, I'll get them together so you can take them with you."

She put down the ornament and rushed into his arms.

"Thank you so much. I love them and yes, I want them on the tree."

"Good."

She looked at him, her mouth curved up in a smile. "That was very thoughtful of you."

He kissed the top of her head. "You're my best girl, no matter how old you are."

He carried the box into the living room and set it on the coffee table. Joylyn sat on the sofa and directed him as he hung all the ornaments. And while he liked that he was making her happy, he wasn't thrilled to know she would be leaving him before Christmas. If he had his way, he would like her to stick around through New Year's.

But he knew that wasn't practical. Once Chandler was home, she would want to get back to Phoenix and have her baby there.

When he'd finished, she took several pictures of the tree. "I'm going to text them to Chandler," she said. "He'll be so excited. I can't believe we're just under two weeks away from him coming back."

"I know you're excited. You'll want him close for sure." He cleared his throat. "If you, ah, want, you two could spend a couple of nights here before heading back to Phoenix. I'd enjoy hanging out with the two of you."

She looked up from her phone. For a second her expression was unreadable and he thought maybe he'd stepped in it, but then she smiled.

"I'd like that, Dad. Let me make sure that's all right with Chandler. I'm sure he'll be happy to stay. With me so pregnant, we can't go see his family this year, so splitting my time between you and Mom makes sense."

"I'd like that," he said, careful to keep his tone happy but not too happy. He didn't want to pressure her.

He held up the empty box. "I'll store this in my office until you're ready to leave. Are you ready for dinner?"

"I am. I already made potato salad to go with the pork chops you're barbecuing."

"Nice. After dinner, I'm going to work in the garage for a little bit." He was nearly done with the bassinet.

She rolled her eyes. "Men and their garages. If we ever have one, I hope Chandler doesn't spend as much time in his as you do."

"It's a guy thing, sweetie. You're going to have to get used to it."

chapter sixteen

Wynn wasn't one to make a public statement, but living in a small town meant it was inevitable. Showing up to The Boardroom with Garrick would definitely get the word out—not that she minded. She liked Garrick and was happy to be seen with him. It was more just knowing that everyone would be looking at them and speculating.

She was not a "center of attention" kind of person. When she'd been dating Jasper, she'd asked that they keep things quiet the first year they were together. But once they'd shown up at The Boardroom together, everyone had known.

Given the fact that the regular Monday night tournaments would be suspended through the first of the year, The Boardroom was offering game night every night this week.

"Nervous?" Garrick asked as he pulled into the parking lot.

"Braced."

He turned off the engine and smiled at her. "If it helps, you look beautiful and every guy in there is going to be jealous as hell."

She laughed. "Most of the guys in there are happily married, so probably not, but you're sweet to say that."

"Just being honest."

He got out of his SUV and came around to her side, then opened the door. When she was standing, he lightly kissed her, then took her hand.

"Best first date ever," he told her.

"We still have hours to go. What if I turn out to be a dud?"

"Not possible."

He was good, she thought, slipping her hand into his. Kind, funny, sexy, great in a bed and thoughtful. Oh, and really good-looking. There was no bad with Garrick—a thought that should have scared her and yet didn't.

They walked inside and were greeted by people they knew. As they chatted, she looked around and spotted Bethany and Cade at a table. Bethany saw her and waved her over.

"We have an invitation," Wynn told Garrick.

"And a serious chance of winning tonight's game," he said with a grin. "They won't last the first round."

"I assume you're talking about them wanting to get home to their daughter and not their lack of skills at—" She glanced at the board games stacked on the bar. "Trivial Pursuit."

"I was. Something tells me Bethany will be great at Trivial Pursuit. I'm guessing her knowledge of world history and geography is better than mine."

"Not good with the rivers?" she asked, her voice teasing.

"The rivers get me every time."

They joined their friends. Bethany shot Wynn a "we'll talk about this later" look before waving over the server in the area.

"We've already ordered." Bethany grinned. "One of the thrills of wrapping up my breastfeeding is I get to have alcohol again. Yay me, especially with them serving all those delicious holiday drinks."

Cade shook his head. "Honey, you don't even finish a glass of wine."

"I know, but I could if I wanted."

Wynn and Garrick placed their drink orders.

"Should we take bets on how long you'll last?" Garrick asked with a grin.

"We're staying for the whole first round," Cade announced firmly. "Maybe."

"Who's home with Addison?" Wynn asked.

"My mother," Cade said.

Wynn tried not to wince. Libby Saunders was a stern woman who frightened most people in town, but she loved her son and adored her granddaughter.

"I think she's trying to get in as much time as she can now," he added. "In case Bethany's folks decide to fly in for the holidays."

"They're not going to just show up," Bethany said.

"You sure about that?"

Bethany hesitated. "Not really."

Wynn laughed. "The king and queen do like to make an entrance."

"My dad likes to make an entrance," Bethany corrected. "My mom just wants to see me and Addison." She glanced at Cade. "And you, of course."

"Of course," he echoed. "I'm the favorite son-in-law. And the only son-in-law."

Bethany laughed. "They love you."

"Your dad told me he'd cut off my head if I ever disappointed you. Not that he would do it himself. I'm sure there's a royal head-cutter-offer somewhere in the palace."

The server appeared with their drinks. Garrick passed them out to the table.

"A royal father-in-law would be tough," he said. "It adds a whole extra layer of pressure."

Cade nodded. "Plus they go crazy with the presents. She's still a baby. She doesn't need a pony."

"They're not giving her a pony," Bethany told him. "They'll wait until she's six."

Wynn smiled at Garrick. "Did you get Joylyn a pony this year?"

"She and Chandler are still in the Marines. They don't have anywhere to put it." He picked up his beer. "He'll have some leave when he gets home. I got them a week at a cabin in Lake Tahoe. They can take the baby and get away for a few days to be a family together."

"That's a great gift," she said. "I'm sure she'll love it."

"I hope so." He glanced at her. "How hard is it to throw a baby shower?"

"You're thinking for Joylyn?"

"Uh-huh. The baby's due on the twenty-fifth. Between her friend's wedding, Chandler coming home and the holidays, I don't think she's going to have one. Doesn't she need a baby shower?"

"It's a tradition for sure," Bethany said. "I wonder why her friends haven't pulled one together."

Wynn thought about the young women who had shown up over Thanksgiving weekend. "Most of her friends are still in college. I doubt it occurred to them. Her other group of friends are Marine wives. While they might want to put one on, she's here and they're in San Diego."

Joylyn might have shown up in Happily Inc crabby and

sad, but she'd changed in the short period of time she'd been here. She and Garrick had reconnected, and she was great with Hunter. The young mother-to-be deserved a baby shower.

"The only dates that make sense are this weekend," she said. "I'm not sure we can pull it off so quickly, but if you want to try, I'll help."

"Let me text Alisha and see what she thinks. She's the mom, after all."

He excused himself and went outside. The second he was gone, Bethany leaned close to Wynn.

"You were holding hands! I saw! Tell me everything."

"Not everything," Cade added quickly, his expression pained. "Garrick and I are friends. There are things I don't want to know."

Wynn grinned at him. "I'll only share the G-rated version."

Bethany clapped her hands. "There's another version? So you're dating. When did this happen? You guys look great together, by the way. So tell me, tell me!"

"I've noticed him for a while," Wynn admitted. "I guess he'd noticed me, as well. Things started happening when he found out his daughter was coming to stay and he asked for my help to get the house ready. Since then we've been hanging out a lot and getting to know each other."

"And the sex part?"

"No," Cade said. "Just no. Please?"

"But she has to tell me now. Joylyn is coming to lunch tomorrow, and I can't ask in front of his daughter."

"Text her later. Just don't talk about it now. Please?"

Garrick returned to the table.

"And?" Wynn asked.

"The shower is on, but Alisha started crying when she

realized she'd totally forgotten to give her only daughter a baby shower."

Wynn squeezed his hand. "That's not your fault."

"I still feel guilty. I don't like making women cry."

"But if you can bring a guy to tears?" Cade asked.

Garrick grinned. "That's different. It shouldn't be but it is. Anyway, I'm going to talk to Joylyn when I get home and ask her if she wants the shower. If she does, Alisha will contact her friends and get it all going."

He looked at Wynn. "It's going to be at my house, and I'll need help pulling it all together."

"I'd love to help." She smiled at Bethany. "With all my friends popping out babies, I'm something of an expert."

"You'll need a theme," Bethany told him. "Once you have that, it helps with all the other decisions."

"Do you know how she wants to decorate the baby's room?" Wynn asked him.

"Light blue and yellow with a lot of Winnie the Pooh."

"There you go," she said. "We have a theme. We'll go online and get some ideas. We can pull it together."

His gaze locked with hers. She felt the connection flow between them and immediately wished they were alone. But they weren't, and this was their first date and she should enjoy it instead of thinking about how much she wanted to make love with him.

The servers walked around, handing out Trivial Pursuit games to every table. As they set up the board, Wynn felt Garrick's leg press against hers. She looked at him and he smiled. She smiled back, ignoring the not-very-subtle aching in her heart.

He got to her in ways she hadn't expected, and she liked how they were together. She had a feeling that while they'd been busy living their lives, she'd been slowly, quietly, falling in love with him. Which meant there was no escaping her feelings. She could only ride them out and hope that he was falling for her, as well.

Wynn left work at eleven thirty. She needed to swing by her place and pick up the Christmas cookies she'd made for the girlfriend lunch. She was also going to get Joylyn, who would be joining her.

She pulled into the driveway and stopped the car. Before she'd even climbed out, Joylyn was locking the front door to Garrick's house and heading her way.

"I'm excited," she said with a sheepish smile. "I didn't want to wait for you to come get me."

Wynn laughed. "Not a problem. We appreciate enthusiasm. I just need to grab the cookies I made for lunch today. Oh, Natalie made enchiladas. Did you take an antacid?"

"Yes. About forty minutes ago. Thanks for the warning. I'm ready for the feast."

Wynn left her car open and hurried into the house. She'd already packed up the cookies in a container. She returned to the car to find Joylyn in the passenger seat.

"Thank you for inviting me to hang out with your friends," Joylyn said earnestly. "It's really thoughtful."

"We're happy to have you join us. You already know me, Silver and Renee. Everyone else is very friendly." She backed out of the driveway. "Usually we have kids running around, but today everyone agreed to leave them at home, so it's just going to be a lot of girl talk."

"I've missed having that in my life," Joylyn said. "Thanks for taking me under your wing and making my stay here so great. My dad's lucky to have you in his life."

"I've been happy to get to know you," Wynn said automatically, trying not to react to the unexpected comment.

Nor was she comfortable asking what Joylyn meant. Have her in his life? As in they were dating? Had Joylyn figured that out? Had she known all along—although technically they hadn't started "dating" until last night. And if Joylyn knew, had she talked about it to Hunter? Should Wynn discuss the situation with him? Not that she knew what she was going to say. Not really. She'd never had a man in her life before—not like this.

She was going to have to think it all through, but not now, she told herself.

"Oh, and thank you for helping my dad with the baby shower," Joylyn added, drawing Wynn back to the present.

"I'm looking forward to it."

Joylyn glanced at her. "I know there isn't much time to pull everything together. Don't worry about everything not being perfect. I'm just happy to have one. Oh, my college friends are all coming." She wrinkled her nose. "They're sorry about what happened the last time they visited and swear this will be different."

"We're not serving alcohol at the party, if that helps."

Joylyn grinned. "I think it might."

"I love your theme. Winnie the Pooh is perfect, and the colors will be so pretty in the baby's room. Plus little Howard won't need a change in decor for several years."

"Howard! We're not calling the baby Howard."

"You won't tell me what names are on the list, so I'm guessing."

Joylyn laughed. "Howard is not on the list."

"It's a perfectly respectable name."

"Still not using it."

Wynn grinned at her, thinking the happy young woman sitting next to her was so different from the one who had arrived a few short weeks ago.

They parked by the Willow Gallery and got out.

"This is beautiful," Joylyn said, taking the grocery bag.

"Natalie used to be the office manager here, along with one of their artists. Now she's doing well enough that she can focus exclusively on her art. The gallery also shows work by the Mitchell brothers. Ronan is Natalie's husband. Pallas is married to Nick, and Carol is married to Mathias. You met Silver and Drew at Thanksgiving."

"I did."

They walked into the gallery. Everyone else was already there. Wynn made introductions.

"We finally get to meet," Pallas said. "Renee's told me all about Holly's wedding. I'm so excited. Everything is coming together."

"Thanks to Renee and the town," Joylyn said happily. "Holly is still stunned by everyone's generosity. I am, too."

"It's fun for us," Pallas said.

Joylyn nodded, then sniffed. "I'm trying not to cry at everything, but it's hard. Thank you again."

Wynn gave her a hug. "No thanks required. Think of the wedding as our way of really celebrating the season. We're excited to help Holly with her wedding, and we're happy to have you here with us today."

Joylyn stood in line with everyone else to fill her plate for lunch. The big table in the center of the gallery was covered with a festive holiday tablecloth. In addition to the enchiladas, bean dip and chips, there were two green salads, a fruit salad and Christmas cookies. Holiday music played in the background.

All the women were so welcoming, she thought. Her friends were nice, but she wasn't sure they would have been so gracious to someone they didn't really know.

"How's it going with Hunter?" Carol asked Wynn as they served each other enchiladas.

"Okay. I think he understands the gravity of what he did. As soon as school's out, he's going to get started on the deck."

"He'll be a busy guy," Carol said. "He's been in touch with me about helping at the animal preserve."

"Make sure he does the grunt work," Wynn said. "It's not supposed to be fun."

"He'll be cleaning out the barns every morning for a week," Carol told her. "And on weekends until he gets his hours in." She smiled. "It's a lot of poop to deal with. I doubt he'll think it's fun."

Everyone laughed and headed for their seats. Joylyn found herself sitting between Renee and Natalie.

"In the end, Hunter did the right thing," Pallas said. "That has to make you happy."

"I'm cautiously optimistic," Wynn admitted. "We'll see what happens over the holiday break."

"Do you think he's going to apply to JROTC again?" Bethany asked.

"I hope so, but that's up to him."

Joylyn thought Wynn had handled the situation with her son really well. She wasn't sure she could have gotten over being mad to act so responsibly. She rested her hand on her belly as she reminded herself that in a few short weeks, she was going to be a parent. At least she wouldn't be alone—Chandler would be with her. They would figure it out together.

Conversation shifted to what was going on in each of their lives. Bethany was still wondering what her parents were going to do over Christmas.

"Like Wynn, I'm cautiously optimistic," she said with a

laugh. "I think we have a good chance of getting through Christmas without the royal family descending."

"When does the king's private jet arrive to whisk you all to El Bahar for New Year's?" Silver asked, her voice teasing.

"On the twenty-seventh." Bethany sighed. "When she gets older, my daughter is going to have a very rude adjustment to normal life."

"You mean like flying commercial?" Carol laughed.

"That among other things. Of course if there's ever a discussion about what everyone's grandparents do, she's going to have a really interesting story."

"The other kids won't believe her," Renee said.

Joylyn listened a lot more than she spoke. She was content to let the words wash over her. She didn't know the details of each life they discussed, but that was fine. Some situations were universal.

She missed this, she thought. Having good friends she could count on. For the hundredth time, she told herself she should have stayed on base where she had support. But this time, instead of feeling sorry for herself, she vowed that she would learn from her mistake and do better next time. She would make sure she had friends she could count on, not ones who showed up drunk and mocked her for not partying when she was nine months pregnant. In return, she saw she had to be a better friend.

A good life lesson, she told herself. One she would hang on to.

"You sure that's not too heavy?" Garrick asked, as Wynn helped him carry the first of five large folding tables through the house.

Wynn, gorgeous as always, in jeans and a T-shirt, her

holiday pinecone charm glinting against her chest, rolled her eyes. "I'm fine. I doubt the table weighs fifteen pounds."

"I don't want you to hurt yourself."

"I'm not infirmed."

"Still."

They reached the patio area by the pool and set down the folding table. He immediately pulled her close and kissed her.

"I wouldn't want anything to happen to you," he told her.

"I appreciate the concern but again, not fragile."

"I agree, but you are special."

Her gaze softened. "You are such a guy."

"That should be good news."

She laughed. "Fine. It's good news and you're very sweet to worry, but please, don't ask me if I'm okay for the twenty minutes it's going to take to unload your truck."

"I'll be quiet if you give me a kiss."

She leaned in and pressed her mouth to his. "No bargaining required for that," she told him.

"I like knowing that."

The light kiss was enough to get him thinking about his bed and them together. He enjoyed the fantasy for about two seconds, then firmly pushed it to the back of his mind. Getting ready for Joylyn's baby shower was the more pressing concern, but maybe later…

Renee and Pallas had loaned him folding tables and chairs for the weekend. The tables he was using were rectangular, and apparently the weddings planned for the weekend were using round tables. Renee had given him more detail than that, but he'd tuned it out. All he'd wanted to know was if he could borrow a few tables or not.

He and Wynn made quick work of unloading the rest of the tables and the chairs.

"Let me show you what I've got so far," he said, grabbing her hand and pulling her into the house.

They went into his office where he'd stacked boxes and shopping bags.

"You are serious about this," she said, looking around.

"It's Joylyn's shower. Of course I'm serious. I went online to figure out what to do and ordered as much as I could."

He pulled out a pad of paper from his desk. "The menu is simple. I checked with all the caterers in town and no one could squeeze in a full meal, so we're doing a high tea. Finger sandwiches from one of the caterers. Different kinds of scones and little petit fours from the bakery. Renee came through with a bunch of teapots, and Silver is going to swing by and drop off a big serving container and ingredients for punch." He looked at Wynn. "Does that sound okay?"

"It sounds great. I'm still pretty impressed you're doing all this."

"I'm getting a lot of help."

"Still, it's a baby shower. That has to be scary."

"I'm a big manly man. I don't get scared."

As he'd expected, she laughed. "Yes, my liege. I bow to your manly man-ness."

He went over his notes. "The colors are light blue and pale yellow. I have yellow tablecloths for the tables. Renee gave me a bunch of white plates to use. I'm picking those up in the morning. Oh, I gave the bakery twenty-four terracotta pots. Little ones. They'll bake cupcakes in them. So an edible party favor."

"You know about party favors from your research?"

"I do now." He scanned the list. "I have blue and yellow balloons on order, the Winnie the Pooh wall decoration for the big wall next to the sliding glass door." He looked at her. "Drinks, food, decorations, games. Oh, prizes."

He crossed to the bags against the wall and pulled out a heavy box. Inside were enamel giraffe key chains.

"I got these from Carol. She sells them at the little shop they have. They're really popular."

Wynn smiled. "You've thought of everything."

"I hope so. You're going to be here, right? To make sure I don't mess up?"

He wanted the day to be perfect for his daughter, and he knew that Wynn would help him make sure that happened.

She wrapped her arms around him. "I'll be here, and Carol's going to stop by to help with the setup."

"Why would she do that?"

Wynn smiled. "Because she's my friend and she's met Joylyn and I asked her. I thought one more body would be helpful. Natalie has a gallery showing in New Mexico, and all my other friends are busy with the snowman wedding."

"She's going to give up part of her Saturday for Joylyn?"

"Don't sound so surprised. It's what friends do."

He knew that. "It's not that Carol's helping, it's that you asked one of your friends to do that for my daughter. Thank you."

"You're welcome."

He kissed her again, liking how her body felt against his. There was something about her, he thought. Something that made him happy. She was caring and smart and funny and sexy and a whole bunch of other things that made him never want to let go.

"Did you buy linens?" she asked, distracting him from his thoughts.

Was she asking about his sheets?

"For the bassinet," she explained.

"I did. They're very Pooh."

He showed her the flat sheets he'd bought, along with a Winnie the Pooh blanket.

"No pillow," he added. "Babies don't use pillows, and we're not supposed to put the blanket in the crib, either."

The corners of her mouth turned up. "I'd heard that. Garrick, I'm just going to say it. You're ready for Joylyn's shower."

"You sure?"

"Yes. You've prepped as much as you can. Saturday morning Carol and I will be here at nine to help you pull it all together. Then there will be nothing to do but get out of the way and watch your daughter have a wonderful time."

"I want that for her."

"I know you do. It's one of your best qualities."

"Yeah? What other qualities do you like?"

She pressed her mouth to his. "Want me to start at the top and work my way down?"

"I do. Very much."

"Even with Joylyn five feet away in her bedroom and my son next door?"

He sighed heavily. "Soon," he said.

"The sooner the better."

chapter seventeen

Wynn opened Garrick's front door to find three young women standing on the doorstep. She'd already let in the three party girls from a few weeks ago, so didn't recognize these friends.

"We're here for Joylyn's shower," the tall, dark-haired one said with a big smile. "We're the surprise." Her smile faded a little. "We told her dad we were coming yesterday, and he said it was fine."

The Marine wives! Garrick had mentioned they were going to try to make it, and here they were.

"It is," Wynn said, stepping back to let them in. "I can't believe you drove all this way for a baby shower."

"We miss Joylyn," a petite, obviously pregnant brunette said. "We're sorry she moved out to live with her mom."

"She misses you, too." Wynn waved them into the house. "We're all out by the pool." She pointed to the hall bathroom, then led the way out to the back patio.

Joylyn looked up and saw her friends, then shrieked as she got to her feet.

"Are you really here? I can't believe it. You came from so far away."

They all hugged, then Joylyn started on introductions. There were her college friends, two of the women from her birthing class and now the Marine wives. Garrick circulated among all of them, getting everyone drinks and putting the presents on a table by the small lawn.

Wynn slipped back into the house just in time to see Carol pull up. She hurried outside to help her friend, who had stopped to pick up the last of the food.

"I drove about five miles an hour," Carol said with a laugh. "I didn't want to ruin anything."

They carried in big pink bakery boxes. Once in the kitchen, Wynn checked the contents. There were dozens of small scones in four different flavors, along with an equal number of petit fours.

"Garrick got the sandwiches this morning," Wynn said. "I was about to take them out of the refrigerator so they can warm up a little. We can put the petit fours in their place."

"Good idea."

Carol helped her take the sandwiches out and put in the little desserts, then they unpacked the small terra-cotta pots filled with chocolate and vanilla cupcakes topped with a little beehive of frosting.

"Too cute," Carol said, setting them on the kitchen table. "Her guests are going to love these. What about drinks?"

"Already done. I put out the two drink servers we borrowed from Silver. One has lemonade and one has a sparkling fruit punch. It's Silver's recipe."

"But nonalcoholic," Carol said.

Wynn nodded. "I think a little vodka would be a nice touch, but of course we're not going to do that." Although if there was any left over, spiking a glass of punch would be a fun reward for the long day.

The doorbell rang. Wynn excused herself to answer it. She opened the door to find a beautiful blonde in her late thirties standing on the porch.

She was well-dressed in black trousers and a deep purple twinset. Diamond studs flashed at her ears. They were about the biggest diamonds Wynn had ever seen in real life, or so she thought until she caught a glimpse of the woman's wedding set.

"You must be Alisha," she said, hoping her tone was warm rather than resentful. Really? Did Garrick's ex have to be gorgeous, well-dressed and perfectly made-up? Couldn't she be just a little frumpy? "I'm Wynn. It's nice to meet you."

Alisha smiled warmly. "I've heard so much about you from Garrick. Thank you for all you've done for my daughter. I hope she hasn't been too…difficult."

"Pregnancy is hard," Wynn said, stepping back to let the other woman inside. Carol joined them and introduced herself.

"The party is just getting started," Carol said. "Why don't I walk you back to the pool area?"

"Thank you." Alisha looked around the living room. "This is very nice. I see Garrick has finally gotten to the place in his life where he wants more than just a sofa and a giant TV. Good for him."

Wynn smiled rather than comment, then returned to the kitchen. There wasn't much for her to do, but it beat watching the reunion between mother and daughter. Not that she cared that Joylyn would be happy to see her mom. And it was nice of Alisha to make the drive. And Wynn really didn't care about her opinion about anything. It was just Alisha was a lot more impressive than she'd imagined.

Garrick walked into the kitchen. "Everything is under control out on the patio. I came to see how I could help you with the food and stuff."

"Alisha's here."

"I saw." He looked at her. "Wait a second. Was that an observation, or was it one of those short sentences loaded with a ton of meaning and I'm about five seconds away from being in serious trouble?"

She drew in a breath. "You're not in trouble. I just thought she would be different."

"How?"

"Less amazing."

He frowned. "How is she amazing? I'm not saying anything bad about her but she's just, you know, a girl I dated in high school."

Wynn appreciated the words and knew he was right, but somehow she'd never expected Alisha to surprise her.

"She's very put together," she said.

He looked confused. "What does that mean?"

"Her clothes."

The confusion grew. "She has on pants and a top thing."

Wynn held in a smile. "It's a twinset and it's lovely."

"But you look better."

Wynn glanced down at her cropped pants and the boat neck T-shirt she'd put on. A step up from her usual at-home uniform of jeans, but not by much.

"Did you see her diamond earrings?" she asked.

"No. Is she wearing earrings?" He shifted uncomfortably. "Wynn, I'm lost here. What's going on?"

She was being ridiculous. Alisha was nothing to Garrick—she hadn't been for decades. There was absolutely no reason to get riled up about her. So what if she was perfectly dressed and more than pretty?

"Sorry," Wynn said, stepping close and putting her hands on his chest. "I had a moment of insecurity. It'll pass."

He drew her against him. "You are the last person who should ever be insecure. You're perfect."

She laughed. "I wish that were true, but I think we both know it's not."

"You're wrong."

He kissed her. She let herself get lost in the feel of his mouth against hers, then stepped back and smiled at him.

"I have pulled on my big girl panties and I'm fine," she said. "Let's head out to the patio. We can get the first couple of games going, then we'll bring out the food. After lunch, another game, then we open presents. Then anyone who wants to leave can, and the rest can stay and visit."

He touched her face. "See? Perfect, just like I said."

Before Wynn could answer, Yolanda strolled into the kitchen. When she spotted them, she waved her half-empty glass.

"So I tried the punch and it's, ah, kind of boring. I was hoping I could get a little something in my drink."

Wynn had to fight to keep from rolling her eyes. "You mean like alcohol?"

Yolanda brightened. "That would be great."

"No."

Yolanda stared at her. "Excuse me?"

"No. This is a baby shower, not a nightclub. I'm confident you can go a couple of hours without alcohol in order to support your friend at her baby shower."

Yolanda's expression turned annoyed. "Whatever." She spun on her heel and walked back the way she'd come.

"See," Wynn said, linking arms with him. "It could be worse. She could be your daughter."

"No, thanks. I'll stick to the one I have."

Joylyn sat in the shade on the patio, letting the conversation flow around her. She was tired, but happy. The shower had been great. She'd enjoyed the games and the laughter. The lunch of high tea had been so special. She still couldn't believe her friends from base had driven all the way out to Happily Inc to spend time with her. The day had been perfect. The only thing missing was Chandler.

They were down to eight days, she reminded herself. He had his flight information, and if all went well, he would be with her a week from tomorrow.

She touched her belly and whispered, "You're going to see your daddy soon, little guy."

Holly was studying the notes she'd made, listing who had given what present. After church tomorrow, Joylyn was going to write the thank-you notes and get them in the mail. Real thank-you notes, she thought with a smile. Not emailed ones. Wynn was going to be so proud.

"Here you go," Holly said, handing over the pad of paper. "I double-checked and I got everything."

"Thank you for helping."

Her friend smiled at her. "What else would I do? You're giving me a wonderful wedding. I'll be grateful forever."

"Not me," Joylyn corrected. "The town."

"I know, but you're the one who made it happen. Rex and I are still in shock."

"It's in a week," Joylyn told her.

Holly grinned. "We're so excited. I can't wait to see how everything turns out. Renee is extraordinary. I loved meeting her and seeing the space in person."

Holly had driven out to Happily Inc early that morning to spend an hour with Renee, going over final details. Joylyn couldn't wait for the wedding itself. Not only because Chandler would be home the next day, but because she wanted to see her friend married to the man of her dreams.

"We're going to head back," Cheryl said, coming to her feet. The other Marine wives nodded and stood as well.

Joylyn hugged them all and thanked them for coming so far. As she walked them to the door, they all promised to figure out a way to get together when Chandler was back.

She stood at the front door and waved until they were out of sight. Her college friends had left right after the presents had been opened. She'd overheard them complaining there wasn't any liquor at the shower. Joylyn had silently shaken her head at the complaint. Hard to believe she was their same age—her life was so different from theirs.

Better, she thought as she returned to the patio, her gait more waddle than walk. She was so lucky. She had family and friends and a wonderful husband and a baby due in the next few weeks.

She sat back in her chair. Her mom was talking to Wynn and Holly. Her dad was picking up the dirty plates and taking them to the kitchen.

He'd really come through for her, she thought. First taking her in when her mom had kicked her out and then totally being there for her through birthing class and her horrible moods. She winced as she remembered how bitchy she'd been when she'd arrived. Part of that had been missing Chandler and part of that had been how hurt she'd been at what her mom had done.

She looked at her mother, wondering what combination of events had caused the other woman to toss out her own daughter. Had Joylyn really been that difficult to live with or were there other forces at work?

Maybe things weren't as good at home as she'd thought. Maybe the boys were getting into trouble or there was tension in the marriage. Joylyn wasn't sure and knew this wasn't the time to ask. While she was still hurt by her mother's actions, she didn't feel quite so raw when she thought about them.

Her dad returned from the kitchen and walked over to stand by her chair. He looked uncomfortable as he cleared his throat.

"I made you something. I was going to bring it out when you were opening the other presents, but then I wasn't sure. I didn't want you to think I was trying to take over the shower or be more important than anyone else, so I waited. But I'd like you to see it."

She laughed. "Dad, I have no idea what you're talking about."

"I know. I'll be right back."

Before he left, he glanced at Wynn, who nodded and got up to follow him.

"What is that about?" Holly asked.

Joylyn shrugged. "They're sure acting mysterious."

She had the brief thought that maybe they were going to announce their engagement, but then told herself it wasn't that. Her dad would never do that at her baby shower. Plus he'd said he made her something. She had no idea what it could be. Her dad didn't…

Wynn returned with a gift bag in her hand. Before Joylyn could ask about it, her father stepped onto the patio, a beautiful, wooden bassinet in his hands. He carefully set it on the concrete, then stepped back and watched her.

Joylyn stared at the incredible piece of furniture. The

lines were simple but elegant. The light stain allowed the beauty of the wood to shine. There was a baby mattress in place.

She got out of her chair and crossed to the bassinet, then ran her hands along the smooth wood. It took only the lightest push to get it to rock.

"Oh, Daddy," she murmured. "I don't know what to say." She looked at him. "You made this for me?"

He nodded. "I wanted you to have something special. You're my little girl."

She thought about all the time it would have taken him to build this for her. She thought about all the years they'd lost because a bitter woman had lied to her and she'd believed her. She thought about her own child and how much she already loved him, then she rushed into her father's arms and hung on tight.

"Thank you," she said as the tears started. They quickly turned into ugly sobs she couldn't control, but no matter how much she cried, her dad didn't let go.

"You're welcome, Joylyn. I love you. I always will."

She nodded, unable to speak. Eventually the waterworks stopped enough for her to catch her breath and dry her face. When she had a little control back, Wynn handed her a bag.

"Your dad got you this, too, but it seems a little anticlimactic."

Joylyn looked in the bag and saw Winnie the Pooh bedding.

"It's perfect," she managed to say, trying her best not to start sobbing again. "I mean it, Dad. It's wonderful."

"Good. I'm glad you like it, little girl."

Everyone took turns rocking the bassinet. Her mother congratulated her on the successful shower.

"It was a special day," her mother said, looking a little emotional. "I'm so glad I was here."

Joylyn hugged her. "Me, too, Mom."

"I hope you're not too angry about me sending you to stay with your dad."

Joylyn didn't know what she was feeling anymore. The anger had faded, but the hurt remained.

"Having me stay here turned out really well for all of us," she said with a smile. "Besides, I'm sure the boys appreciate not having to be quiet in case I'm resting."

Her mother bit her bottom lip. "They do miss you. I miss you, too. If you want, I can take some of the baby's things with me so you have less to transport when Chandler gets home."

"That's okay. Dad's going to drive back with us. What we can't fit in my car, we'll get in his SUV. It's really big."

Her mother looked at her. "Joylyn, did you want to come home now? I keep thinking you should be with your family when you're so close to giving birth."

A month ago Joylyn would have jumped at the chance to leave Happily Inc, but not anymore. "I want to stay here," she said easily. "I'm settled with my dad, and there's Holly's wedding next week and my last birthing class. I'm good, Mom, but thanks for thinking of me."

"You are still mad."

"I'm not." She drew in a breath. "We will have to talk about what happened, but not today, please. It was a perfect day. I love that you came to my baby shower. Can't that be enough?"

Her mother studied her. "You've changed. You're more grown-up."

"Don't you think it was time?"

"I don't want to lose you, Joylyn."

Joylyn thought about how her mother had let her walk away from her dad. How she'd taken the easy road, rather than make her daughter do what was right, which was so different from how Wynn had handled the situation with Hunter. Joylyn supposed everyone was flawed and made mistakes. She sure made plenty herself, so she couldn't judge.

"You're not going to lose me, Mom. I'm right here." Joylyn hugged her. "I'll see you soon."

Alisha didn't look convinced, but she nodded. Joylyn sank back in her chair and thought that she was pretty darned proud of herself for how she'd handled that. Maybe this acting more mature thing was going to work for her.

Monday at eleven, Wynn left her office for the final girlfriend lunch of the year. They would take off the last two weeks of the year to accommodate the craziness of the season. She drove home to collect what she'd made and to wait for her ride.

Unlike the other lunches with a haphazard potluck menu, this meal was planned and everyone had a part. Silver provided a fun cocktail, while the food duties were shared. Wynn, who was still in a holiday baking frenzy, had offered to take care of dessert.

She'd decided on a cookie-based treat, mostly because everyone loved her sugar cookies. After playing with a couple of frosting variations, she ended up with a sugar cookie fruit tart. The sugar cookie stood in for the crust and the frosting—a custard buttercream—was the filling. She topped each cookie with blueberries and raspberries, along with a bit of sugar glaze.

She'd saved the largest bakery box from Joylyn's shower

and had put the tarts inside. Now she carefully carried them to the door and waited.

Right on time a large black limo pulled up. The plan was to enjoy the cocktails and not go back to work afterward. The limo was going to take them home, so no one had to worry about driving.

Natalie jumped out of the car and hurried up the front path to help with the box while Wynn closed the door behind herself and made sure it was locked.

"Hi," Natalie said cheerfully. "I'm ridiculously excited about our lunch."

"Me, too. I love our regular get-togethers, but this one is special."

Natalie glanced at the house next door. "I wish Joylyn had been able to join us."

"Me, too. I texted her this morning, just to confirm she was still tired. She said she was feeling too lazy to get herself together enough to come with us."

The driver held open the back door for them. Wynn took the box from Natalie so her friend could slide in.

"She's really pregnant," Natalie added, when they pulled away from the curb. "That has to be exhausting."

Wynn was sure that was most of the reason Joylyn had elected to stay home, but she also had the thought that her new friend didn't want to intrude on what was a special event. Wynn had told her she was more than welcome, but Joylyn had insisted she was not up to the day.

They drove to the animal sanctuary and picked up Carol, then made their way to Weddings Out of the Box, where the lunch would be held. Drew was dropping off Silver with her supplies, and Cade had agreed to deliver Bethany to the lunch.

When they arrived, they found Silver, Bethany, Renee

and Pallas in the large open area where most of the weddings and receptions were held. A long table had been set up by the windows. A green, red and black plaid table runner topped a white tablecloth. Long, low centerpieces of red and white roses were accented with pinecones and greens.

A second table had been set up to hold the Secret Santa gifts.

Wynn carried her cookies to the kitchen area. Servers were at work, getting the prepared food ready for the lunch. She returned to the main room and greeted her friends before adding her gift to the pile. The rules of Secret Santa were simple—the gift had to be inexpensive and fun. Everyone drew numbers out of a hat, and that was the order the gifts were chosen. If you were last and ended up with your own gift, you got to take a gift from someone else in exchange for yours.

Wynn had found a cute wooden penguin at an estate sale. The little guy looked like he was about to burst into penguin laughter at any second, and she knew he would be right at home on anyone's desk.

"This is so fun," Pallas said. "Merry Christmas, everyone. As you can see, we're going to have a delicious lunch. We'll start with Silver's cocktail. I can't wait to find out what it is. Then butternut squash soup with cheddar biscuits. Blueberry chicken salad with more biscuits, and Wynn's sugar cookie tarts for dessert."

Everyone moaned.

"That sounds amazing," Bethany said. "I'm not sure my soup is up to the challenge."

"At least you got to bring something," Natalie said with a pout. "I didn't bring anything."

"You were away at a show," Renee pointed out. "You

got home at midnight last night. When were you going to make a dish?"

Wynn patted Natalie's shoulder. "Next year you'll get the entrée."

Natalie brightened. "I'd like that."

"Cocktails," Silver said, picking up a tray of champagne glasses. "This is called a Wallaby-Darned."

Carol laughed. "Seriously?"

"That's what they tell me." Silver served each of them. "The basic ingredients are champagne, vodka and peach schnapps."

Renee leaned close to Wynn. "That explains why we all have rides home," she murmured.

Wynn laughed. "They sound delicious."

They took their seats at the table to talk for a bit before the meal service began.

"I heard the baby shower was so fun," Pallas said. "I wish we could have been there."

"It was great." Wynn took a sip of her cocktail and decided it was so good, she was going to have at least two. "Joylyn was so appreciative of everything. Thanks again for the loan of the table and chairs." She looked at Carol. "And thank you for helping me."

Carol waved away the words. "It was fun. I never get to do the party stuff. Plus we never get to help you. You're always helping us."

The comment surprised Wynn. "You help me."

"We don't," Silver told her. "You're so together all the time. You rarely need anything." She held up a hand. "I'm not complaining. I love that my friends are all self-sufficient, but it's nice to be able to give a little something. Like Holly's wedding."

"That's coming together," Renee said. "I met with her

Saturday morning and she is such a sweetie. I can't wait for her big day. The wedding is going to be perfect."

Bethany asked if everyone had already decorated for Christmas and the conversation shifted, but Wynn didn't join in. She didn't think of herself as particularly together, but it was nice that her friends viewed her that way. She tried to be a good person and take care of business. She loved her friends and her son and her life.

Only it was no longer enough. She wanted more. She wanted love and more babies, and she wanted them with Garrick.

The truth had been standing in front of her for a while now. Yes, they hadn't known each other that long, but it wasn't as if she didn't know a lot about him. His past, his work, his daughter all spoke to the kind of man he was. He loved deeply—the question was, did he want to love her?

"You okay?" Natalie asked.

Wynn smiled. "I'm great."

She turned her attention back to her friends and the fun of the day. She would think about Garrick, and what she wanted, later. She would come up with a plan to tell him how she felt and then hope he wanted the same things she did.

Doing so meant risking her heart, but she knew it was time for her to take a chance. She'd forgiven herself for her past—now she had to be willing to embrace her future and all the possibilities it offered.

chapter eighteen

Wynn pointed to the counter. "Just dump them there," she said, setting down a box containing ribbon, gift tags and tape. Garrick did as she requested with a half dozen rolls of wrapping paper. When his arms were free, he grabbed her by her jeans belt loop and pulled her close before lowering his mouth to hers.

Her body, still humming from her recent orgasm, responded immediately. A reality that made her smile. While she was certainly interested in round two, she knew that Garrick would need at least half an hour to recharge. Men were so delicate.

"Why are you smiling?" he asked, cupping her butt and squeezing.

"Because this is nice."

"It is." He kissed her again. "How late is Hunter going to be?"

"It's dinner while watching a basketball game," she said, glancing at the clock. "We have maybe an hour, but I wouldn't want to push it past that." She glanced past him to the piles of presents stacked on several chairs around her dining room table.

"And we really do have to get going on the wrapping."

He nodded, kissed her one last time before stepping back. "Chandler's coming back late Saturday or early Sunday. They'll head back to Phoenix on Tuesday, so I do need to wrap everything before he gets here."

"Have you asked her to stay through Christmas?"

He looked at her. "No. I don't want to pressure her with that. She and Chandler are spending a couple of extra days with me and that's enough."

"I know you want more," she said gently.

"I do, but it's not practical. She's getting close to her due date. She'll want to be home with her regular doctor."

Wynn was less sure about that. From what she'd seen at the baby shower, Joylyn was still figuring out how she felt about her mom and all she'd learned about her past—not to mention the fact that she'd been kicked out of her own home. Joylyn might not have wanted to come to her dad's place, but everything had changed.

"She's been happy here," she said, walking over to the gifts. "I would suggest letting her know she always has a place with you."

"I'll think about it. So how do you want to do this?"

"I like to sort through the presents. See how much I have to wrap, then decide which ones get what paper. I bought a couple of rolls of really pretty paper for Joylyn. There's the cartoon print for the baby and Hunter."

"Hunter's fourteen. Isn't he too old for cartoon Christmas wrap?"

She laughed. "Yes, and that's the point. He rolls his eyes at me and complains, but I think he secretly likes it."

They went through the presents, separating them by

recipient. Garrick had bought Chandler a tool kit and a leather jacket.

"Joylyn helped me pick it out," he said. "Apparently it's one he's been eyeing online for a while."

He'd gotten Joylyn pearl earrings accented with a small diamond.

"They're beautiful, and I'm impressed with your ability to walk into a jewelry store and not freak out," Wynn said, teasing him. "It's a skill."

"Jewelry stores don't intimidate me," he told her. "Although having seen your latest piece, I wouldn't know what to buy."

She grinned as she fingered her puka shell necklace. "Are you saying bad things about my Secret Santa gift?"

"Not at all. It's lovely."

"I know it's silly, but I like it." She shifted a few bags to the "Chandler and Joylyn" pile. "I don't know Chandler at all, so I went with a family gift."

"You didn't have to get them anything."

"I wanted to." She tapped the bag. "It's an electronic picture frame. They can hook it up to their Wi-Fi and send new pictures anytime they want." She pointed to the large boxes next to the chairs. "Those are diapers."

"For Christmas?" He sounded disappointed.

"Trust me, she'll be grateful. No one got her diapers at the shower, and babies go through dozens every week. The cost adds up. They're a huge expense. However many I buy, she's going to need so many more."

"I hadn't thought of that. Maybe once they're settled I can get them some kind of service."

"Aren't you already giving them a week in a cabin in Lake Tahoe?" she asked. "And going in on a meal delivery service with Alisha?"

He shifted his weight. "She's my baby girl."

"I get it," she said softly. "You have a lot of Christmases to make up for."

"I know. I keep telling myself that I gave her gifts those years, even if she wouldn't see me, but it's not the same. I didn't see her, so I had to guess what she wanted. I never knew if she liked them or not."

"I think she liked them even if she wouldn't admit it to anyone."

They went through the rest of the gifts. The last bag held baby clothes. Wynn pulled out a couple of pairs of footie pajamas and a little T-shirt that said *I'm New Here.* There was a cute hoodie with matching baby-sized sweatpants.

She remembered how little she'd had when Hunter had been born and how she'd been terrified they weren't going to make it. She'd felt alone and lost, and if that lawyer hadn't shown up with the unexpected inheritance, she didn't know what would have happened.

Things were different now, she thought as her heart ached with longing. She was different. Settled, mature and with a support network she could count on. She was still in her midthirties. Biologically there was no reason to think she couldn't get pregnant and have a baby. Maybe even two.

"Wynn, are you all right?"

Emotions filled her, making it hard for her to breathe. The need grew until it was bigger than anything she'd ever felt.

"Wynn?"

She looked at Garrick. "I want to have a baby."

His eyes widened and he immediately took two steps back, putting one of the chairs between them.

His reaction was so honest and male that she couldn't help laughing.

"Don't freak. I was making a statement, not asking for a donation."

His expression turned from panicked to wary. "It's an unexpected statement."

"Sorry." She held up one of the footie pajamas. "How can you resist something this sweet?"

"Buy all the baby clothes you want."

"It's not the clothes." She smiled at him. "Relax. This isn't about you. It's about me and the choices I made. How I cut myself off from a part of who I am because I felt I had to be punished."

"Because of what you did with Chas?"

She nodded. "I was wrong. If he was still around, I would tell him that. I made a mistake, but I learned from it. Things are different now—*I'm* different."

She folded the pajamas. "I like kids. I like being a mom. I always wanted more than just one child. Hunter's nearly grown. In a few years, he'll be heading off to college and then what? I've lived with regrets for too long. I don't want to do that anymore. I want kids."

She also wanted Garrick in her life, but thought going there now was probably a little too much information for him to take in. She had no idea how he felt about her. Oh, she knew he liked her and wanted to have sex with her, but what about beyond that? What about the next step?

That was where everything got fuzzy. They hadn't been together long enough to have that kind of conversation. Should they reach that point, she wanted him to know her plans for the future. She wanted more children, and if he didn't, well, she wasn't sure how that would work out.

"Like how many?" he asked, still looked shell-shocked.

"Two."

He relaxed. "That's manageable."

"I'm a realist." She walked around the chair, placed her hands on his chest and stared into his eyes. "I'm not asking you for anything, Garrick. Please believe me. I wasn't hinting." She might have been wishing, but he didn't have to know that. "I like what we have."

She felt him relax.

"I like it, too."

"Good." She raised herself on tiptoe and kissed him. "Now let's wrap some presents."

Thursday after work Garrick drove up the mountain to watch football with his friends. As he navigated the route, he tried to settle his mind, but there was too much going on. Holly's wedding was Saturday, Chandler was due back right after that, then Joylyn would be heading back to Phoenix to await the birth of her baby.

Garrick still wasn't sure what he was going to do. He had some time off around the holidays. He supposed he would get a hotel room in Phoenix and spend Christmas there so he could be with Joylyn. It was the plan that made the most sense—only he didn't want to be that far away from Wynn and Hunter.

Adding to the confusion was the fact that he couldn't forget what she'd told him last night when they'd been wrapping presents.

She wanted to have more kids.

The statement had thrown him. He believed her when she said she wasn't hinting at anything. Wynn was straightforward and open. She didn't play games. Still, the statement had been unexpected, and he'd been unable to let it go.

Did she want kids with him? He believed she hadn't been hinting, but still, they were a thing and he liked what they had together. And if so, how did he feel about that?

While he wasn't opposed to marriage, he'd always assumed he wouldn't do it again. His relationship with Sandy had been a disaster, for the two of them and for him and Joylyn. He didn't want to take any more risks like that. But kids were different. He liked kids. But how to have one without the other?

He parked in front of Jasper's house and walked to the front door. Seconds after he knocked he heard Koda barking. Jasper let him in.

Garrick handed him the six-pack of beer he'd brought, then dropped to a knee to greet the old dog who circled him, tail wagging.

"Hey, you," he said, rubbing Koda's ears. "How you doing, big guy?"

Koda woofed his answer, before swiping Garrick's face with a quick lick. Garrick stood and greeted his friend.

"You don't have to rub my ears," Jasper said dryly, leading the way to the family room where a large Christmas tree, decorated in red and silver ornaments, dominated the space.

"Good, because I was going to say you don't have to lick my face."

Cade sat on the sofa. He looked at them both. "Do I want to know what you're talking about?"

Garrick laughed. "Nope."

Cade grinned. "Now I'm worried."

Garrick took one of the beers and opened it, then settled on the far end of the huge sectional. The game was on, but the sound was muted.

"Where's Renee?" he asked.

"Prepping for the wedding tomorrow," Jasper said, stirring the contents of the Crock-Pot. "I guess it's a big one. Then Saturday is Holly's wedding, which should be easier."

"She still taking off the rest of the year?" Garrick asked as Jasper joined them on the sofa.

"She is." Jasper reached down and patted Koda.

"So where are you two going?" Cade asked. "You said somewhere tropical. Hawaii's nice. So's the Caribbean."

"We're staying here." Jasper raised a shoulder. "Renee just wants us to hang out here and do nothing. To be honest, I don't care what we do, as long as we have a couple of weeks together."

A sentiment Garrick understood. He would like that with Wynn. Just the two of them somewhere quiet. The location wasn't important. It was more about the time and the company. Not that he minded having Hunter around. He was a great kid. But a little one-on-one with Wynn would be great. Just them and zero complications.

Only she wanted more children. Did it change anything? While they were involved, neither of them had ever mentioned having a future. Still, he wasn't the kind of guy who went from woman to woman. He liked being with Wynn. As for his worries about getting married again, he knew she wasn't like his ex at all. So what did that mean?

"Earth to Garrick," Cade said, waving his beer. "You still with us?"

Garrick nodded. "Just got a couple of things on my mind."

Jasper looked at him. "Want to talk about it?"

Cade raised his eyebrows. "When did you turn into someone with a soft, gooey center?"

"I'm a writer, my friend. I'm allowed to be intuitive and sensitive."

"You say that like it's a good thing," Cade muttered.

"You act tough, but the truth is you're just as much of

a wuss as the rest of us," Garrick said. "We can't help it. We've evolved."

"And the world is better for it," Jasper said, his gaze still on Garrick. "Is that you avoiding what's on your mind or do you really not want to talk about it?"

"Aren't those the same things?" Garrick asked, his tone light as he considered the question. He drew in a breath. "Wynn wants more kids."

Jasper surprised him by smiling. "Good for her. I'm glad she got there."

Got there? Why would Jasper put it that way? But as soon as he asked the question, he realized he knew the answer. Wynn and Jasper had dated for a couple of years. They'd broken up about the time Garrick had moved back to Happily Inc, so he'd never seen them together, but they'd been a thing.

He found himself wanting to stand up and challenge his friend. The need was accompanied by a jolt of jealousy and he ignored both. Whatever had happened was long done. Jasper was married to Renee, and Wynn was obviously not longing for the other man. But the surge of emotion was unexpected.

"Kids are great," Cade said. "But your daughter is grown. Are you done with that part of your life?" He held up a hand. "Or are we assuming too much about your relationship with Wynn?"

Jasper nodded, but didn't speak, leaving Garrick to figure out what he wanted to say.

"I don't know," he admitted. "About kids. I never thought about it. Joylyn's all grown up."

But he'd enjoyed all the stages of her life, and he'd been devastated when she'd refused to see him for all those years. A do-over would be great. Only there was no way to go back in time and get back those years. Which only left him with the future.

Not that he would have a kid to make up for what had happened with Joylyn. The reason had to be about himself and what he wanted, along with what he could give to a child. But was he looking for that?

"Wynn's a great mom," he said, more to himself than them. He could see her with a couple more kids. Maybe girls. He knew most guys would want a son, but he was happy with the idea of girls. He'd enjoyed watching Joylyn move through the various stages of growing up. From the little girl who hung on to her stuffed pig to the fearless ten-year-old who'd raced around on her bike.

Did he want to do that again? Did he want to start over with Wynn? Did he want to be a part of her life and have her be a part of his? He knew he didn't want to let her go. He liked what they had together. Liked her. But that was a long way from "Hey, we should talk about having kids together."

"Let's change the subject," Jasper said easily. "Cade, what are you getting Bethany for Christmas?"

"A custom saddle," Cade said with a grin. "She's going to love it. There's this old guy who lives in El Bahar. He's done work for the royal family for years, and Bethany always admires his work when we are back there. I talked to him the last time we visited and arranged for the saddle. At first he didn't want to make a saddle for a woman, but when I told him who I was giving it to, he changed his mind." His expression turned smug. "She's known as an excellent horsewoman."

"The leather guy didn't know who you were when you talked to him?" Garrick asked.

"He gets customers coming to him from all over the world, so to him, I was just another American."

"I'm still wondering about a man who won't make a saddle for a woman," Jasper said. "Don't tell Bethany. She wouldn't be happy."

"Not just Bethany," Garrick pointed out. "I'm not thrilled, either."

"Social evolution takes time. They'll get there." He took a drink of his beer. "I'm giving Renee a girls' weekend with all her friends at a spa."

Cade groaned. "Man, no. You'll make the rest of us look bad."

Jasper grinned, then reached out to pet the orange tabby cat that jumped on the back of the sofa and walked toward him.

"That's just a bonus," he joked.

"A girlfriend weekend is a really good gift," Garrick admitted.

"What did you get Wynn?" Cade asked. "Or are you not at the gift-giving stage?"

"We are. At least I hope we are." He hesitated. "She's not easy to buy for. She isn't into fancy things, and she has her life together."

He'd thought for a long time, trying to find something she would enjoy that wasn't dumb or predictable.

"I got her a cleaning service. They'll come every two weeks and clean the house."

Jasper chuckled. "That's perfect. It takes away a chore she doesn't like, and she'll think of you every time they show up."

Garrick exhaled. "Good. I wasn't sure. I got Hunter a drone. I figured he would fly it up here and take pictures and stuff. Joylyn was easy. Alisha and I are going in on a meal service for her and Chandler when they get settled, and I'm giving them a week at a chalet in Tahoe."

"So you have it all figured out," Cade told him.

Garrick nodded, wishing that was true. Having it figured out would mean knowing what to do next. He liked Wynn—he liked them. But liking her a lot was different than wanting forever. Did he? And what about kids? He was still in his thirties, so age wasn't an issue. But it was a big step, and he had a lot to consider before he could make up his mind. And once he knew what he wanted, there was also the issue of finding out where she was. It would be a hell of a thing to decide he was in love with her only to have her tell him she wasn't that into him.

This was why he'd avoided relationships, he thought, turning his attention to the game. Because there were always complications. In the past he'd assumed being alone was just plain easier. Only now that he and Wynn were involved, he wasn't sure he could say that anymore.

chapter nineteen

Joylyn was determined to get through Holly's wedding without bursting into tears. Her hormones had settled down a little, so she thought she might have a chance, but it was going to be difficult, especially when the day was going to be so beautiful.

She had a quick moment to text with Chandler before he headed for the airport to start his long trip home. With luck they would be back together late that night—otherwise in the morning. Either way, she had less than twenty-four hours to go, and that was its own miracle.

Holly and Rex had arrived the night before, getting two rooms at the Sweet Dreams Inn. The ceremony would be at four with cocktails from five to six and the dinner after that.

Joylyn had picked up her friend at the inn and driven her over to Weddings Out of the Box. Even though it was only eleven in the morning, Renee was already there, with her team hard at work.

"You're here!" Renee said, hugging them both before smiling at Holly. "How do you feel?"

"Excited. Happy." Holly blinked back tears. "Grateful. I still can't believe everyone did this for me."

"We are very special people, so let's accept that and move on. I want to show you everything we have. Your wedding is going to be even more beautiful than you imagined."

Joylyn squeezed her friend's hand. "Aren't you excited? I can't wait to see how it all turned out."

"I'm still having trouble believing this is real," Holly admitted. "But I'm also thrilled to be here."

"Good."

Renee led them into what Joylyn remembered as the main open area. Only now it had been partitioned in several smaller rooms. A pretty foyer had been decorated with Christmas trees and lanterns filled with large, white candles.

"Guests will be directed through there," Renee said, pointing to an open doorway.

Joylyn and Holly walked through and found themselves in a big room. There was a center aisle with wooden chairs on either side. Sprays of white roses and red dahlias, accented with seasonal greens, were attached to the chairs on the aisle. Long red and green ribbons trailed to the floor. At the far end of the center aisle stood a stone fireplace. It was huge—maybe ten feet square, with logs piled in the opening. Twinkle lights lined the mantel, while two Christmas trees stood on either side.

Joylyn stared at the fireplace. "I don't remember seeing that before."

"It's portable," Renee said.

Holly stared at her. "How is that possible? A portable fireplace?"

"I know. A gentleman in town called last week. He heard

about your wedding and offered it to us. The whole thing is on wheels and runs on propane. There's a venting system out the back." She grinned. "We've tested it twice and it works great. It gets a little toasty so we'll wait until the last minute to turn it on, but it's going to be so beautiful."

Joylyn hugged her friends. "The pictures will be amazing."

"I can't believe all this is happening."

From there they walked over to where the reception would be held. The tables were set with white tablecloths with a Christmas plaid runner down the center. Dahlias and roses and greens covered the plaid runner. Votive holders of different heights were nestled in with the flowers. A gold charger anchored every place setting.

"And the cake will go over here," she said, pointing to a smaller, square table at the far end of the room.

They saw the bowls of red ornaments decorated with Holly's and Rex's names, along with the date. In the kitchen, they peeked in the large refrigerator and looked at the simple white four-layer cake.

"The caterer will get it in position in about an hour," Renee told them. "She'll add a cascade of red roses down one side and then let it come to room temperature. By the time you and Rex are ready to cut it, the cake will be ready."

"You've thought of everything," Holly told her, brushing away tears. "I can't thank you enough."

"Oh, we thought of a little more," Renee said, grinning at Joylyn.

Holly looked between them. "What is she talking about?"

"I have no idea."

Renee led them to the Bride's Room where two massage tables were set up and two masseuses were waiting for them.

"Welcome to your own spa day," Renee said. "First a massage, then mani-pedis, then you get your hair and makeup done. There will be a light lunch at one, so don't worry about that."

Renee smiled at Joylyn. "I had your dad check with your doctor, and you're good to go with a massage. Moira, your masseuse, is very experienced with pregnant women."

Joylyn was thrilled by the surprise, delighted for her friend and not sure she could even get on the table. "I'm pretty pregnant," she said. "With my belly…"

Moira moved the sheet aside to show a cut-out in the table. "We like to think of everything," she said with a smile.

Holly started to cry in earnest, and Joylyn couldn't help joining in. People who didn't know her or her friend had gone to so much trouble to make everything perfect.

"You're being so nice to us," she said, reaching for Renee. "I don't know why, but thank you."

Renee hugged her. "We want you to be happy. Both of you. Now go enjoy your spa afternoon. By the time everything is done, it will be time for the wedding."

Joylyn couldn't remember ever being pampered so much. The massage was perfect. The table took all the weight of the baby without mushing her, and she loved being able to stretch out on her front after so many months of having to wrestle with her stomach in the way.

After their mani-pedis, they got their hair and makeup done, then Wynn showed up to help get Holly into her dress.

"I did a quick walk-around," Wynn said, steaming the hem of Holly's dress. "Everything looks stunning. The cake came out so amazing. I love the simple design, and the white on white with the frosting makes the roses stand out."

"I couldn't be happier," Holly told her, looking beautiful with her makeup done and her hair in curls, piled on her head.

Wynn and Joylyn helped her into her dress, then Wynn began the laborious process of fastening all the little buttons.

"Just remember, you need to give yourself an extra five minutes every time you need to pee," Wynn teased. "Someone has to undo the buttons, then redo them. Unless you want a couple of us to come in with you and hold the dress."

Holly winced. "I'm not really comfortable having my friends do that for me."

Joylyn rubbed her belly. "I wouldn't have wanted to do that, either," she said. "But I think after going through childbirth where everyone is standing around looking at my girl parts, I'll be a lot less modest."

She moved to a chair and sat down. Her back was aching. She'd noticed it that morning. The massage had helped but now the dull but steady pain was back. No wonder, she thought. There was too much baby and not enough her.

The photographer came in and took pictures of Holly, and then a few of Holly and Joylyn together.

At almost four, Renee appeared, a tablet in her hand. She paused to smile at them both.

"So beautiful," she said with a happy sigh. "All your guests are here, the caterer is busy with the food, Silver is getting ready for the postceremony drink rush and I have triple-checked everything. There are six handsome men waiting by the minister." She smiled. "I assume you only want to marry Rex, but the other five are tempting, too. Ready to get married, Holly?"

"I am."

Joylyn took her bouquet of flowers and started for the

door. The pain in her back seemed to circle around to the front and squeeze.

Not now, she told her baby. She was a week from her due date and knew that false labor could happen at any time. *Give me about three hours and then you can fake labor all you want.*

Amazingly the pain went away.

"I have superpowers," Joylyn murmured to herself as she walked toward the foyer.

Ninety minutes later, she stood with the five co–best men, talking about how beautiful the ceremony had been. The bride and groom made a wonderful couple, and by the time they exchanged rings nearly everyone had been fighting tears.

"I can't believe how fast this wedding got pulled together," Will said.

"It took a village," Joylyn told her.

Servers circulated with trays of champagne and appetizers. The guys helped themselves. Peter got her a glass of juice, while the two Bens and John offered her food. Joylyn smiled at them and tried to participate in the conversation, but couldn't seem to follow along. She'd been hungry before, but since the earlier cramping, she'd kind of lost her appetite. Plus the pain was back, but with a little more intensity. She was just about to go look for a place to sit when she felt her insides twist with so much intensity that she nearly doubled over from the pain.

The shock of it was followed by bone-numbing fear. Nothing was supposed to hurt that much. What if something had happened to the baby?

She no more than thought the question when the pain returned, sharper this time—a rip cord circling her belly, wrapping tighter and tighter. Panic joined fear. This was bad. Really bad.

She looked around at the party going on and had no idea what to do. She didn't want to create a scene but knew she couldn't stay standing much longer. She was breathing in pants and she'd broken out in a cold sweat. She had to—

Her mouth literally dropped open as the truth dawned. Nothing bad had happened. She was in labor!

Her dad walked up and put his arm around her, while smiling at the guys. "This is about the prettiest wedding I've ever been to. You did good, kid. Holly's going to remember this day for the rest of her life."

Joylyn stared at him. "That's true, Dad, and for more reasons than you think."

He frowned. "What are you talking about, sweetie?" He studied her more closely. "Are you all right?"

Before she could answer, she felt a rushing wetness between her legs. It was as if she'd peed herself, only she hadn't had to go to the bathroom. She stared down at the dampness on her pink dress, then at her father.

"I'm in labor."

His eyes nearly bugged out of his head. "What?" he demanded in a loud voice. "Now? Are you sure?"

His freak-out had a calming effect on her. She motioned to the front of her dress and managed a smile. "Pretty sure, Dad."

"Okay." He put his still-full glass of champagne on a table. "We can do this. It's early, but not too early. You'll be fine."

"I know."

"Your mom's in Phoenix. We'll call her on the way to the hospital. Chandler's on a plane, so that's more complicated." He took her hands in his. "Joylyn, I'm going to be here for you. I want you to believe me. We've taken the classes together, and we both know what to do. I won't leave your side, little girl. I'll be right here, taking care of you."

She smiled. "I know, Dad. I trust you to take care of me. Now let's go home so I can change and get my bag, then we'll drive to the hospital."

Garrick held his newborn grandson in his arms. Despite the swaddling and the cap, he was so small. Technically, he was perfectly healthy and a good weight at seven pounds, nine ounces, but all wrapped up like that, he was impossibly little.

"You're going to be growing," Garrick told him in a low voice. "One day we'll all look back at the pictures of you, and we won't believe how much you've changed."

He glanced across the room where Chandler lay stretched out beside Joylyn in the hospital bed, their arms wrapped around each other. He knew he should get going and give the new family some time together, but he wanted just a few more minutes with his grandson.

"Your mom did an incredible job," he continued. "She was so strong. I was the one who was scared."

Giving birth was not for the faint of heart, he thought, remembering how Joylyn had clutched his hands, breathing and pushing, delivering her first child with more bravery than he'd ever seen before. As promised, he'd been with her every step of the way. During the various exams, he'd offered to step out of the room, but she'd asked him to stay by her side and he had.

It didn't make up for what they'd lost—nothing could do that—but it had given them new memories.

Chandler carefully slid off the bed and joined him.

"She's asleep," he said in a low voice. "She's got to be

exhausted." He looked at Garrick. "I want to thank you for taking such good care of her."

"I'm her dad. Taking care of her is all I ever wanted to do." He smiled. "Now it's your job, and I expect you to do a good one. Just remember that I loved her first."

"I will."

Garrick kissed the baby's forehead, then passed him to Chandler. "Years from now it will be your turn to tell someone you loved this little guy first."

Chandler held the baby gingerly. Garrick wanted to offer advice, but told himself the kid would figure it out as he went. Babies were a lot tougher than they looked.

Easy for him to say, he added silently. He got to be the grandfather, with only part-time responsibility. He had a feeling Chandler was going to be doing some soul-searching as he assessed his ability to be a father. Holding your child in your arms was a hell of a wake-up call.

He crossed to the hospital bed and smiled down at his sleeping daughter.

"I'm proud of you, baby girl," he whispered before returning to Chandler. "I'm going to head home for a little while. You have my number if you need anything. And when these two can check out, just let me know and I'll come get all of you."

His chest tightened as he thought about what would happen after that. Now that little Elijah had been born, staying a few extra days would be out of the question.

"You'll want to head back to Phoenix as soon as you can. You know, for the holidays."

"Joylyn and I were just talking about that. We were wondering if we could stay with you through Christmas. Her mom has the boys running around, and a newborn might be a bit much when those three are so excited about their presents." Chandler raised a shoulder. "Plus she's been talking about how much she's been enjoying her time with you. We'd like to stay—if that's all right with you."

Stay with him? For Christmas? Garrick had to clear his throat before he could speak.

"I'd like that very much."

Chandler grinned. "Us, too."

Garrick patted him on the back, touched his grandson's cheek and walked out into the hallway. He'd barely gotten to the lobby when Alisha raced toward him.

"I just got here," she said, pressing a hand to her chest. "Are they all right? Chandler called to say they were fine, but are they? I can't believe I missed it. Our little girl, Garrick. She has her own baby."

Garrick hugged her. "She's doing just fine, and the baby is healthy and handsome."

"Have they named him yet? We can't keep calling him 'the baby.'"

"Elijah."

"Oh, I like that," she said.

"Me, too." He gave her the room number. "She's sleeping, but I know she'll want to see you."

Alisha started for the elevator, then turned back to face him. "Did you stay with her while she was in labor?"

"I was with her until the baby came." He thought about hanging on to his daughter's hands and telling her she could do it. "I'd taken the classes with her, so I had a fair understanding of what was going on." He chuckled. "The trick is not to look."

Alisha laughed. "No, Garrick. The trick is passing something the size of a bowling ball."

She stepped onto the elevator and waved.

He went outside and was surprised to see the sun was

up. A quick glance at his watch told him it was just after nine. They'd left the wedding around five thirty last night, so they'd been in the hospital just over fifteen hours. He had a strange sense of being out of space and time.

The drive home was quick. As soon as he pulled into his driveway, Wynn burst out of her house and raced toward him.

"How is she? How are you? The pictures were beautiful. I can't believe he's here. How was it? Were you scared? Oh, Garrick, what a wonderful experience to share with your daughter."

She threw herself against him. He caught her and held her tight, needing to know she was close to him.

"I missed you," he said, surprising himself with the words. "I missed you a lot."

She wrapped her arms around him. "I was thinking about you all night. How did you do?"

"I hung in there. Joylyn did the work."

They walked into the house. Wynn started coffee while he leaned against the counter and tried to process his emotions.

"I thought she would be a wreck," he said. "She's been so upset all the time, but she wasn't. She was calm and just seemed to know what to do. It was incredible. I was right there when he was born."

He thought about the stillness in the moments after the baby had entered the world and the collective sigh of relief when he'd started to cry.

"He's healthy?" Wynn asked, turning to face him.

"Ten fingers and toes, along with everything else. He's already started breastfeeding. Chandler got there about twenty minutes after he was born. Joylyn was so happy to see him."

"Her family is complete," Wynn said with a smile. "What an amazing couple of days."

"How was the rest of the wedding?"

"Lovely. The dinner was fantastic. Holly and Rex had the best time, and everyone appreciated the updates. The crowd cleared out about midnight. I got a little sleep, but I was mostly waiting to hear that he'd been born."

"Thanks for that."

"I didn't do it for you. I care about Joylyn. She's going to be a great mother."

He knew Wynn meant what she said—that Joylyn was important to her. Because she was someone who cared about other people.

The coffee finished brewing. Wynn poured them each a cup, then urged him to sit at the table.

"Are you hungry? Or do you want to just get some sleep? I know you were up all night."

"I'm not hungry," he said, although he thought he would be later. Right now he wanted to understand everything that had happened. There was a feeling inside him—one he couldn't name—but it was big and getting bigger.

"She wants to stay here for Christmas," he told Wynn. "Chandler told me. The three of them are going to be with me through Christmas Day."

Wynn reached across the table and squeezed his hand. "I know you'll like that."

"I will. Can we do something together? Have a big dinner or something? Or am I asking too much?" He frowned. "Do you already have plans?"

She smiled. "I'd like us to spend Christmas together. I was going to make a turkey anyway and share the meal with a few friends. It's Christmas—the more people at the table, the happier I am. Especially if you'll be there."

He stared at Wynn. She was so beautiful, he thought. But more than that. She was strong and kind and sexy and giving. She was a good mom. A great one. He thought about what she'd said about wanting more kids. He thought about how Joylyn had stared at him, telling him she needed him to be there while she had her son. He thought about the responsibility and joy and how being his daughter's father was the best gig ever.

"We should have kids together," he said abruptly.

Wynn stared at him, her eyes wide. "What did you say?"

"We should have kids together. You and me. I want to give that to you, Wynn. It's what you said you wanted, and I can make it happen. You're a great mom—look at what you've done with Hunter. I'm a decent father, but I can do better. You want more children. You told me, Wynn. I'd like that, too. With you." He reached for her hands and squeezed them. "Let's do it. Let's have a couple of kids together."

She pulled back. "I don't know what you're saying."

"I don't know exactly, either. But we can make it work." He motioned to his house. "We already live next door to each other—that's convenient. We can have a couple of babies and raise them together. Fifty-fifty. You know, co-parent or something. I know you want this, and now I want it, too."

Her expression was unreadable. He had no idea what she was thinking, but she didn't look happy.

"You want to have children with me," she said slowly. "So we would share parenting responsibility, but we won't be involved. We wouldn't be in love or get married or anything. Is that right?"

When she said it like that… "You're making it sound bad," he complained. "Don't be like that. You said you wanted more children. I'm suggesting a way to make that happen. We're a terrific team. We trust each other—that's a big thing. We both want a bigger family and now we can have that."

"Co-parenting?"

"Yes."

"Because we live next door?"

"Not just because of that. You're taking it wrong. I thought you'd be happy. That this solved all the problems. We're good together and…"

There were more reasons, but suddenly he couldn't think of any—not with her looking at him like he'd just kicked a kitten. Why was she making him the bad guy?

"No," she said, coming to her feet. "Just no. I could never do that with anyone. It's not what I want, and I can't believe you suggested it. How could you?"

With that, she turned and ran out of the kitchen, leaving him alone with a feeling that he'd just screwed up in more ways than he could understand.

chapter twenty

After Garrick left, Wynn stood in her living room, not sure what to do or how to feel. Hurt and disappointment tightened her chest until it was difficult to breathe.

She pressed a hand to her stomach and told herself she was fine. Yes, Garrick had said something ridiculous, but so what? It didn't mean anything. Only she knew it had meant something to her—something awful and sad.

The pain increased until it became too big to hold inside. She knew she was seconds away from breaking down into ugly, loud sobs that would terrify her son. Doing her best to keep it all inside, she grabbed her handbag and moved into the hallway.

"Hunter, I'm going to run a few errands," she said, grateful her voice wasn't shaking.

"Okay, Mom," he called back. "I'm going to finish my history paper, then watch that documentary on NASCAR."

"I won't be long," she said, before hurrying to her car.

She carefully backed out of the driveway, then headed for town. The pressure built inside until she knew she didn't have much more time. Should she go find some quiet place to park where she could cry in peace?

Three blocks later, she pulled over and reached for her phone. She scrolled through her list of contacts, pausing at each of her friends before pressing the call button.

"Hi," Silver said, sounding cheerful. "Do you have a baby update?"

Wynn felt herself starting to lose control. "Can I come see you?"

Silver's voice was instantly concerned. "Of course. I'm home."

"Give me five minutes."

Wynn managed to make her way to the upscale neighborhood by the golf course. She pulled into Silver and Drew's wide driveway, then stumbled out of her car. Silver met her at the door.

At the sight of her friend, she gave in to the sobs and let them overtake her. Silver pulled her close and held her tight.

"I'm here," her friend said. "Whatever it is, we'll get through this. I have some contacts. We can arrange for a big burly guy to beat the shit out of Garrick if necessary."

Wynn wiped her face. "How did you know this was about Garrick?"

"It's Sunday morning, so it's unlikely you heard bad medical news, and if it was Hunter, you would have said that up front. A town-based disaster, like your business burning down, would have meant calls from more than just you. That leaves a man."

Silver led her into the living room where they settled on one of the overstuffed sofas. Drew was nowhere to be seen—a fact for which Wynn was grateful. She liked Silver's husband just fine, but didn't really want him around when she was so vulnerable.

Silver disappeared for a few seconds, then returned with a box of tissues.

"Do you want something to drink? Coffee? Water? Tequila?"

"I'm okay," Wynn said, struggling to get control. "I don't like being this way. I'm not a crier."

"It's an involuntary physical response. We all do it."

"You're saying I'm ordinary?" Wynn asked with an attempt at fake humor.

"Practically mundane." Silver rubbed her back. "Tell me what happened."

Wynn blew her nose, then quickly recounted the conversation from a week or so ago, when she'd confessed that she wanted more children.

"I didn't mean to say it," she added when she was done. "I wasn't hinting at anything."

"You were hinting," Silver said gently. "Or at least testing the waters."

Wynn started to protest, then stopped herself. "Maybe," she admitted. "I do want more kids, though."

"Sure, but not on your own. You want them with Garrick."

"Is it that obvious?"

"No, but I know you."

Wynn sighed heavily. "I guess I was hoping he would be excited, too. That he would start thinking about us being together and what that would be like. I was hoping he would see that we're really good as a couple and that we could have so much more. A blended family, more children."

"Love?"

Wynn twisted the tissue and nodded. "Love," she whispered. She turned to Silver.

"But that's not where he went at all. When he got home

from the hospital, he started talking about us having a couple of kids and co-parenting together. That I wanted more kids and he could make it happen. How it was superconvenient because we lived next door." The tears returned. "He's not in love with me. He doesn't want to have a family together—he wants me to be some kind of baby mama with a co-parenting agreement and maybe some sex on the side."

"Baby mama?" Silver asked, her voice teasing.

"You know what I mean."

"I do, and I'm sorry."

Wynn looked at her. "I'm in love with him, and he's not in love with me."

"You don't know that."

Wynn thought about what had happened…and what hadn't. "I do know that. He's not in love with me. I've already learned this lesson. You can't force a man to care about you, and you can't trap him into loving you. After everything I've been through, I'm back where I was fifteen years ago. Loving someone who doesn't love me back."

Three days after the fact, Garrick realized that maybe giving Wynn time had been a bad decision. He hadn't seen her at all, and the only response to his text suggesting they talk had been a quick *This isn't a good time for me.*

He knew he'd screwed up big time, but he didn't know exactly what he'd done. Was it wrong to want to have kids with her? Shouldn't she see that he was trying to give her exactly what she wanted? He thought she was amazing and wanted to raise children with her. How was that bad?

He decided enough was enough and went next door to talk to her. Whatever was going on needed to be fixed. He missed her and wanted them to go back to where they had been.

But when he knocked, Hunter answered the door. A Hunter who seemed older and bigger and didn't look happy to see Garrick.

"Is your Mom around?" Garrick asked, offering an easy smile.

"She doesn't want to see you," Hunter said flatly. "So you can't come in."

The slightly threatening tone was nearly as surprising as the message itself. Wynn didn't want to see him?

"She's still upset?" he asked.

Hunter rolled his eyes. "Yes, she's still upset. I don't know what you did, but it's bad. My mom cried. She never cries. Even when I totally screw up, she doesn't cry. When she found out about what I did with faking her signature on the JROTC application, she didn't cry. So whatever you did, you'd better fix it and fast."

With that, he closed the door in Garrick's face.

Garrick stood on the porch for at least a minute, trying to figure out what had just happened. He'd known Wynn was upset, but he hadn't realized how serious the situation was. Hunter was right—he had to fix it and fast. But first he had to figure out what he'd done wrong.

Women, he thought grimly, as he made his way back to his house. What had God been thinking?

He sat on the top step of his front porch and replayed his last conversation with Wynn. He'd said only nice things about her, he'd offered to have children with her—children that she wanted. So why wasn't she speaking to him? No, why was she crying?

The front door opened and Joylyn came out. "Hey, Dad. Elijah's finally sleeping, so it's safe to come inside."

He glanced at her. "That's okay. I'm going to sit here and think."

Joylyn sat next to him, wincing slightly as her butt hit the wooden porch. "Fresh air. This is nice. I'm not sure I've been outside since we left the hospital. Maybe tonight we'll sit out back by the pool."

"Sure. Good idea. We can barbecue something for dinner, if you'd like."

"Water buffalo?"

He stared at her. "What?"

She smiled. "Just making sure you're listening." The smile faded. "Dad, what's going on? You've been acting weird for a couple of days now, and I haven't seen Wynn even once. Did you two have a fight?"

Interesting question, he thought. "I don't know."

She rolled her eyes. "That is such a guy answer. What did you do?"

"Maybe I didn't do anything. Maybe I was just being a great guy and she completely overreacted."

Joylyn stared at him without speaking.

"Fine," he said between gritted teeth. "A week or so ago Wynn mentioned that she regretted not having more children. There were reasons, but now with Hunter growing up, she wishes she had a bigger family."

"And?"

"And after you had Elijah, I came home and told Wynn I wanted to have children with her. I said she was a great mom and I would like the chance to be a father again and we should have a family."

Joylyn drew her brows together. "So you proposed?"

"What? No. I said we could co-parent. We live next door, and it would be easy for us to…" His voice trailed off as he realized how ridiculous he sounded.

His daughter stared at him. "You offered to co-parent with her?"

"It's what she wanted."

Joylyn waved to the house next door. "Based on the fact that you're sitting here and she's in her house, it wasn't what she wanted. Really, Dad? Co-parenting? Not, 'I love you more than life itself, let's get married?'"

He'd been able to ignore the proposal comment, but this one required a response. "Why would you say that?"

"Because you're hanging out together all the time and you're sleeping together and—"

"How do you know we're sleeping together? We've been discreet."

"Oh, please. You whistle after you two have had sex. If you were anyone but my father, it would be cute, but it's not." She angled toward him. "Dad, do you really not get what you did? You're in a committed relationship with a great woman, and instead of telling her you love her and proposing, you suggest some ridiculous co-parenting arrangement. She wouldn't want that. She doesn't need you to have more kids. She's more than capable of doing that on her own. She has a steady income and lots of friends for support. What she doesn't have is a partner to love her and have her back. That's what she wanted."

Before he could absorb what she'd said, let alone figure out a response, he heard Elijah crying.

"I need to go check on him," Joylyn said, standing. "Dad, you have fix this. Either tell her you were a fool and of course you love her and want to marry her, or end things. You don't get to have middle ground on this one."

With that, she turned and walked back into the house.

Garrick stared after her, then faced front and waited for his world to stop spinning.

Love Wynn? This wasn't about love, it was about having kids together because that was what Wynn—

He blinked, then swore under his breath. No. No! He'd completely and totally blown it. Joylyn was right—Wynn didn't need him to co-parent. She could easily have more kids on her own. She wanted to be a part of something. She was amazing and incredible and a woman like her would demand it all.

He'd been so sure he was giving her exactly what she wanted, and instead he'd been an idiot and possibly hurt her in the process.

Joylyn was right—he had to do right by Wynn, and that meant committing to her in a meaningful way or walking away. There wasn't going to be any middle ground.

Jasper's office was separate from the house up on the mountain. It was a big, open space with lots of windows and room to pace. There was also a sofa against one wall.

Wynn sat there, her feet tucked under her, an untouched mug of coffee on the table in front of her. Jasper was in his desk chair, waiting patiently for her to explain why she'd shown up with no warning and asked him if they could talk.

He was a good-looking man, she thought absently, taking in the dark hair and green eyes. He'd been a magnificent lover. She'd spent hours in his bed and had enjoyed herself, yet there wasn't a single part of her that regretted the fact that they'd ended things.

"We were never right for each other," she said.

One eyebrow rose. "We were right in the moment," he corrected, "but it was never going to be anything more than that."

"I wasn't willing to trust you."

He smiled. "You weren't willing to trust yourself."

"Yikes, that's too insightful. It makes me uncomfortable."

Instead of replying, he waited. This was her party, she reminded herself.

"When I was nineteen, I fell in love with a guy named Chas," she began. "He was a professional surfer, and he made it clear ours was just an off-season fling. When it was time to go back on tour, he would be gone and there was nothing I could say or do to change his mind."

He watched her without speaking.

She sighed. "I got pregnant on purpose to trap him into a relationship. He took off anyway, leaving me alone and pregnant." She held up a hand. "I don't blame him. It was all on me. But it was hard, and there were times I wasn't sure I was going to make it."

Emotions flickered through Jasper's eyes. Emotions that she couldn't read, or maybe she didn't want to.

"Has Hunter ever met him?"

She shook her head. "Chas died. I didn't know until his lawyer showed up to tell me about a life insurance policy. I was the beneficiary." She waved her hand. "It's how I bought the business and you know the rest."

His expression sharpened. "So that's the guilty secret? You wouldn't let me in because you were punishing yourself? You couldn't have a real relationship because you'd tried to trap Chas? Self-punishment when there was no actual punishment to help you atone?"

She groaned. "I really hate that you're a writer."

"It can be inconvenient for other people. While I appreciate you telling me what happened, it doesn't explain why you're here now. Oh, wait." He nodded. "This is about Garrick."

She covered her face with her hands. "I hate my life."

"No, you don't."

She wished Renee would return from wherever she'd

gone and interrupt them. She wished she'd been able to figure this out on her own so she wouldn't have to talk about it with Jasper of all people. Yet her gut told her he would have answers she couldn't find anywhere else.

"He knows about Chas," she said. "He seems okay with the information."

"Most people will be." His voice was gentle. "Wynn, you were a kid. You made a dumb mistake and you regret doing it. You've learned from it, which is even more important. You need to forgive yourself and move on."

"I have. I've been working on it for a while, and I've put it behind me. But while working through all that, I realized that in punishing myself, I've kept myself away from something I really want." She looked at him. "A family. I want more kids."

He smiled. "You're a great mom."

"Thanks. The information has been slow in coming, but seeing all my friends have babies and getting to know Joylyn has made me wish I could have a couple more babies. Which I mentioned to Garrick, too."

"What did he say?"

"Not much. I assured him I was sharing information, not hinting."

"So you lied."

"What? No! Why would you say that?"

His gaze was steady.

She flushed. "Fine. Maybe I was trying to find out how he felt about me and us and a future."

He held up a hand. "I get it. No one likes to put themselves out there. It's scary to expose your heart without knowing if it's going to be trampled on. Which apparently is what he did. What happened?"

She leaned back against the sofa. "He offered to have

children with me. Not as a couple, but as co-parents. He mentioned how convenient it would be because we lived next door to each other."

"Ouch."

"Yeah."

"Did you tell him you're in love with him?"

"No. I can't tell him that. I won't try to trap another man. I've learned my lesson on that one."

"Wynn, loving someone isn't a trap."

"That's not what Chas thought."

"There's a big difference between getting pregnant on purpose and telling someone you love them." He leaned toward her. "Love heals. Love makes us better than we ever thought we could be. Loving someone, the act of loving, is a generous gift. True love is our greatest calling. Not just romantic love, but all love."

She blinked at him. "Wow. Renee's a lucky woman."

"I'm the lucky one. Tell Garrick how you feel. It's not trapping him, Wynn. He deserves to know what's on the line. And you need to be able to share your feelings."

She nodded and rose. He stood and pulled her close, then hugged her. She hung on for a second, wondering what twist of fate made one person right and another person not the one.

"You give good advice," she said when she stepped back. "Thank you for that."

"Anytime."

Christmas Eve day was slow at the Happily Inc police station. Even those in town for holiday weddings seemed to be on their best behavior. Garrick had planned to use the time to catch up on his paperwork, but ever since he'd talked to his daughter about what had happened with Wynn he'd been unable to put their conversation out of his mind.

Joylyn had assumed he was in love with Wynn and he'd assumed he wasn't. Only one sleepless night and an unproductive morning later, he knew that his daughter had been right and he'd been a fool who might have lost the woman of his dreams.

Wynn was great. He'd thought that from the second he'd gone to ask for help and she'd jumped right in to make sure his house was warm and welcoming for his daughter. He admired her enough to offer to have kids with her—a reality that made him cringe every time he thought about it. Because if he really was in love with Wynn, then he'd pretty much done everything possible to mess up what could have been an incredible moment.

Co-parent? Had he really suggested that? What kind of moron offered to have children with a woman before talking about how he felt? He wasn't interested in a business arrangement. He wanted a forever thing. Love, marriage, a family. But instead he'd hurt her, and now he had absolutely no idea how she was feeling or if he'd screwed up everything between them forever.

Shortly after eleven, he couldn't stand it anymore. He told his assistant he was going to be gone for about an hour and drove the short distance to Wynn's store, taking a chance that like most of the businesses in town, she would be open until at least one in the afternoon.

Sure enough, the lights were on and a couple of customers stood at the counter. Garrick walked in and looked around but didn't see Wynn. One of her employees glanced up and smiled.

"She's in her office, Garrick."

"Thanks."

He made his way down the hall and then stepped in through the open door.

Wynn was on her computer, staring intently at the screen.

She was so beautiful, he thought, coming to a stop. She had on a red sweater with little reindeer across the front. Her long curly hair was pulled back, and there was a slight frown line between her eyebrows.

Warmth swept through him. Not just the sexual kind, which was nice enough, but the loving kind. This woman was exactly who he'd been looking for. He could only hope he hadn't figured that out too late.

"You have a second?" he asked.

She jumped and turned to him. "Garrick, hi. I wasn't expecting you."

"I know. I just need a minute of your time." Maybe two minutes. He wasn't sure how long it was going to take him to tell her how sorry he was to have been so stupid and how much he loved her.

"It's okay." She stood and smoothed her hands down her jeans. "I wanted to talk to you, as well. I was waiting until this afternoon when I thought you'd be home."

That was good, right? Her wanting to talk to him? Unless she was planning on telling him he was too stupid for the likes of her and to get lost.

He swallowed. "Do you want to go first? I can, if that's better."

She smiled. "I'll go first." The smile faded. "Garrick, I'm sorry about how I acted before, when you mentioned co-parenting children together."

He winced. "Not my best move. I'm sorry about that."

"It's okay. I said I wanted more kids in my life, and you came up with a way to make that happen. I was just surprised because, well, I guess I was surprised and hurt, which I didn't want you to see."

"I didn't mean to hurt you."

"I know. It's on me, not on you." She squared her shoulders and looked at him. "I was hurt because I don't just want children with you, Garrick. I want a real relationship. I'm in love with you, and I want everything that goes with that."

She was in love with *him*?

He circled the desk and pulled her against him, then pressed his mouth to hers. Her arms came around him, and she kissed him back.

"I had more to say," she mumbled against his lips.

He drew back an inch. "Like what?"

"I had a whole speech about how I'm not trying to push you or make you uncomfortable, but that I wanted you to know how I felt."

He kissed her again, then leaned his forehead against hers. "I'm sorry I was an idiot. It was a dumbass thing to say. I love you, Wynn. Of course I want kids with you, but I also want to marry you and have us be a real family. All of us. You, me, Hunter, Joylyn, Chandler, the baby, our kids and maybe a few pets." He paused to stare into her eyes. "If any of that interests you."

She smiled at him. "We would need a much bigger house."

"I have some savings."

"Me, too. Plus if we sell both our houses and pool the money, we'd have enough."

He tightened his hold on her as the love washed through him. "That sounds a lot like a yes."

"It does, doesn't it?" She kissed him. "Garrick, I love you."

"So you'll marry me?"

"I will."

"Woo-hoo!"

He picked her up and spun her around, as best he could in the small office, before putting her down.

"Do you want to wait?" he asked. "We can. It's up to you, if you think a long engagement is a good idea. Or we could get married sooner."

She smiled. "Sooner works."

"Great." He released her. "So I need to go get you a ring and you need to tell Hunter not to be mad at me anymore and I want to let Joylyn know she's right."

He stopped. "Wait a sec. If it's okay with you, I'd like to talk to Hunter first. Explain what I did and then ask his permission to marry you."

Wynn blinked several times, as if holding back tears. "That would be great."

Garrick pulled her close again. "I'm going to spend the rest of my life having your back, Wynn. You have my word on that."

"I'll have yours, too," she whispered. "Always."

chapter twenty-one

Wynn woke up early Christmas morning. There was no reason not to sleep in, but at quarter to six, her eyes popped open and refused to close again. After a few minutes, she gave up trying to fake sleep and got up. She shrugged into her robe, then made her way to her kitchen where she started coffee. While that brewed, she pulled out the breakfast casserole she'd made the night before. She would let it warm up a bit before popping it into the oven.

The shelves of the refrigerator were overflowing. Her turkey was next door at Garrick's, but all the ingredients for the side dishes were in hers. The chocolate cream pies that were a holiday tradition at her house had the place of honor on the top shelf.

She poured herself a cup of coffee, then walked into the dining room. All the extensions were in the table, and the special holiday linens were waiting to be put in place. The house would be full today, she thought happily. Full of family and friends and soon-to-be family. Jasper and Renee would join them for dinner, along with Joylyn, Chandler and their baby. Hunter, of course, and Garrick.

Just thinking about him made her glance down at the sparkling diamond on her left hand. She and Garrick were engaged—a happy truth that still made her giddy. The knowledge that he loved her as much as she loved him warmed her. They were blessed, she thought.

This weekend, Wynn, Hunter and Garrick were going to spend more time looking at houses online. Monday she and Garrick had an appointment with a mortgage broker to discuss financing for the house they wanted to buy. Tuesday they were going out with a real estate agent to look at the houses that fit them best. Hunter already had a wish list that included a bonus room big enough to be converted into a media room, and a pool. She wanted a big kitchen with plenty of storage, and Garrick wanted a garage with a workshop area.

She went into the living room and turned on the tree lights before sitting on the sofa. Happiness bubbled through her. She'd come a long way from that scared single mom she'd been fourteen years ago. Finding where she belonged had taken a lot of work and some patience, but it had been worth it in the end.

"Hey, Mom," Hunter said, stretching as he walked into the living room.

"Merry Christmas," she said, standing and hugging him.

He hugged her back, all long, skinny arms and bony ribs. He was still growing and already taller than her. When had that happened?

"Merry Christmas," he said as he slumped down on the sofa. "You're up early."

"So are you."

He grinned. "I couldn't sleep." He pointed to the pile of presents under the tree. "Santa came."

"Yes, he did."

Her son stretched again. "You know, Mom, it's okay for Garrick to spend the night. I'm not a kid or anything."

"Thank you for that, but we're going to wait to live together. The wedding is only a few weeks away."

They were getting married at the end of January, hopefully right around the time they closed on their new house. They would get settled and then take a delayed honeymoon in February or March. Hunter would stay with Jasper and Renee while Wynn and Garrick were gone.

Until then, she and Garrick would steal their moments together. Once Joylyn and Chandler returned to San Diego, Garrick would have his house back and they could have a little privacy.

Not that she minded having the young family with them. She and Joylyn had become friends, and Chandler was good company. Elijah was an added bonus, giving Wynn a little baby practice. She and Garrick had agreed they would start trying to get pregnant over the summer. They wanted a few months to settle into married life before the excitement and yes, stress, of a baby.

"Garrick and I have been talking about what kind of car I'm going to get when I turn sixteen," Hunter said.

"Have you."

Her son grinned. "Uh-huh. We talked about buying an old junker and restoring it, but decided that wouldn't be the best choice. We'll get something safe for me and then get an old junker to restore for fun."

She sipped her coffee. "This all assumes I'm ready to think about you learning to drive. You're still only fourteen."

"And a half. I can get my learner's permit in a year."
Hunter gave her a winning smile. "You said I could work
for you this summer. I'm going to save all the money and
put it toward a car."

He was a kid with a plan, she thought, both pleased by
his maturity and horrified that he was that old. What he
didn't know was that she and Garrick had already talked
about enrolling him in a driver's education class over the
summer, so he could get the twenty-five-hour requirement
out of the way before he joined JROTC in the fall.

As for buying a car, Garrick had some ideas about a safe
vehicle for a sixteen-year-old. And when she'd started to
hyperventilate about her little boy being all grown up, he'd
reminded her that they still had plenty of time.

But she knew how quickly that time would pass. With
luck, a year from today, she would be several months pregnant. Even if she wasn't, she would still have Garrick, and
that was more than she'd ever hoped for.

There was a knock at the front door, then the sound of
a key in the lock. Garrick let himself in. He smiled when
he saw them on the sofa.

"Merry Christmas," he said as he walked toward them.
"Joylyn and Chandler have just put the baby down and are
hoping to grab a couple of hours of sleep before breakfast,
if that works for you."

"I said about eight thirty or nine," Wynn told him, coming to her feet as he pulled her close. "They must be exhausted."

"They are, but they're happy, too."

Mindful of Hunter in the room, Garrick kissed her
lightly, then greeted her son.

"Excited about your presents?" Garrick asked.

Hunter eyed the impressive pile. "I am." He yawned.

"Maybe I'll go back to bed for a couple of hours, too." He glanced at her. "If that's okay, Mom."

"Sure."

He got up and ambled toward the hall. When his bed-room door closed, Garrick pulled her close again and kissed her with a little more passion.

"How are you feeling?" he asked.

"Happy. What about you?"

He smiled at her. "The same. So much so, I woke up early and couldn't get back to sleep."

"Me, too."

"Let me get a cup of coffee, and we can go look at more real estate listings together."

His offer might not sound romantic to some women, but for her, it was magical. Garrick took care of the details and worried about the people he loved. He'd promised to always have her back, and she knew that he would.

"Real estate listings sound like fun," she said.

He put his arm around her and together they walked into the kitchen. Behind them the Christmas tree lights glowed, and in front of them was a happy future full of promise and love.

* * * * *

#1 New York Times *bestselling author*
Susan Mallery delivers a warm and witty new novel
about two sisters, their parents' vow renewal and
wedding, and a Christmas they'll never forget.

Enjoy this preview of
The Christmas Wedding Guest

one

"It's a vacuum," Reggie Somerville said, trying to sound less doubtful than she felt. "You reinvented the vacuum?"

Gizmo stared at her, his hurt obvious, even behind his thick glasses. "It's a *smart* vacuum."

"Don't we already have those round ones that zip across a room?"

"They're not smart. They're average. Mine is smart."

Reggie was less sure about the vacuum's intelligence than her client's. Gizmo had a brain that existed on a different plane than those of average humans. His ideas were extraordinary. His execution, however, wasn't always successful. A basic knowledge of coding shouldn't be required to work any household appliance—a fact she'd tried to explain to him about fifty-seven thousand times.

She eyed the triangular-shaped head of the vacuum. The bright purple casing was appealing and she liked that it could roam on its own or be a regular stick vacuum if that was what she wanted. The printed instructions—about eighteen pages long—were a little daunting, but she would get through them.

If the trial went well, she and Gizmo would discuss the

next steps, including her design suggestions. Once those were incorporated, they would start beta testing his latest invention. In the meantime, she would be doing a lot of vacuuming.

"I'll get you my report in a couple of weeks," she said.

Gizmo, a slight, pale twenty-year-old who lived with his extended family just north of Seattle, offered her a small smile. "You can have until the first of the year. I'm going to be busy with Christmas decorations for the house. We started putting them up just after Halloween and it's about to get really intense. I've worked out some of the kinks from last year, so the animatronics look more real. It's taking a lot of time. My grandma's really into it."

"Sounds like fun."

"We're launching the Friday after Thanksgiving, but we'll be upgrading everything through December. Come by close to Christmas. You'll be blown away."

"I can't wait," she said with a laugh.

She and Gizmo talked for a few more minutes before she walked him out of her home office. When the door closed behind her client, Belle, her one-hundred-and-twenty-pound Great Dane, poked her large head out from behind the desk.

"You didn't come say goodbye to Gizmo," Reggie said. "I thought you liked him."

Belle shifted her gaze to the purple vacuum sitting in the middle of the area rug, obviously pointing out that potential death still lurked.

"It's not going to hurt you," Reggie told her. "It's not even turned on."

Belle's brow drew together, as if she wasn't willing to accept the validity of that claim. Reggie tried to keep from smiling. Belle made a low sound in her throat, as though reminding Reggie of Gizmo's last invention.

"Yes, I do remember what happened with the dog walker robot," Reggie admitted.

The sturdy, odd-looking robot had started out well enough—walking a very concerned Belle around their small yard. Unfortunately, about ten minutes in, something had gone wrong with the programming and the robot had started chasing her instead. Belle, not the bravest of creatures, had broken through the screen door in her effort to escape the attack, hiding behind Reggie's desk for the rest of the day.

Gizmo had been crushed by the failure and had needed nearly as much reassurance as the dog. Sometimes, Reggie thought with a sigh, her job was the weirdest one ever.

"I'm going to leave this right here," Reggie told Belle. "It's turned off, so you can poke at it with your nose and get used to it."

Belle took two steps back toward the desk, her body language clearly saying she would never get used to it and why couldn't Reggie have a regular job that didn't threaten the life of her only pet?

"Or you could sit on it," Reggie pointed out. "The robot weighs about ten pounds. You're more than ten times that size. You could probably crush it like a bug."

Brown eyes widened slightly and filled with affront.

Reggie held in another smile. "I'm not commenting on your weight. You're very beautiful and way skinnier than me."

She settled on the sofa and patted the space next to her. Belle loped all of three strides before jumping up and leaning heavily against Reggie. The soft rose-colored sweater Belle wore to protect herself from the damp cold of mid-

November looked good on her dark gray fur. Reggie put an arm around her dog and pulled her phone out of her pocket. A quick glance at the screen told her she'd missed a call. From her mother.

She tried to ignore the sudden sense of dread. Not that she didn't love her parents—she did. Very much. They were good people who cared about her. But they were going to insist she come home for Thanksgiving and Christmas, and she couldn't think of a single reason to refuse.

Last year had been different. Last year, she'd stayed in Seattle, with only Belle for company, enduring the holidays rather than enjoying them. She'd given herself through New Year's to mourn the breakup and subsequent humiliation that went with the man of her dreams proposing on the Friday after Thanksgiving, arranging an impromptu celebration party on Saturday and then dumping her on Sunday.

After sharing her happiness with nearly everyone she knew, having her friends coo over her gorgeous ring and ask about wedding plans, she'd had to explain that Jake had changed his mind. At least that was what she'd assumed had happened. His actual words, "I can't do this. It's over. I'm sorry," hadn't given her much to work with.

Hurt and ashamed, she'd buried herself in work and her life in Seattle. She hadn't returned home to Wishing Tree even once since it had happened. She'd told herself she was healing, but Reggie knew the truth was less flattering. She was hiding and it was time to suck it up and get over herself. Thanksgiving was next week. She was going to go home, like she did every year. It was past time. Besides, it wasn't as if she was still mourning Jake. She'd moved on and now it was time to demonstrate that to her hometown.

"At least that's the plan," Reggie told her dog and pushed the button to phone her mother.

"Hey, Mom," she said when the call was answered.

"Reggie! It's you. You'll never guess. It's so wonderful. Your dad and I are getting married."

Reggie blinked a couple of times. "You're already married. Your thirty-fifth wedding anniversary is coming up next month. I thought we'd have a party or something." She and her sister had talked about the possibility a couple of weeks ago.

Her mother laughed. "You're right. Technically, we're married. We eloped, and I have to tell you, I've always regretted not having a big wedding. Your father pointed out I've been upset about that for the last thirty-five years, so maybe it was time to do something about it. We've decided we're renewing our vows with a big wedding and a reception afterward. It'll be the Wednesday before Christmas."

"You're having a wedding?"

"Yes. Up at the resort. We're inviting everyone. It's been so much fun, but the planning is getting a little out of hand. I was hoping you could help me."

"With your wedding?"

"Yes, dear. Are you feeling all right?"

"My head's spinning a little."

"I know it's a surprise, but I'm so happy. You're coming home for Thanksgiving, aren't you?"

"I am."

"Good. So I was thinking you could just stay through Christmas. There's plenty of room down in the basement for you to work. You could handle your business in the morning and help me in the afternoon. It's only five weeks, Reggie. You have a job that lets you work from anywhere."

While technically true, Reggie wasn't thrilled at the thought of packing up her life for over a month and moving in with her folks.

"What about Belle?" she asked, hoping bringing up that subject would help shift things.

"You know we love her."

"She's afraid of Burt."

"Oh, they're fine together. It's all a big game."

Reggie thought about how Belle quivered with fear every time she saw her father's small dachshund in the room. Burt was normally good-natured, but he'd never taken to Belle and spent most of his time running after her and biting her ankles. Belle, for her part, tried to keep out of his way, frequently traversing a room by going from tabletop to sofa to chair, often with disastrous results.

"I want her to be a flower girl," her mother added. "We'll get her an adorable dress and she can have a basket of rose petals hanging around her neck."

Reggie rubbed her dog's back. "She'd look good as a flower girl."

"See? Say you'll come home and help me with my wedding, Reggie. I need you. Dena's busy with school and she's developed terrible morning sickness. I have no idea where she got it from. I was fine with both my pregnancies, but she's wiped out. You've been gone too long. It's time to come home."

Almost the exact words Reggie had told herself, minus the wedding guilt.

"Mom," she began, then held in a sigh. Why fight the inevitable? Once she was home, she would be happy she'd done the right thing. Plus, it was Wishing Tree at Christmas—nowhere else in the world came close to that little slice of magic.

"Sure. I'll be there. Belle and I will drive over the day after tomorrow."

"I'm so happy," her mother squealed. "Thank you. We're

going to have so much fun. We haven't had the first snow-fall yet. Maybe you'll be home for that and you can go to the big town party. All right, now that I know you're going to be home for the holidays, I have yet another favor to ask you."

Reggie wasn't sure if she should laugh or moan. "What did you do?"

"Nothing, really."

"It has to be something or we wouldn't be talking about it."

"Yes. Good point. Dena's class is going to do a knitting project for their holiday charity this year. Normally I'd be happy to manage it for her, but this year with the wedding and all, I just don't have time. I was hoping you could do it for me."

Reggie closed her eyes. "Mom," she began, then stopped, knowing she was going to say yes in the end, so why fight it?

Every year students at the local elementary school came up with several charity projects to do in December. Since Dena, Reggie's older sister, had started teaching there, the family had also gotten involved. For the past couple of years, Reggie's mom had been in charge of that project, organizing supplies and students, paving the way for their good deed.

"This is why I've avoided coming home," Reggie said weakly.

"No, it's not. You avoided coming home because Jake Crane was too stupid to realize what he had with you. I hope he spends the rest of his life regretting his decision and fighting a very painful rash."

"Go, Mom."

Her mother laughed. "I can be supportive."

"You always are." Reggie smiled. "Fine, I'll be the knitting queen."

"Wonderful. I'll email you the information you'll need to get up to speed. You're going to have a great time with the kids. In the meantime, think about wedding favors. Something we'll make ourselves so it will be really special. I was playing with the idea of painted coasters, or we could make soap. I've always wanted to learn how to do that. We could go botanical or floral."

They were going to make soap? "You know you can buy really cute little soaps, Mom. They sell them online."

"I'm not buying the favors. I want this to be a project for us to do together. Anyway, I'll see you soon. Let me know when you leave Seattle so I can start worrying when you're not here on time."

"How about if I just show up unexpectedly so you don't have to worry at all?"

"Where's the fun in that? I can't wait to see you. I'll give Dad your love."

"Thanks, Mom. And congratulations on the wedding."

Dena Somerville had known being single and pregnant would offer challenges, but she'd never thought she would be sick every second of every day. *Her* mother had always talked about how easy her pregnancies had been and the fact that the women in their family popped out babies with barely a pause in their days.

Sitting on the floor in her bathroom, leaning against the wall, while wondering if she was done throwing up for this hour, Dena decided either her mother had been lying or Dena had been adopted.

It wasn't supposed to be like this, she thought, turning over the damp washcloth on the back of her neck and wishing she could magically transport herself eight weeks into the future, the time her doctor had promised the nausea and subsequent vomiting would finally end. Alas, she had yet to figure out how to move through time at will, so she was stuck with the unpleasant reality of knowing that, in an hour or two, the waves would return and three times out of five she would oh, so elegantly puke with little or no warning.

What really got her was the fact that she'd had a plan. A good plan, a sensible plan. A plan that could almost be called superior. She'd always been the girl with a plan and she'd always done the work to make it happen. She didn't believe in luck or fate—she put in the time and effort required, even when it was hard.

She'd fulfilled her childhood dream of being a teacher and she loved her job even more than she'd thought she would. When her grandmother Regina had passed away, dividing her estate between her two granddaughters, leaving stocks and bonds to her namesake Reggie and the Wishing Tree B&B to Dena, she'd moved into the spacious apartment above the old carriage house and had spent her summers updating the place.

Although Dena had been less than successful in the romance department, she'd kept putting herself out there. She'd signed up for a dating service and had traveled to Seattle every other weekend for five months in an effort to meet *the one*. She'd used three different dating apps, had told anyone who would listen she was on the market. She'd gone on group dates, blind dates and double dates.

After two years of honest effort, she'd accepted that she wasn't likely to find Mr. Right, or even Mr. Good Enough. At that point, she'd had to start asking herself the hard question: Did giving up on love also mean giving up on having a family? The answer had come quickly enough and it had been a big fat no. She loved kids and she wanted kids of her own.

Being a logical, fact-driven person, she'd taken an entire year to research IUI—aka intrauterine insemination, or what her sister referred to as the turkey baster method of getting pregnant—and another six months to make the decision to have the procedure. She'd scheduled the first such that her due date would align with the end of the school year, thereby giving her the whole summer to spend with her baby.

She'd picked out colors for the nursery, she'd investigated the best day care options, and she'd typed up notes for when she sat down with her family and told them what she wanted to do. She had a wonderful support system, including her parents, her sister, Reggie, and the staff at the B&B, all of whom had become like family to her. She'd even managed to get pregnant right out of the gate.

She'd tried to think of everything, but she'd never considered the possibility she would be laid low by morning sickness.

The combination of the cool, damp washcloth and the cold tiles beneath her butt seemed to ease the nausea enough for her to risk standing. When she was on her feet, she paused to see if her stomach would punish her, but all seemed calm. With a little luck, she would get through the next couple of hours without the need to barf.

Tightening the belt on her robe, she walked to her balcony and stepped out into the freezing, dark morning. As always, the sharp, cold air shocked her lungs and made her shiver, but the last whispers of nausea faded in the chill.

It was barely six in the morning and much of the world was still asleep. This far north and only a month from the shortest day of the year, daybreak was nearly two hours away. She looked up at the bright stars twinkling overhead. Although it was cold enough to snow, the weather had been remarkably clear. The mythical first snowfall had yet to occur.

Soon, she thought with a smile. Soon there would be snow and the celebration that went with it, because Wishing Tree was that kind of town.

She glanced toward the main building of the B&B and saw the kitchen lights were on. Ursula, their gifted but snarky chef, had already gotten to work on breakfast. Once that meal was done, she would put together box lunches for any guests who had ordered one. That endeavor was followed by batches of cookies, brownies and scones that they sold in the lobby every afternoon. Ursula's last task before heading home was to create appetizers for their evening wine and snacks event.

Sometimes she made little quiches or put together a really great cheese plate. Her stuffed mushrooms were popular, as were the crab puffs. And the wine. All beautiful Washington wines from the great wineries: L'Ecole, Painted Moon, Northstar, Lake Chelan, Doubleback and Figgins.

"Ah, wine. How much I once loved you," Dena murmured, then laughed. At least she could still eat the food— or most of it. Soft cheeses were a no-no and these days olives made her gag, but otherwise she was all in.

A light clicked on, illuminating the back patio of the unit below. The ground floor of the carriage house had been split into a storage room for the B&B and a stand-alone suite for guests who preferred something more upscale and private. The space came at a premium, but they rarely had trouble filling it—especially during the holiday season.

The current resident, a ridiculously good-looking guy who had arrived two days ago, was booked through the day after New Year's. Dena was nearly as excited about the thought of all those weekly charges filling up her bank account as she was by the eye candy. Most of her guests were couples and families. Attractive single men didn't often find their way to her B&B.

Not that his marital status mattered to her. Not only had she accepted that love wasn't in her destiny, she was pregnant, and getting involved with a guy made no sense. Oh, and there was the added fact that, based solely on looks, he was miles out of her league. Still, an expectant mother could look and admire, she thought with a smile.

So far, he was a quiet neighbor who didn't slam doors or play his TV too loud. Last night she'd heard music coming from his place—a song played several times in a row. The soft rendition had lulled her to sleep, so she wasn't about to complain.

The cold seeped through her bathrobe and made her shiver. Dena sucked in one more breath before heading inside to start her morning. She brushed her teeth, then dressed quickly. Once in the kitchen, she ate the only breakfast she was able to keep down these days. An avocado and egg salad sandwich on rye bread. Possibly gross in most circumstances, but her doctor had given it a thumbs-up.

She glanced longingly at her coffee maker, thinking how incredibly close the two of them had been, back before her life had been defined by something the size of a lima bean. Not that she had regrets—giving up coffee was so worth it for her baby's sake, but at least she'd known that deprivation was coming. It was the morning-slash-afternoon-slash-early-evening sickness that was going to do her in.

But for now, her tummy was quiet, so she filled her water bottle, retrieved her lunch from the refrigerator and headed downstairs to her car. If she could get a little cooperation from her body, she was going to have a good day—mostly because every day she was teaching was a good day. Plus, there were so many things to look forward to. On Friday she would be announcing the charity project chosen for the third-grade class, then next Monday they would have their monthly career day presentation. If she remembered correctly, they were hosting a plumber, a veterinarian and a Christmas tree farmer. So many possibilities, she thought as she walked to her car. She was, in every way possible, the luckiest person on the planet, and she had the life to prove it.

Need to know what happens next? Pick up your copy of The Christmas Wedding Guest *today!*